MISS ME FOREVER

— A NOVEL —

EUGENE CROSS

DZANC
BOOKS

2580 Craig Rd.
Ann Arbor, MI 48103
www.dzancbooks.org

First Edition: November 2023
Cover design by Steven Seighman
Interior design by Michelle Dotter

ISBN: 9781950539789

Printed in the United States of America

10   9   8   7   6   5   4   3   2   1

MISS ME
FOREVER

For all those in search of a home
And for Kelly, who gave me mine

PART ONE

Dear Brother,

How do I say what is in my heart? How do I tell you those things now clouded by distance?

I have known you in your earliest hour. I have watched you come into the world.

Brother, you are gone from me. For the first time your life has parted from my own. Who shall I watch over? Who shall I protect if not you?

You were the smallest baby any elder in our camp had ever seen live. A miracle, they said. A nub of a child swaddled and hidden at our mother's breast. There were times I thought you did not exist, so small I could not see you among your blankets or slung against our mother's back. How is it that something I once scarcely believed was real has left such an absence? A void I feel more urgently than my own beating heart.

Brother, I have wanted the world for you. And it is the world that has taken you from me.

Susmita

OCTOBER 2008

TULSI IS DREAMING OF OCEANS when he hears the explosion, a thundering boom that rattles the casement windows of his grandfather's apartment. For a moment he is back in Nepal, in Camp Goldhap, the bamboo walls of his sister's hut casting a ladder of light across the packed earth floor. When he opens his eyes, he sees his grandfather at the front door, waving the broom he uses to clean the stoop.

"Poor boys," he yells through the screen. "Poor boys."

It is the night before Halloween, Tulsi's first holiday in the United States. It is a festival he does not yet completely understand. From what he has gathered it involves human skeletons, candy, and the decoration of giant gourds, which are then blown up by the neighborhood boys for sport. Twice this week, Tulsi has heard the explosions and peered out the window to view the orange carnage in the street. Once, while dozing on the pullout that serves as his bed, he was awakened by the splatter of an egg against the window. Tulsi does not like Halloween and will be happy when it has passed.

Tulsi hurries across the apartment, his sandals slapping the plank flooring. He steps behind his grandfather and takes the broom from him. A piece of stringy pulp sticks in the screen.

"Bad boys, Hajurba," Tulsi says as he places his hands on his grandfather's bony shoulders and guides him to his chair. "Here, they are named bad boys."

"Poor in spirit," his grandfather says. He lowers his wiry frame into the tattered La-Z-Boy and with a sudden yank lifts his bare feet into the air. Their soles are the deep red brown of mahogany and just as hard. "You must not be like them," he says, closing his eyes. "You are Nepali. Always remember this."

Tulsi hears the boys laughing, their expensive sneakers pounding the sidewalk as they run away, and he thinks, it is impossible not to remember.

•

Tulsi arrived in the United States two months ago, on an afternoon so impossibly damp and gray he wondered if he'd landed on the underside of the world. Three days after leaving the transit center in Kathmandu, sleeping on planes and buses and in airport terminals, Tulsi picked his bag off a rotating conveyor belt that slid past his feet like a long steel snake. Outside the airport a husky man with spiked blond hair held a cardboard sign that read *Tulsa*. A black headset hung from one ear, and he appeared to be talking to himself. When he saw Tulsi staring at the sign, he touched something on the cellular phone attached to his belt and extended his hand. He pulled Tulsi into a half embrace until their shoulders met.

"You've come a long way, brother," he said, "but your journey is only beginning." Tulsi was not quite sure what the man meant. He was clean-shaven with features like a baby's, soft and rounded. His chin protruded only slightly farther than the roll of fat at his neck. He took Tulsi's bag and introduced himself as Pastor Ken, a youth pastor and volunteer for the International Institute. "Call me PK," he said. "That's my nickname. Do you have nicknames in Nepal? We'll get you one pronto," he said and smiled.

On the ride to Tulsi's grandfather's apartment, the man spoke endlessly, describing the high school where Tulsi would be enrolled as a sophomore, the area of town where Tulsi's grandfather had just recently been relocated, the amount of rain they'd had that summer, and a list of other topics Tulsi only partly understood. Tulsi kept his eyes trained on the world unfolding around him. Four-lane highways divided by concrete slabs, rows of brick factories and warehouses that seemed completely empty, vehicles the size of boats with wheels that spun even when they stood still.

He wished his sister Susmita were with him. She would be able to explain this place, help him understand. She had remained in Goldhap, teaching at the one-room school where Tulsi himself had been a student. That spring she had married another teacher, a kind man named Purna who was so quiet you had to lean toward him when he spoke, as though his voice held magnetic properties. Tulsi had lived with them until his grandfather was settled in Pennsylvania, a place Tulsi's friends had assured him was governed by vampires. Purna's family would be relocated as well, and once they were, Susmita would travel with them as was their custom. Their new home could be anywhere: Canada, Australia, New Zealand. Tulsi knew it might be months before he heard from her, years before he saw her. He knew he might never see her again.

•

The Tuesday after Halloween, Tulsi takes the bus to Pastor Ken's church, a huge white building with a giant cross on the side and the biggest parking lot he's ever seen. Inside is a chapel, gymnasium, full kitchen, nursery, and a dozen classrooms. By the time Tulsi finds the one where the ESL class is being held, many of the students are already seated with notebooks spread open before them. Most are dressed in jeans and sweatshirts. Tulsi was unsure what to wear for a class being held in a church, and so he has on khakis, beige socks beneath his leather sandals, a white dress shirt, and a tie his grandfather bought him. The tie is pale blue. Stitched onto the front is a giant whale swimming vertically toward Tulsi's face, mouth spread open as though it means to devour him. Pastor Ken spots Tulsi from across the room and jogs over.

"Oklahoma," he says, placing a meaty hand on Tulsi's shoulder. "We'll call you Oklahoma. You know, because I thought your name was Tulsa, but it's not." Tulsi nods uncertainly. While they're speaking, a slender woman in jeans and a T-shirt appears. Tulsi is suddenly very aware of the whale on his tie and crosses his arms over his chest to hide it.

"You must be Tulsi," the woman says. She has the blondest hair he has ever seen. Her eyes are the color of copper. "I'm Abigail, Pastor Ken's wife. I'm here to help out as a conversation partner." Tulsi shakes her hand while keeping one arm crossed over his chest.

"How's Oklahoma?" Pastor Ken asks his wife, wrapping an arm around her waist. "We're trying to figure out a nickname."

Abigail smiles politely as though she's meeting the man standing beside her for the first time. "A bit long. Nicknames are supposed to be easy."

"It's because I thought his name was Tulsa."

Abigail pats her husband's hand where it holds her. "We'll give it some thought," she says.

Pastor Ken opens the ESL class with a prayer. Through a sort of miming routine he instructs everyone on the correct posture: hands clasped, heads bent, eyes closed. Partway through, Tulsi peeks around the classroom. The other students have followed Pastor Ken's instructions with the sort of fervor they all feel is necessary to fit in. Their hands are folded and outstretched before them. Their heads appear glued to their desks. Pastor Ken's eyes are squeezed shut, and a strained expression covers his face as though he is lifting a heavy object. He is saying something about trials and sacrifice. Across the room Tulsi sees Abigail watching her husband, looking serious. She is the only one beside himself who does not have their eyes shut. Before Tulsi can put his head back down, Abigail turns and locks eyes with him. For a moment he worries he's in trouble, but then Abigail smiles.

The class is taught by Dr. Malak, a local professor who is also a member of the church. A tall man with a long gray ponytail, he conjugates verbs on a dry-erase board and makes jokes Tulsi does not understand. The Asian man next to him fills his notebook with furious scribbles even when the professor is not speaking. Tulsi has not brought a notebook, and instead repeats in his mind over and over what Dr. Malak has listed on the board. *I am being. I have been. I will be.*

·

While he waits at the bus stop, Tulsi leafs through the free Bible each student received after class. He can hardly believe how thin the pages are, like the wings of an insect. Across the highway, a construction crew digs a trench beside the road. A yellow car shaped like a helmet pulls near to where Tulsi waits. Abigail waves him over.

"Ken meets with the youth group on Tuesday nights, but I'm headed home. Need a ride?" The air smells of burning leaves and diesel fuel. A dump truck beeps as it backs toward the trench. Abigail reaches over and pushes open the passenger door. "Come on," she says, glancing at his sandals, "your feet must be freezing."

A hymn plays on the radio. For the first few minutes they listen silently. The sky is a metallic blue with dark clouds that crop up like distant mountains. Tulsi wants to make conversation, but it is hard to think of something to say. Before he can, Abigail says, "I like your tie." Tulsi had momentarily forgotten about the stupid whale tie and looks down to find it clearly visible between the nylon straps of his seatbelt. He cannot imagine why, out of all the ties in their new country, his grandfather chose this one. He almost didn't wear it, but there was his grandfather, smiling his partially toothless smile, holding the tie out in both hands like an offering. Tulsi does not think Abigail is being sarcastic, though sarcasm is something he has trouble detecting, especially female sarcasm, which is somehow subtler.

"My grandfather buys it for me," he finally says. Abigail nods as though she knew this was the case.

"Well, it's very nice. It reminds me of the story of Jonah."

"I am not familiar," Tulsi says, surprised to hear himself do so. Normally when he doesn't know what people are talking about he smiles, like at school when the boys in his class argue the finer points of Ultimate Fighting, referencing things like cage matches and grappling, submission holds and fish-hooking, razor elbows and Brazilian Jiu-Jitsu. Tulsi wants to argue with them, wants to say he's seen some of the fights on late-night cable, but joining their conversation is like jumping on a moving train. Instead he remains silent, listens to their words as they rumble past.

"Jonah and the whale," Abigail says. She reaches over and touches the Bible in Tulsi's lap. "It's in there."

"I am looking before," he says, "very small print." He makes a gesture with his thumb and forefinger like he's crushing a bug, and instantly feels stupid. "It's surprising me. Everything else in the United States is very big."

Abigail laughs a deep laugh. "I guess that's true," she says, and then her face goes serious. "It must be a lot different here than in the camps. Do you miss Nepal?"

They are heading north along Peach Street. Below them Lake Erie makes a second, bluer horizon beneath the sky. Tulsi wants to explain the situation as best he can, wants to tell her how the Bhutanese government kicked out all the ethnic Nepalese long before he was born, how the refugee camp was the only home he ever knew. When he was very young his mother died from infection, and then his father left. He wants to tell Abigail how his grandfather and Susmita raised him, how Susmita chose to stay behind, and now he only has his grandfather who is getting older and older, dark spots appearing on his skin like the water stains on the ceiling of their apartment. He wants to tell her how his grandfather works the overnight shift at the juice plant, how tired he looks when he gets home, but how he still waits until Tulsi has finished his breakfast and left for school before he'll sleep. Tulsi wants Abigail to know he'll never be able to repay his grandfather for this.

Abigail's car rocks over a pothole. In the distance the faint outline of the moon sits atop a ribbon of clouds. Somewhere on the other side of the world, Tulsi thinks, Susmita is sleeping, her shiny black hair covering her pillow like spilled ink.

"Some things I miss," he says.

•

That night Tulsi lies awake on the pullout. His grandfather was already gone when Abigail dropped him off, and the apartment feels even emptier than it normally does. A streetlight shines through the yellowed blinds, throwing stripes across the bare walls. Somewhere a siren blares, and a few blocks up, a freighter rumbles along the tracks above Fourteenth Street.

Before he shut off the light, Tulsi read the story of Jonah, how he disobeyed God and ran away from him, how the ship he escaped on was struck by a terrible storm. He read how, after casting lots to see who brought this misfortune upon them, Jonah asked to be thrown overboard into the angry sea. Lying on the mattress, Tulsi imagines himself sinking slowly through dark water, his limbs weightless. He imagines a whale, as big as a mountain, swallowing him whole, the great rush as he's sucked into the belly of the beast. He closes his eyes, sealing in the darkness of that place, feels the creature descending, swimming through deep oceans, until after three days it spews him onto a distant shore, far from the land he calls home.

•

Wednesday is the first day of Tihar, and Mr. and Mrs. Bhandari, an elderly Nepalese couple resettled nearby, come over to celebrate. Together they light small clay lamps and pray that good will always triumph over evil. Mrs. Bhandari is kind and smiles at Tulsi, her face so full of wrinkles her features seem lost between them. Her husband ignores Tulsi altogether. He speaks to his grandfather about America as though it is another planet.

"I am not liking it here," he says. "This place is not good for Nepali people. It is making them forget our home country and our values." He glances in Tulsi's direction. "Especially young Nepali," he adds. "I try not to leave my home, *ever*. This is my first exit since Monday, when we were required to meet with the worker from the resettlement committee."

They are sitting at the kitchen table. It is covered with half-empty dishes, a plate heaped with roti, a pot of curried vegetables, and another of spicy dal, bowls of fermented pickles and chutney, and sweets made of almonds, pistachios, and coconut. Tulsi can still taste the burn of the chutney and wets his lips to reignite it. At school they serve mashed potatoes, lukewarm spaghetti, chopped steak in thick brown gravy, food so bland Tulsi eats it only to keep from fainting.

"And if there was a fire?" Tulsi's grandfather asks Mr. Bhandari. "Would you leave then?" He nudges Tulsi below the table with his knee. Tulsi hides a smile, grateful to be the grandson of this man and not the one across the table.

Mr. Bhandari considers the question seriously. "Yes," he finally says, "if there were a fire, *then* I would leave."

Sunday is Bhai Tika, the final day of the Festival. It is the day sisters bless their brothers and pray for their well-being. Every year, for as long as his memory permits, Tulsi recalls Susmita drawing a tika of rice paste on his forehead, Tulsi touching her feet as she prayed that he would live a long and happy life, free from the evils of this world. The night before, Tulsi slept with the phone cradled on his chest. All day he waits for the phone to ring, waits to hear his sister's voice as she asks these things for him once again. But the day drops from beneath him like a trapdoor, and his grandfather leaves for work and the phone does not ring. Tulsi sits in the empty apartment and wonders who will bless him now.

●

The next Tuesday, Tulsi is the first to arrive at the ESL class. He is wearing a hooded sweatshirt and jeans. He brings a notebook, half a dozen pens, a bottle of water, and a PowerBar. He finds a seat near the front of the class and arranges these items at even intervals before him like a shrine. When Pastor Ken says the opening prayer, Tulsi keeps his forehead pressed against the cool plastic of his desk. Tulsi listens to Dr. Malak intently as though he were offering the key to happiness, for in a way, Tulsi thinks, he is.

Twenty minutes into the class, Abigail arrives and takes the open seat beside him. Tulsi smiles at her. She has brought nothing but herself. Taking care to be as quiet as possible, Tulsi tears three sheets from his notebook. He places them on her desk along with a pen.

The instructor makes a list of questions on the board and asks the students to find a conversation partner. They are to take turns interviewing each other.

When Abigail asks him the first question on the list, his favorite food, Tulsi says Philadelphia cheesesteak. Tulsi has never tried one, but has seen them prepared and eaten on the Food Channel and Philadelphia is the biggest city in his new state.

"*Really?*" Abigail asks. "I love those."

"Yes," Tulsi says. "Delicious." All around him he hears his peers struggling with their responses, their thick accents filling the air like a toxic gas.

"You know," Abigail says, "for how long you've been here, your English is very strong."

"I study before leaving," Tulsi says, "at Blooming Lotus English School in our camp. But there we study British English." A look of recognition lights up Abigail's face. She puts her hands over her heart and pretends to swoon.

"That's it," she says. "I thought I heard a bit of a British accent from you. I adore it. It's so official-sounding."

Tulsi's cheeks flush with heat. He picks up a pen, sets it down again. He is flattered and embarrassed. He knows it was meant as a compliment, but still, this is not why he has come to class.

"I want to sound American," Tulsi says, looking away.

•

After class Abigail offers Tulsi a ride home. He thanks her, but says he is planning on making a stop first and doesn't want to delay her.

"I'm in no rush," she says. "Just tell me where we're headed."

•

It's past eight, but the Walmart lot is filled and they have to park next door at the giant Cineplex built to look like a castle. Inside Walmart, an elderly employee in a cowboy hat and suspenders greets them and pushes a cart toward Tulsi. Fluorescent light reflects off the waxy floor. They pass barrels brimming with discounted DVDs and display cases filled with MP3 players and cameras. There are pyramids of junk food and rack upon rack of clothing. The front left wheel on the cart jiggles incessantly, pulling Tulsi toward aisles he has no wish to enter. There's a vision center, a tire display, a wall of freezers, a lawn and garden department. Finally they reach the shoe aisle.

Tulsi lives at the corner of Eleventh and Ash. The kids on his block all wear Nike Air Yeezy's and Reebok G-Unit's. He's taken the bus to the Millcreek Mall and wandered through The Finish Line and Foot Locker, eyeing the wall displays, but all these sneakers are too expensive. Even if he had the money, Tulsi knows he would feel guilty buying a pair. After weeks of saving what his grandfather gives him for lunch, eating nothing but hot dogs, the cheapest thing in his school cafeteria, and drinking only water, he has managed to scrape together thirty dollars. Just enough for the newest pair of Champion C9s. He finds them in black then searches for a pair of eights. The closest he can find are nine and a half's. He slips them on and laces them up.

"Better try them out," Abigail says. At the end of the aisle a mother pushes her cart and yells at her lagging daughter to hurry up. Once they turn the corner and disappear, Tulsi and Abigail are the only two around. Tulsi drops into a sprinter's stance and takes off, running up and down the aisle while Abigail watches and laughs her deep laugh. The sneakers feel like they're going to slip off at any moment, but Tulsi figures he can double up on socks. Better too big than too small. He can grow into them. Abigail leans over the edge of the empty cart, applauding.

"Well?" she asks. "How do they feel?"

"Perfect," Tulsi says. He places them back in their box exactly as he found them and puts it in the cart.

In the checkout line Tulsi recognizes another student from the ESL class, a Middle Eastern man named Aban. He is holding a giant package of diapers, and when he sees Abigail and Tulsi, he steps out of line and walks back to them.

"Hello, friends," he says, smiling. He has on a faded turtleneck beneath his coat, the collar frayed by his thick beard. "A good class tonight." He hefts the package of diapers. "I buy for my baby. Only three weeks old."

Abigail smiles politely and offers a quiet, "Congratulations."

"It is wonderful surprise for me." He looks at Tulsi and asks, "You are student?" It is almost their turn at the register and people are already waiting. Tulsi wishes Aban would not have seen them.

"Yes," he says, inching the cart forward, "at East High School."

"Excellent. Maybe you become doctor, or minister like PK." Aban's brow wrinkles and for a moment he looks as though he might cry. He turns to Abigail and says, "Your husband is wonderful man."

Abigail nods. "He's very fond of you as well." Her voice sounds flat, distant. Tulsi thinks she's acting strangely and wonders if it's because they have been seen together in public, if this is somehow improper.

Aban's face lights up. He clutches the diapers to his chest and nods toward them. "You have?" he asks. "Baby with PK?"

The cashier is waiting for them to step up. Tulsi can feel the eyes of the other people in line. Impatience, he has learned, is something of a birthright in his new home. Abigail is silent. She reaches out and taps her fingers against the handle of the cart, as though checking for stability. She shakes her head.

"No," she says.

•

The car ride home is silent. Abigail grips the wheel like it's something alive she is trying to subdue. Tulsi holds the shoebox in his lap. The clerk did not offer him a bag. He listens to the wind as it sails over the hood. The road they are on cuts through a rising valley Tulsi has never seen before. They might be headed downtown where he lives, but he can't be certain. He wants to check with Abigail, but something tells him he should keep quiet. A line of clouds floats past a bone-white moon, and in the distance, below the rise of the road, Tulsi spots the oily black surface of a pond. Abigail is staring straight ahead and suddenly she says, "Why did he have to ask that?" Her voice sounds different and Tulsi feels the tiny hairs on the back of his neck prickle. A home for the elderly sits in a clearing above the road. It is built low and wide, and some of the windows are lit up like portholes on a ship. "What kind of a question is that?" Abigail says.

Tulsi is unsure what to say, and so he says nothing. Abigail is still not looking at him, and he senses that she does not expect him to answer. The road descends into the valley, where the shadows of trees have darkened the asphalt, and for a moment Tulsi feels the sensation of being submerged.

Abigail cranks down her window and the car floods with a sudden rush of freezing air, the sound it makes deafening. Tulsi keeps his head lowered, his eyes trained on the lettering of the box, which seems even more unfamiliar to him now. After a moment Abigail turns to him, surprised, it seems, that he is sitting beside her.

"I'm sorry," she says. "It's been a long day, a long couple of days, and I'm very tired."

Tulsi nods. Slowly he is beginning to understand. Abigail offered him a kindness and he made a mistake. He took too long at the store and now it is late.

"I'm sorry for this," he says, patting the box. "It is dark out and I am keeping you."

"No," Abigail says. "That's not it at all. I'm glad you found your shoes. I'm glad you like them."

She pats his hand and instantly Tulsi forgets the guilt he was just feeling. Abigail rolls her window back up and adjusts the heater so that it blows a steady stream of warm air.

"If you're happy I am too," she says. She turns to him and smiles. "You're happy, aren't you?"

Tulsi pulls the shoebox closer, feels the warm air from the heater wash over him. Abigail is driving him home and he trusts she knows the way. "Yes," he tells her. "I am happy."

•

A few days later Tulsi sees snow for the first time. Fat flakes descend from bulging clouds and cover cars and benches, the naked branches of trees. For three days it does nothing but snow, and for three days Tulsi watches. Giant yellow plows fight through the drifts, forming banks along the sides of roads, building tiny mountains at the edges of parking lots. Tulsi is afraid to go outside, afraid to touch it. The temperature continues to drop and the snow glazes over with a thin coat of ice that sparkles like crushed glass. At night his grandfather wraps shopping bags over his socks and sandals and ties them with twine. Tulsi watches him slip and stumble along the sidewalk on his way to work. Tulsi tells his grandfather he is sick and cannot attend school. Tuesday comes and he skips the ESL class. He stays inside the apartment all day wrapped in a thick shawl Susmita made for him before he left. When he first arrived, it smelled like her, like cardamom and lavender, but now when Tulsi holds the shawl to his face and inhales he smells only the cold. He wonders if Purna's family has been issued their resettlement orders, if Susmita has left Nepal. He wonders if it is snowing where she is.

•

On Thursday there is a knock at the door. Tulsi walks across the room, the shawl draped over his shoulders like a cape. He opens to find Abigail standing in the snow. She is wearing a bright red winter coat, a yellow scarf, and a green knit cap. She reminds Tulsi of a rainbow. He wants to say so, but instead invites her in.

"You weren't in class the other night," she says. "I was worried." She is holding a large brown package tied with string. "Are you sick?"

Tulsi shrugs his shoulders and the shawl slips from one, dangles to the floor.

"It's beautiful," Abigail says, pointing at it.

"My sister makes it for me," he says, surprised to hear the words come out of his mouth. This is the first time since arriving that he's spoken of Susmita to anyone but his grandfather.

Abigail looks intrigued. "I didn't know you had a sister," she says. "What's her name?"

"Susmita," he says. "I live with her before I come here."

"You must miss her very much," Abigail says. Tulsi lifts the shawl from the floor and begins to fold it.

"She wanted me to come here," he says, "to live with our hajurba." Tulsi points toward the bedroom. "He is asleep." Lately his grandfather has been picking up extra shifts, volunteering to fill in when other employees request off for the holidays. He arrives home exhausted, too tired even to eat.

"I'm sure she thought it was for the best," Abigail says. Tulsi nods. He remembers how in the weeks leading up to his departure, Susmita would only speak with him in English. She wanted him to be prepared, to be ready for his new home. If he tried to engage her in Nepali, she would cover her ears and hum. He remembers his frustration, trying to communicate at such an important time in a language not his own.

"I brought this for you," Abigail says, handing him the package. Tulsi accepts it hesitantly.

They sit across from each other at the kitchen table. Tulsi unties the string taking care not to rip the brown wrapping paper. Inside is a navy-blue winter coat and matching hat. Both feature the trademark Nike swoosh in stark white. Tulsi runs his fingertips over the cool nylon.

"I wasn't sure if you had any winter clothes," Abigail says and smiles. "I know the weather here isn't quite the same."

Tulsi touches the smooth fabric once more, then folds the wrapping paper over it. "I am sorry. I cannot accept," he says and slides the package across the table.

Abigail looks confused. "You don't like it?"

"I like it very much, but I cannot repay you."

"You don't have to," Abigail says and pushes the package back toward Tulsi. "It's a gift." She smiles and motions toward it. "Take it. It's nothing."

Tulsi sits quietly for a moment. He knows he shouldn't, but finally he lifts the package and holds it to his chest. "It *is* something," he says.

•

Outside it is still snowing. The sidewalks have not been shoveled, and so they walk along the icy street, snow crunching beneath Tulsi's C9s. He is wearing his new coat and hat. The air is crisp against his skin. He feels better than he has in days. Abigail asks him why he skipped the ESL class and he tells her.

"This," he says, pointing at the bank that comes up to his waist. "It is something new to me."

Abigail laughs. "You'll have to get used to it, living here. Besides, it's not so bad." She kicks at a pile of powder and Tulsi watches it explode in the air like smoke. The sun shines above the apartment complexes to the west and makes the snow glimmer. Tulsi leans down and scoops up a small handful. It looks like a mound of cotton, wet and cold in his bare palm. Abigail scoops some up as well, then crunches it in both hands. "Perfect for snowballs." She winds up and tosses it toward a stop sign but misses to the right.

Tulsi makes his own and hits the sign above the *P*.

"Nice shot," she says. The two of them stand there tossing snowballs, seeing who can get theirs nearest the middle of the sign.

The light begins to fail and the streetlights switch on and after a while Abigail says she has to go. Tulsi thanks her for the coat and hat and watches her walk back to her car. He waves as she drives by. For a long time he stays there, pitching snowballs at the sign until the fingers of his throwing hand go numb.

•

The Tuesday before Thanksgiving arrives, and in lieu of a lesson, the ESL class has a party in the church gymnasium. Dr. Malak has asked the students to bring a dish native to their home country. He has told them this is called "potluck." Tulsi arrives late wearing his C9s and his Nike coat and hat. He is carrying a bag of Doritos he bought at the corner store near the bus stop. The others have all dressed up. The men wear threadbare sports coats from Goodwill. Their slacks are mismatched and too short, revealing white tube socks and scuffed dress shoes. Some of the women sport saris while others have on secondhand dresses. Everyone is smiling and laughing, holding plates of food and glasses of punch, but somehow, all of it strikes Tulsi as sad. He walks directly to the long folding table to set down his chips. He scans the gym for Abigail but sees no sign of her or PK. Dr. Malak is standing at the far end of the basketball court talking to Aban. Tulsi walks over and interrupts them.

"Is Abigail been here?" he asks. Dr. Malak looks down and smiles.

"*Has* Abigail been here," he says. Tulsi repeats it and he nods approvingly, the way he does during class. "They were here earlier, but only to say goodbye."

"*Goodbye?*" Tulsi asks. Across the gym, two Sudanese women from class break into song. They sway side by side, arms around each other's waists. Tulsi watches momentarily and then says again, "*Goodbye?*"

"PK has been offered the senior pastor position at another church. Unfortunately, he and Abigail will be leaving us soon."

"PK *was* very excited," Aban says while looking at Dr. Malak.

"Yes, he *was*, Aban. Nice job."

"I am confused," Tulsi manages to say. His heart is beating fast as though he's just finished running. His head is suddenly dizzy, his legs weak. "How can this be so?"

"We hate to see PK and Abigail go, but the Lord has called them elsewhere. It's *His* will."

Tulsi feels a rush of panic, the same way he felt as he climbed into the van that took him from Goldhap, everything he owned packed into a cloth duffel bag in his lap. He remembers Susmita calling his name, waving to him as the van pulled away until she was nothing more than a faceless onlooker in the crowd. Sometimes, when he tries to think of her now, he cannot picture her face.

"It's bittersweet," Dr. Malak says. "Do you know that word? Bittersweet?" Tulsi shakes his head. "It's something good that also makes you sad. Do you understand?"

"No," Tulsi says and turns to go.

At the information booth in the lobby, Tulsi finds a church directory. The first few pages contain pictures of the ministry staff with their families, smiling couples flanked by children in tiny suits and ruffled dresses, God's workers in miniature. On the last page are PK and Abigail. PK's hair looks extra spiky, his doughy face stretched into a smile. He is standing behind a seated Abigail, his big hands resting on her shoulders. Abigail is wearing a white dress with black flowers on it. She is beaming, her hands folded in her lap. Her dress swells at the stomach, a prominent bump that cannot be mistaken. Tulsi runs his fingers over the picture, the page glossy and cool. Finally, he thinks, he is beginning to understand.

Beneath the picture is a phone number and address. Tulsi writes them down on a piece of church stationery and leaves.

The first bus driver tells him to wait for the Number 17 and get off at the third stop. When it arrives, Tulsi takes a seat alone in back. It's only five o'clock and already the light is failing. A thin haze of violet rests above a line of trees. The air looks smoky, and the driveways and lawns on either side are covered in white.

By the time Tulsi gets off the bus it is full dark and beginning to snow. He walks east until he reaches Costa Drive. Most of the houses are lit up. Tulsi reads the numbers on the mailboxes until he finds 112. It's a tiny two-story home with a shoveled stone walkway and lavender window boxes. Abigail's car sits in the driveway covered in a shell of snow. The house is set back from the road. Tulsi wants to go right up and knock on the door but senses the impropriety in this. He was not invited. He has never visited their home. He worries how he will answer if PK opens the door, what he will say if asked how he's found their address. Instead, Tulsi cuts through an adjacent yard, taking care to stay close to a row of evergreens that runs parallel to a darkened garage. His sneakers crunch through the icy snow. Somewhere nearby a dog barks. Tulsi ducks against the hedge and waits for it to quiet. He jams his bare hands deep into the pockets of his coat. His feet are freezing and as he waits snow begins to cover his sleeves. He can feel the flakes settling in his collar. He tries to keep from shivering but it's hard. He's never felt so cold in his life.

When the barking stops, he continues to move, staying low to the ground. After what seems like forever, he reaches the end of the hedge and cuts through an opening into PK and Abigail's backyard. A clean sheet of snow covers the frozen grass. Unlike some of the other yards on the street, theirs is empty. No grill, no bird feeder, no swing set. Behind a sliding-glass door, the dining room is lit up. The light casts a bluish sheen over the snow before dying into darkness. Abigail and PK sit side by side at the table, their hands clasped together, their eyes closed. They are facing him, and from where he stands, Tulsi can see PK's lips moving, the urgency with which he speaks. His face looks the way it does when he prays in class, full of pain and wonder. Abigail's face is blank, her mouth set in a rigid line. After a while PK stops speaking and leans against Abigail until their cheeks touch. He kisses her on the temple, stands and leaves the room.

Tulsi looks up and follows the snowflakes as high as he can before they disappear in the dark. It isn't that far. A wind comes rushing down the yard and cuts straight through his coat, chilling his skin. He wants to step closer, wants to stand where the light touches the snow. He takes a step, then another. Abigail has her elbows on the table and is holding her head as if it weighs a thousand pounds. Her shoulders heave, but Tulsi can't tell if she is crying or coughing. He wants to know. He takes another step and when he does a motion light clicks on, bathing the yard in light. Abigail looks up and Tulsi stands perfectly still, unable to breathe. Abigail tilts her head from side to side, rushes to the window and cups her hands to the sides of her face. Tulsi is unsure if she can see him. She raises her hand and bangs her knuckles against the glass as though to frighten an animal. Tulsi hears the dog barking again, this time closer. Another light goes on in a neighboring yard. Tulsi turns and runs.

He goes back the way he came, his feet crashing through the crusty snow. When he reaches the front of the house, he realizes he's lost one of his sneakers. He keeps running down the sidewalk, his socked foot pounding against the cold concrete. Behind him there are headlights. He cuts through a yard, and then across the road into a stand of woods. He stumbles over snow-covered underbrush, his hands held out before him like a blind man. Branches whip at his face. A car door slams. He stops, falls to the earth and crawls behind a nearby tree, sits with his back against it. He cannot be sure but he thinks he has made it deep into the woods, too deep to be seen from the road. For a moment there is nothing. And then there is Abigail.

"Tulsi," she yells. Her voice sounds far away. "Tulsi, I know it's you. I saw you in the yard."

Tulsi doesn't move. He cannot feel his fingers. His sock is soaked through and his foot throbs.

"Listen," Abigail says, "you don't have to come out, but just *listen*." Tulsi leans back hard, feels the bark press into his spine. He does not want to listen. He does not want to hear a word. He wants to cover his ears, jam them with dirt, scream until his lungs burn and set fire to his frozen body. He rests his chin against his sternum, and then, with as much strength as he can manage, slams his head backward against the trunk. He does this again, keeps his eyes open so that the world jars as though trying to right itself.

Susmita is gone forever. Her children will never know him. His grandfather will work himself to death in this cold place where no one waits for anything. Abigail is leaving.

"I know you're upset," she says, "that you think you're being abandoned. I've felt that way too."

Nearby a branch cracks and falls under the weight of the wet snow. Something warm trickles down the back of his neck and soaks into his shirt. He thinks about running farther into the woods. He imagines living in the hollowed-out center of a giant tree, surviving on nuts and berries, drinking water from a clear stream, never again speaking to another living soul. It is a crazy, childish fantasy. But people have done things like this. He stays still and holds his breath. His head is spinning, white dots float near the edge of his vision. Abigail has left the headlights on and thin cuts shine through the branches. It reminds him of Susmita's hut, the way the morning light filtered through the bamboo slats. He remembers waking late, the rib work of wood beams above him, Purna and his sister already gone for the day. He remembers dressing in the stifling heat while dust particles fell through the hazy light, pulling on his sandals before rushing outside to find his friends.

The morning he left Camp Goldhap, he wanted so badly to speak to Susmita in Nepali, but even then she refused, told him it was more important than ever. He remembers standing in line beneath the scorching sun, UN volunteers helping the elderly and very young as they boarded the vans that would take them away. Soon it would be his turn. Soon he would be gone. What he wanted to tell Susmita was to never forget him, to always remember him, her brother. He recalls the frustration he felt at trying to translate the words in his head. In the end, he said nothing.

A strong wind rushes through the trees. Tulsi's entire body aches, stung by the cold. Slowly, he rises to his feet in the darkness. Abigail is calling him but instead of turning toward the direction of her voice he moves away from it. He walks carefully, feeling for branches with outstretched hands, lifting his feet high to keep from tripping.

He does not know the proper way to say goodbye, does not have the words. He moves deeper into the darkness, brushing past trees on either side, the headlights dying out among them. All he has to do is keep moving, past the pain and fatigue. Somewhere the woods will end, and the world begin.

Dear Brother,

I awoke today to find you gone. It is not new, this revelation. Weeks have passed since your departure, and yet still I search for you. In the muddy fields behind the clinic where once you gave chase with friends. Among the faces waiting to fill bottles at the cistern. In the dusty classroom of Blooming Lotus School. I do this unwittingly, knowing that you have left. It is foolish, and still, habit dictates.

Last week the monsoons reached their peak. For two days it rained, flooding the camp's pathways until they were as streams. In Venice, I've read, they have gondolas. Here the children tug one another down the muddy canals on sheets of cardboard slicked with palm oil. Their laughter is the only thing that makes the rain tolerable.

I write with prayers that this will reach you. I have inquired at the camp office as to your exact address but they are uninformed and provide only the resettlement state. They tell me they have filed a search. They say I must wait. The IOM visits the camp infrequently and my requests for information have gone unanswered. Please do not think I have forgotten you.

I wonder what your new country looks like. If it is cold. If its people treat you kindly. I pray they do. I find myself imagining you as you watch this new world. Even as a child you were observant and alert. You were always looking. Though I cannot picture it, I pray that all you see brings you peace. I send blessings to you and our hajurba. Make certain he rests. If you can, limit his tobacco.

I will write again soon, but be secure in knowing that all is as you left it. Be assured in your new home and do not worry over me. In time your absence will register. For now, I'll stop short of calling your name at the forest's edge. My little brother.

Blessings, Susmita

SEPTEMBER 2009

THE FIRST THING TULSI NOTICES about Malcolm are his fingers, dark and slender and smooth, as though sculpted from clay. It is the beginning of junior year, and they are seated across the aisle from one another in Honors Algebra. At the front of the room, their teacher, Mr. Brezicki, has shared his expectations for the quarter and has begun speaking forcefully on the perils of cheating.

"You take your lives into your own hands, people. Your lives into your own hands."

In addition to teaching algebra, Mr. Brezicki is the junior varsity baseball coach. He has brought his habits from the practice field into the classroom and pauses at intervals to spit tobacco juice into a Styrofoam cup.

Tulsi is trying to pay close attention but keeps finding himself glancing at Malcolm's hands. The nails look shellacked, as though covered with some sort of clear polish. They shine dully, like a freshly waxed floor. They are a woman's fingernails, filed and trimmed meticulously, as neatly maintained as the lawns Tulsi has passed in the rich sections of town.

Malcolm is new; a transfer student from some other city school Tulsi is unfamiliar with. Still, it would not matter if he'd been there all along. Almost a full year of attending East High School and Tulsi has yet to make a single friend. Sophomore year was spent sitting alone in the backs of classrooms, eating alone at the ends of lunch tables, rushing through the halls anonymously, arms crisscrossed over his chest, clutching his book bag straps as though they belonged to a parachute. Hallways, Tulsi believes, are the most dangerous place in school. Overexposed and unprotected, Tulsi feels not unlike a boy riding a bicycle on a freeway, the groups of friends that overtake him like semis roaring past. Only when he has arrived where he's going does he feel safe, and even then, one wrong glance and it's ruined. He has a habit of staring, born of curiosity, born of awe. And though he's tried to break it he still catches himself, and in turn is caught, gawking openly at things that intrigue him or that he does not understand. He's been called many names since coming to East. Some he knows. Some he does not.

Even now he cannot help it. The rest of Malcolm makes sense. His tight buzz cut, freshly lined so that the edges of hair look penciled in. His oversized jeans and tan Timberlands, the striped polo that does not violate the school's clothing policy. No solid reds. No solid blues. All of it makes sense to Tulsi. Everything but those hands: too perfect looking to exist on a boy, or a human being for that matter. A doll's hands. A mannequin's.

Mr. Brezicki scrawls an equation on the board. A triangle of sweat works its way up his enormous back. Tulsi opens his notebook, uncaps his pen, and then glances over at Malcolm once more.

Malcolm is staring at him.

Malcolm is smiling.

Slowly, almost imperceptibly, he leans into the space that divides Tulsi's desk from his. He keeps staring, keeps smiling. Tulsi understands that he is to lean in as well. He does so, his eyes fixed on the oxidized steel legs of Malcolm's desk. Mr. Brezicki's chalk strikes the board, scratching out numbers and letters. When Malcolm speaks, it is in a voice so low it is barely a whisper.

"Keep staring," he says, "and I'll chop your fucking balls off."

•

On Tuesdays, Tulsi's grandfather picks him up from school. Mondays are his night off at the juice plant, and though Tulsi has asked him not to, he insists. He waits in the park across the street from East's main entrance. Sometimes Tulsi finds him there feeding the pigeons that gather near the park's gazebo, tearing hunks of bread from a day-old loaf. Other times he stands at the park's edge smoking one of his rolled cigarettes. Today, Tulsi discovers him sitting alone on a bench, staring absently through the turning leaves, the look on his wrinkled face one of worry.

"Hajurba," Tulsi says, approaching him. For a moment his grandfather looks at him blankly as though they are strangers. Then the glazed expression breaks and he stands to embrace him.

"Scholar," he says, "how are the studies?"

"Good so far," Tulsi says. His grandfather lifts the bag from Tulsi's shoulder and sets it on the ground. "Things will get more difficult," Tulsi adds.

"This is always the way."

They sit for a while watching the sunlight break upon the shimmering leaves. His grandfather removes a leather pouch from his shirt pocket, pulls pinches of tobacco, and sprinkles them neatly down the center of a rolling paper. In the States he is unable to find the Suryas he smoked in Nepal and so he's taken to making his own cigarettes using a blend he buys at the Pakistani market in their neighborhood. Tulsi watches the process, the care with which his grandfather rolls the cigarette. It is his one vice, and even then he smokes no more than two or three a day, a ritual of relief. His grandfather strikes a match. The closed end of the cigarette blackens and curls. The tobacco holds a spicy sweet smell Tulsi finds comforting.

"Have you found many friends?"

It is the part of their conversations that Tulsi has come to dread.

He knows it stems from goodness, his grandfather's dutiful soul, but he has grown tired of lying. Abigail and Pastor Ken left in January, taking with them the nearest thing he'd found to friendship.

"Some," he says now, looking away.

In Camp Goldhap Tulsi had endless friends, a group who would wait for him to emerge from his sister's hut. He remembers dusty afternoons spent chasing each other through the camp's narrow paths, returning home exhausted, his legs stained to the knees with red earth. His best friend, Kiran, left before he did, resettled with his family to New Zealand. They had known each other all their lives, had grown up in that place like brothers. Here, if he looks at someone too long, he is threatened with castration. How can he possibly explain this to his grandfather?

"It is still early in the year," his grandfather says. "There is still time." He licks his pointer finger and thumb and extinguishes his cigarette, then places the butt in his shirt pocket. All around them are crushed filters and debris. His grandfather cannot comprehend littering, this carelessness of others.

On their way out, they pass a statue of the park's namesake, Brigadier General "Mad Anthony" Wayne, hero of the Revolutionary War. The statue is carved from an entire chestnut tree, its bottom still covered with bark. It depicts a stunted version of the general in a three-cornered hat, clutching the lapels of his waistcoat and staring victoriously into the breach. His grandfather stops to admire it.

"This is what I like best about America. Here they do not forget their ancestors. They honor their heroes." He smiles and wraps his arm around Tulsi's shoulder. "Maybe," he says, "they will one day build a statue of you."

•

At home, while his grandfather sleeps, Tulsi watches television. The ancient wooden console had been sitting in a corner of the apartment when his grandfather moved in, abandoned by a previous tenant. It is a Sanyo, wood-paneled and so dense it's nearly impossible to move. His grandfather never even turned it on, but when Tulsi arrived last year he was mesmerized. He has never had a TV before. For ten dollars a month, their downstairs neighbor split his cable line and runs it upstairs through an air vent. Tulsi knows this is wrong, knows that technically, when he slides the crumpled ten-dollar bill below the man's door every month, he is partaking in something illegal. But he can't help himself. Without TV, what would he know of American sports? The Cleveland Indians and Buffalo Bills, Pittsburgh with its Penguins, Pirates, and Steelers. When his grandfather is at work he watches Ultimate Fighting and *Diners, Drive Ins, and Dives*; he makes mental notes of cities he wants to visit, foods he wants to eat. He does not care much for reality television with its generic romances and embarrassing extravagance. He feels guilty even to watch. Tulsi prefers reruns of classic American sitcoms: *Full House, Boy Meets World, Friends*. They have helped to improve his English, the endless idiomatic expressions and colloquialisms. They keep him company in the evening hours. He sits entranced on the sofa, which he folds back into itself every morning after he wakes.

His favorite show, the one he watches religiously every day, is *Saved by the Bell*. He knows it's outdated, knows that people no longer dress in blinding neons and acid-washed jeans, but he doesn't care. That's not why he watches. At first he liked the show for its simplicity. There was little nuance, few jokes that he could not comprehend. But even after he started to see the same episodes replayed, he kept watching. What he likes now is the show's order, the way everything at Bayside High seems to fall into place. No matter what trouble is stirring in the show's opening scenes—Slater's underage drinking, Lisa's cruel gossip, Jessie secretly indulging in diet pills—things always fall into place by episode's end. The gang heads over to the Max for milkshakes and fries, no one's feelings are hurt, Zack stares right into the camera and smiles that impossibly perfect smile. It gives Tulsi a feeling not unlike relief. All the characters, despite their differences, remain friends. Jocks, overachievers, fashionistas. In this world it doesn't matter. Still, he's aware of the role popularity plays, how powerful a thing it can be. Some mornings when he waits for the bus, the cold lake wind cutting through his jacket, he reminds himself that this is how you make friends. Be a Zack, he thinks. Do not be a Screech.

•

Varsity soccer tryouts are being held that Saturday at Family First Sports Park. Tulsi arrived in the States too late to play as a sophomore, but has promised his grandfather he'll try out this year. He played on a team at Camp Goldhap and was regarded a solid defender, quick to the ball and persistent. Even so, he has his doubts. He hasn't been on a soccer field since leaving Nepal, hasn't run outside of gym class.

He takes the bus to Family First and arrives half an hour early. The complex is huge, a concrete maze of indoor basketball courts and AstroTurf soccer fields and a giant domed bubble that serves as a year-round driving range. Out back are tennis courts, a baseball diamond, and another soccer field where the tryouts will be. A few boys pass a ball near the far goal; others stretch. A group of parents linger near the bench. It is early September but the mornings are already cool, the sun barely visible above the distant tree line. Tulsi jogs toward the field. Sport duffels and bags of gear cover the grass near the bench. Tulsi has brought nothing but his old cleats, swinging by their laces from his shoulder.

He is sitting on the ground slipping them on when a shadow settles over him.

"What the hell are you doing here?" Malcolm asks. He's dressed in wind pants and a faded Arsenal jersey.

"I'm here for the tryouts."

"These aren't *real* tryouts," Malcolm says. "Everybody makes the team. It's just to see who's gonna start. To figure out a depth chart."

A fist of relief opens in Tulsi's chest. He's made the team simply by showing up.

"Position?" Malcolm asks.

"Sweeper, but I can play fullback and midfield too."

Malcolm stares at him, a look of confusion plastered on his face. He sits down and strips off his wind pants to reveal a pair of old aqua Umbros. Even compared with Tulsi's weathered blue mesh shorts, they are ridiculous. They look like something someone on *Saved by the Bell* would wear. Malcolm is skinnier than Tulsi thought, long legs lean and hairless. He has not brought a bag either, and this makes Tulsi feel better. He has, however, brought a pair of shin guards, which he pulls on over his cleats. He reaches into the pocket of his wind pants and takes out a set of padded gloves.

"Are you a keeper?" Tulsi asks.

"Damn right," Malcolm says without looking up. "At least I used to be. That's the position I played at my old school."

Tulsi has avoided Malcolm since the last time they spoke, refusing to let his eyes wander over in Mr. Brezicki's class and generally keeping to himself the way he always has. He's surprised to hear Malcolm speaking so openly to him now, impressed by the easy confidence of his voice.

"I was a starter," Malcolm says. He smooths the shin guards with his manicured fingers.

"What was your old school?"

"Central," Malcolm says. He squints as though the sun is in his eyes. "East plays them the second-to-last game of the season. Payback's a bitch."

"What happened?" This is the most Tulsi has spoken to another student all year. He's afraid he's overstepping some invisible boundary, but Malcolm intrigues him. From the outside he seems somehow fragile, but when he speaks there is an anger Tulsi recognizes.

"Long story." Malcolm pivots the lower half of his right leg behind him and leans over his left thigh, stretching. "But let's just say I'm not welcome back anytime soon. Some people there chose to fuck with the wrong guy." He grips his calf, lowers his head. "What about you?" he asks. "What's your story?"

A year ago, this question would have baffled Tulsi. *What's your story? What's your deal? What's up?* The phrases sounding related and yet each cloaked in its own unique meaning. TV has prepared him for all of this.

"I didn't play last year," Tulsi says. "I started school too late. But I played in Nepal, in a camp there. That's where I'm from."

Malcolm, still stretching, looks up and smiles. "I don't know about all that," he says. "Just be happy you're not a keeper, cause that shit is mine." He lowers his head and stretches the fingers of his left hand toward the toe of his cleat, their pinkish tips falling just short.

●

The tryout begins with running, an easy jog at first and then wind sprints that light a blaze like burning tinder in Tulsi's chest. The coach is a stout Englishman who looks better equipped for rugby than soccer. His accent reminds Tulsi of the UN volunteers from Goldhap. After a while, the coach says it's time for suicides. Tulsi knows what this word means. The image of a ruined banker stepping from a ledge flashes in his mind. He is confused until it is his turn to run. Afterward he is no longer confused. They take turns dashing to cones set fifteen meters apart, touching the ground and returning to midfield after each interval, repeating this until they have reached the goal line. They double over and gasp for air until it is their turn to sprint again. The morning chill has worn off and the sun is high and bright above them. One boy vomits and Tulsi turns away, thankful it was not him. Occasionally he catches sight of Malcolm running, his gait upright and awkward.

They dribble through cones to test their agility and handling skills. It's been so long since Tulsi played that even the touch of the ball feels strange. Soon it comes back to him, though, and in no time at all it becomes an extension of his foot, an object attached to him by a string. He keeps the ball slightly out in front of him as he was taught, his gravity low and centered for cuts. For a moment, as he dribbles between the sidelines, his cleats biting into the soft turf, his head on a pivot scanning the anonymous field, he forgets that he is at Family First Sports Park in Erie, Pennsylvania. He forgets he is not surrounded by the friends who learned this game beside him, friends he's lived and played with all his life, friends now scattered across the world like ash. Tulsi reaches the far sideline and delivers a swift pass to the boy waiting there.

●

When practice is over, Coach Davies eyes Tulsi inquisitively.

"Not bad," he says, rubbing a stubby-fingered hand over his crew cut. "Not half bad. Your endurance needs work, but that goes for the lot of you. Stick with it and you'll have a shot at first team."

Tulsi nods and straightens his aching back. He does his best not to smile until the coach turns.

On his way toward the parking lot, Tulsi sees Malcolm standing near the batting cages.

"How was your practice?" Tulsi asks.

Malcolm shrugs. "I'm already behind 'cause I didn't play here last year. Seems like they're pretty settled on that Kolwitz kid."

Tulsi knows Kolwitz from school, a smug senior who has never so much as acknowledged his existence. While practicing, players were separated by position, but during a break Tulsi watched Malcolm defending shots in goal. His style was unorthodox but effective, his lankiness helping him deflect high kicks to the corners.

"Maybe the Kolwitz kid will get hurt," Tulsi says. He is surprised by himself, but even more surprised that he generally means it.

"Yeah, he's a cocky prick," Malcolm says. "Swift kick to the nuts might do him some good." They both laugh before Malcolm's expression goes serious. "I'd just like to get a fair shot, you know?"

"Yes," Tulsi says. And he does.

●

Tulsi is almost to the bus stop when he hears someone calling from behind. It is Malcolm, standing beside a light blue Buick LeSabre, one arm on the passenger side roof, the other beckoning Tulsi.

Malcolm sits up front with his mother, a heavy Black woman with an abundance of dark layered hair. She smiles at Tulsi in the rearview mirror and Tulsi smiles back. Sunlight has baked the interior, and he can feel the warmth of the flaking leather seat through his T-shirt. The car smells like old McDonald's and wintergreen gum. A pop song plays low on the radio.

"How was practice?" Malcolm's mother asks, tapping out the rhythm against the steering wheel. Tulsi waits for Malcolm to respond but when he doesn't, Tulsi says, "Good, ma'am. We had to run a lot."

"You're sweet, but none of this ma'am business," she says. "I'm Rachel. Plain old Rachel."

Tulsi cannot imagine calling this adult woman by her first name, but he thanks her regardless. The windows are open just a crack, letting in the afternoon air. They drive down upper Peach Street, below the I-90 overpass. A casino and racetrack have been built one exit east and industry has sprung up in accordance: hotels and chain restaurants and gas stations, even an indoor water park with a covered slide that juts out like an appendage.

It is sunny and warm. Soon September will turn on them, and it is as if the whole city knows it. Brewster's Ice Cream is packed, weekend shoppers wheel brimming carts through the Walmart parking lot. Rachel drives slowly and Tulsi takes it all in. A pair of motorcycles rumbles past.

"You boys must be famished," Rachel says. "They feed you?"

Malcolm hits the seek button and the music vanishes. "No," he says.

"Good," his mother says. "I don't want you eating junk anyway. I'll fix you both something at home. That sound good to you, honey? Can you eat?" Tulsi waits again for Malcolm to answer but then catches Rachel's eyes fixed on him in the rearview. She is speaking to him. He is *honey*.

"Yes," Tulsi says. "I can eat."

•

Malcolm's house is not far from where Tulsi lives with his grandfather on Eleventh Street. It is a small split-level with aluminum siding. Inside, it is warm and smells of incense and cooking oil. A ceiling fan circulates the still air. Tulsi feels the coziness of the home immediately, the sensation of it enveloping him. It's a far cry from his grandfather's apartment with its threadbare rugs and chipped white walls, the vinyl plank flooring scratched and cold. Rachel disappears into the kitchen while Tulsi and Malcolm sit on the living room couch watching the Indians game. The TV is a Sony, its flat screen the size of an oven door. The picture is incredibly clear, not at all the pixilated glow of the Sanyo.

"Who are your teams?" Malcolm asks.

"I like them all," Tulsi says, and he does. He admires every aspect: the grace of the athletes, the pristine fields on which they perform, even the umpires and referees with their unmistakable authority. When one team is behind, Tulsi favors them. If that team overtakes the other by a sizeable score, he shifts allegiance again.

"You can't like them *all*," Malcolm says. "Erie's in between Cleveland, Buffalo, and Pittsburgh. You gotta choose one and stick with that city."

"How do you choose?" Tulsi asks.

"You gotta have a reason, but it doesn't really matter. Like me, for instance. My mom lived in Cleveland when she was in nursing school, so I root for all Cleveland teams. Browns, Cavs," Malcolm points at the screen. "Indians."

Tulsi nods as he takes this in. It's yet another lesson he's learning about his new home: the importance of choosing sides. He hears Rachel humming a soft tune in the kitchen and then the sound of something sizzling. A door in the back hallway closes shut. A moment later a tall girl emerges wearing black slacks, a white button-down shirt, and a green tie. Her hair is braided into a ponytail and hangs over one shoulder down her chest.

"Tell Mom I'm headed to work," she says, rummaging through her purse.

"Tell her yourself," Malcolm says. "She's in the kitchen."

The girl looks up and acknowledges Tulsi's presence with a nod. Her dark eyes are rimmed in purple mascara, her lips shiny with pink gloss. A gold stud peeks from one nostril. Tulsi is frozen by her beauty and must reckon with it. If he stares slack-jawed or looks away too quickly he's caught. Ignoring it out of hand is even worse. He turns to the game and then back to the girl, then back to the game once more. Stupid, he thinks, so stupid.

"Who's your friend?" the girl asks. "And why are you trying to act hard? You showing off?"

"Tulsi, meet my sister, Kyla, future Olive Garden lifer."

Kyla steps forward and shakes Tulsi's hand, then delivers a halfhearted slap to the back of Malcolm's head. "Let me know when someone's willing to hire your sorry ass," she says. And then she is gone.

Rachel emerges from the kitchen a few minutes later carrying two plates of hot dogs slathered in a sweet chili she calls Greek sauce. Chopped onions and melting cheddar cheese sit atop the steaming buns. Tulsi and Malcolm eat in front of the TV. In the ninth inning, Jhonny Peralta hits a walk-off single that gives the Indians the win. Malcolm jumps off the couch and pumps his fist. Tulsi is excited as well, returning Malcolm's high five. When the game is over, he walks home, the hand that Kyla shook buried deep in his pocket.

•

Tulsi arrives home to find his grandfather on the stoop speaking with their neighbor, Mr. Bhandari. In the year Tulsi has lived here, Eleventh Street has become something of a tiny global village. It is the area most utilized for resettlement by Erie's International Institute, and so their neighbors are from all over: Somalia, Sudan, Bosnia, Syria, Iraq. Tulsi cannot always pinpoint someone's country of origin, but he can spot those who have just arrived. There is a bewildered, uncertain look to them that is always the same. It is like staring into a mirror and seeing himself a year ago.

"How was your practice?" his grandfather asks. He is dressed in his rest clothes: a weathered pair of olive-green cargo pants and a long white kurta that has been with him since the camps, its fabric yellowed with age. When Tulsi first arrived, he found that his grandfather would sometimes walk through the neighborhood in nothing more than sandals, an undershirt, and a pair of pajama pants. Tulsi had to explain to him that things were different here, that this was not acceptable.

"I made the team," Tulsi says. For a second he considers telling him that everyone makes the team but his grandfather's smile is so wide that he dismisses the thought. His grandfather pulls him in for an embrace and Tulsi inhales the sweet scent of tobacco and tea leaves.

"Little Beckham," his grandfather says. "Look at my star footballer," he tells Mr. Bhandari, his arm snug around Tulsi's shoulder.

"Here they call it soccer," Tulsi says. His grandfather releases him and pats his head as he has done since he was a boy.

"Ah, soccer," he repeats, testing the sound of it. "Even better."

Mr. Bhandari nods. He is stoic and wary of all things American, but even he seems a bit proud.

"It was a long practice, no?" his grandfather says. "Did you take the bus?"

"We finished at noon. My friend Malcolm gave me a ride. His mother, actually."

My friend Malcolm. The words roll strangely from his tongue. He is not certain that he and Malcolm are technically even friends. Still, he knows his grandfather will be pleased. More than anything, this is what he wants in this moment.

"You must be careful accepting rides from new people," Mr. Bhandari says, his voice stern. "They told us this when we arrived."

"He's a classmate of mine."

"No matter," Mr. Bhandari says. "Do not forget that there have been attacks against us outside this neighborhood."

Tulsi's grandfather releases a sigh and looks at his friend in exasperation. "Kazi," he says. "You could steal the joy from your own daughter's wedding."

"I am only being truthful, and you know it. There are some who do not like us. I have met many who are unhappy we are here."

"Right now, Kazi, *I* am unhappy you are here."

Tulsi tries to suppress a laugh as Mr. Bhandari huffs and walks away.

●

That night, to celebrate, Tulsi and his grandfather order pizza and chicken wings from Lucchetti's. Wings are among Tulsi's favorite American foods, the spicier the better. They set up folding chairs on the stoop and eat outside, passing a two-liter of soda back and forth between them and taking slices right from the box. The air is only slightly chillier than it was all day and both Tulsi and his grandfather have put on sweatshirts. Music is audible from an open window down the block and a cluster of fireflies works its way through the strip of grass near the sidewalk.

It is at times like these when Tulsi thinks of his sister. If he allows it, he will find himself imagining not only where she might be and with whom, but whether or not she fits there, whether or not she has achieved any harmony with the world.

It is not that he is unhappy in this moment. It is just the opposite, his happiness laced with something like guilt. He tries to convince himself that Susmita would want him to be content. It is an argument he holds with himself over and over.

A pair of moths waltz near the porch light, darting in and out of its ambient glow. His grandfather closes the lid on the pizza box and scoots it beneath his chair. In the distance Tulsi hears children laughing.

•

Over the next few weeks Tulsi and Malcolm establish a routine. After school they ride the bus together to Family First for practice. Once it's ended, they wait until Rachel finishes her afternoon shift at Hamot Hospital and comes to pick them up. Sometimes, if it's empty, they sneak out onto the putt-putt course. The balls and putters are locked in a shed once the paying customers leave so instead they play with pebbles, rolling them toward the hole and counting each roll as a stroke, competing against each other while keeping score in their heads. Other times they shoot baskets on the outdoor courts or watch people hit golf balls at the driving range. But most of the time, they keep practicing alone, borrowing a soccer ball from the front desk. Tulsi lines up penalty shots and Malcolm tends goal, and they continue that way—Tulsi working his placement, Malcolm stalking beneath the crossbar—until they see the blue LeSabre pull into the parking lot. Malcolm is quick but Tulsi can usually beat him with a kick to the upper corners. Even so, for every goal he makes, there's another that Malcolm blocks or that sails wide. They are both improving, Tulsi can sense it. He hopes the extra work will not go unnoticed by their coach.

Sometimes Rachel has to stay late at the hospital. The days are growing shorter, and if she's delayed long enough it becomes too dark to keep practicing. On these nights, sitting beside one another on the empty field, Tulsi and Malcolm talk.

For a long time Malcolm hadn't asked about anything that had happened before Tulsi arrived in the States, their conversations centering on sports and school gossip. And so Tulsi had not volunteered his stories. Then one day, unprompted, Tulsi began to tell of his time in the camps, the memories pouring forth as though they'd been stopped up for too long. He found once he began that it was hard for him to stop, and to his surprise, Malcolm showed a sincere interest, as though he'd secretly wondered all along.

Now when they talk, Tulsi describes the identical rows of thatch-roofed huts, the endless lines for rations at the distribution center and for water at the cisterns. He recounts playing in the forests that surrounded the camp, he and his friends chasing each other through the thickets of trees. He even tells Malcolm about Abigail and the English class he took upon first arriving, how Abigail left Erie so her husband could be the head pastor in another church, in another city. How he has not heard from her since. He tells Malcolm the things he likes most about living here, and those that still confuse him. He shares many things, but even when he feels the urge, he never mentions his sister, or his worries about whether she is okay. He never reveals his secret hope to one day find her. These are things he can barely admit to himself.

•

One night Malcolm tells Tulsi that his father died in a car wreck when he was very young. He describes his memories of his father, a sequence of blurred snapshots: a hunched silhouette lacing up his winter boots in the front hallway, a slender man wrapping his arms around Rachel while she stands at the kitchen sink, a figure shutting off his bedroom light and closing the door.

"My aunt told me that for a long time my mom couldn't get out of bed in the morning. She hardly left her room, let alone the house."

"What happened?" Tulsi asks. "How'd she get better?"

"I'm not sure. One day she just did. I guess it was like she understood or something."

"Understood what?" Tulsi asks. A breeze works its way across the field, bending the taller grass of the sidelines.

"I don't know. That life keeps going, I guess. That you can't just say 'Fuck it.' She had us to take care of. She moved on."

Above the trees the sky is a soft purple, some stars already visible in the early evening. The parking lot behind them is empty but in the distance there is the hum of semis traveling along Interstate 90. *Moved on*, Tulsi thinks, weighing the words in his mind, sensing their finality.

•

On most nights, Rachel invites Tulsi to stay for dinner and though he feels guilty for not eating with his grandfather and is perpetually afraid of accepting too much hospitality, it is hard for him to say no. Rachel, he has learned, is an excellent cook, and some nights, if she is not working, Kyla is there as well. A tension exists between Kyla and Malcolm that is as obvious to Tulsi as the food they eat, but he attributes this to sibling rivalry. Rachel dotes on each of them and even Tulsi cannot help but crave her affection and approval. For her children it must be worse, both wanting their fair share and more.

The four of them sit at the circular wooden table in the kitchen and eat. Rachel always begins by saying grace. Tulsi bends his head along with her though neither Malcolm nor Kyla does. It is a habit Abigail instilled in him, though after she left Tulsi quit praying. He still thinks about God but not as he once did.

At the dinner table they talk about their days and Tulsi listens and answers when spoken to. Afterward he helps Rachel clear the table and load the dishwasher. These dinners are exceptional in their normalcy, Tulsi understands, but not for him. For him, they are something else altogether, a routine that fills him with gratitude, a glimpse at something he cannot quite name.

•

After dinner they play Xbox in Malcolm's bedroom. Malcolm is a gamer and belongs to several online teams. Most of the time Tulsi doesn't play but simply watches as Malcolm navigates his avatar, speaking into his headset to coordinate moves with other players who could be anywhere. After a while Malcolm shuts off the Xbox and opens his laptop.

"What is this?" Tulsi asks, pointing at the screen. "This program?"

"You don't have Facebook?"

"I don't have a computer," Tulsi tells him.

"You don't need one. I mean, you can use mine and the ones in the lab at school."

In half an hour they have created him an account. Using his cell phone, Malcolm takes a picture of Tulsi and then uploads it for his profile picture. Tulsi is still dressed in his soccer clothes: a sweat stained T-shirt and crinkled wind pants, his silky black hair a peaked mess, but Malcolm insists.

"Everyone has Facebook," he says. "This is how you keep up with people. It's the only way to know if anybody's talking shit about you." In the past few weeks, Tulsi has come to understand that Malcolm is at best highly concerned with how others view him and at worst completely paranoid. He suspects there is much more to the story of why Malcolm left Central, but he does not want to ask. He does not want to upset the first real friend he's made since arriving.

Malcolm leaves to use the bathroom while Tulsi regards his profile page, his disheveled self staring back at him. So far his account has only one friend, Malcolm. Tulsi is still happy, even more so for seeing it spelled out onscreen, as though this somehow makes it official. He is exploring the News Feed when Malcolm rushes back in.

"Something's up," he says. "I heard Kyla talking on the phone. She's headed out."

"To work?" Tulsi asks.

"No," Malcolm says as if Tulsi has missed the entire point. "*Out* out. To a club."

"Oh, cool," Tulsi says, still confused. Kyla passes the open door. Malcolm calls to her and a moment later she reappears.

"What?" she asks. She's dressed in her Olive Garden outfit; a bulging purse dangles from her shoulder. Tulsi is still smitten but knows he doesn't stand a chance. Kyla is a senior at Central and, Tulsi suspects, popular in a way he cannot compete with. Tulsi, not knowing what else to do, raises his hand in a half-hearted wave.

"Where you headed?" Malcolm asks.

"Where's it look like? I have the dinner shift, then I'm spending the night at Laurel's."

"Cool," Malcolm says. "Have fun." Kyla rolls her eyes and turns to leave. Before she's out the door, Malcolm says, "Maybe I'll ask Mom if we can stop in for dessert. They have that tiramisu." Malcolm looks at Tulsi. "You ever had tiramisu, man? It's this delicious Italian dessert they make with coffee and whipped cream. My mom loves it."

Kyla spins around. "Don't be an idiot. Mom's not gonna drive your lazy ass up Peach Street on a Friday night all so you can get some dessert."

"Yeah, you're probably right. Maybe I'll have her call the restaurant and ask if you can bring some home." Tulsi senses the dynamic of the conversation changing in front of him. He wishes he were still in the kitchen with Rachel, or out on the couch watching TV. Kyla narrows her eyes.

"What did you hear?"

"Nothing. Just sounds like you have a big night planned."

"Keep your mouth shut, okay?"

Malcolm takes a seat on the edge of his bed, his hands folded before him thoughtfully. "What's in it for me?"

"How about absolutely nothing," Kyla says. "Let's start there."

"Fuck you," Malcolm says, "you're on your own."

"All right, fine. What do you want?"

Malcolm looks at Tulsi, then back at his sister. "We want to go with you."

"No way," Kyla says, waving a braceleted arm in front of her face.

"Fine," Malcolm says, "maybe I'll tell Mom she should call Laurel's house to see what you two are up to. You know, since you're *staying* there."

Kyla rests her hand on her hip and stares at Malcolm, her forehead creased. "What are you going to tell Mom *you're* doing?"

"I'll tell her I'm sleeping over at Tulsi's."

Kyla turns to Tulsi then back to her brother. "You can't even get in."

"Bullshit," Malcolm says. "*You* can get us in."

Her dark eyes are hard with anger, but Tulsi can tell that she is trapped. He does not want to be part of anything that upsets her, but knows his allegiance is to Malcolm.

"Fine," she says, "but get him out of those fucking soccer clothes. I'm not taking either of you dressed like that."

•

From outside, the King's Rook is built to look like a castle. A narrow parapet lines the front of the building and rounded stone turrets sit at either end of its façade. Situated near the train tracks at Eighteenth and Peach, it's in an area of town Tulsi has never been to before. They park a block away and Kyla tells them to get out of the car. From the corner of his eye Tulsi sees Kyla changing in the front seat, undoing the green tie and sliding out of her pressed black slacks. Malcolm talks excitedly and doesn't notice Tulsi's glance as Kyla opens her bulging purse and pulls out a bright wad of fabric. When she finally exits the car, she's wearing a slinky purple dress with thin straps. Tulsi can feel his pulse quicken. It is cold outside but sweat beads his brow.

"Man, I can't believe this is really happening," Malcolm says as they trail Kyla. He has still not explained what exactly the King's Rook is or why they're going there, but Tulsi knows it is something they are technically not supposed to be doing. His thoughts move to his grandfather, who is just now starting his Friday night shift at the juice plant. He will not be home until nine tomorrow morning and so they have the whole night ahead of them. Tulsi's stomach sways with a mix of nervous anticipation and guilt.

"So listen," Kyla calls back to them. "Just act cool. I'll take care of it, but if I can't get you in, you're on your own." She walks briskly, her high heels nearly skipping along the sidewalk. Tulsi is dressed in dark jeans and a black T-shirt Malcolm loaned him. The jeans are slightly too small and so Tulsi has left the button undone, pulling the bottom of the T-shirt down to hide it.

"And if anybody asks," Kyla says, "you're both freshmen at Clarion home for the weekend."

The three of them wait in a line that stretches halfway down the block. Kyla stands in front, a few steps ahead to make it look as if she is not with them. She scans the line anxiously, then pulls her cell phone from her purse and texts.

"It's college ID night," Malcolm says. "You've got to be eighteen and over, but Kyla can get us in."

At the door a muscular man in a graphic T-shirt sits on a stool checking IDs. His hair is buzzed, and a sleeve of tattoos covers his right arm from elbow to wrist. The skin of the other is bare save the splintering of veins beneath it. Kyla leans in and hugs him and the man rests one hand on the lowest part of her back. Tulsi's cheeks grow warm and he looks away.

"Kyla," he says, "long time, no see. You getting too good for us?" A full suit of armor adorns the wall behind him. Loud music plays from inside. Tulsi can feel the bass thumping through the soles of his sneakers.

"Been crazy busy," she says, laying an arm across the man's bulging shoulders and turning around. "Clyde, this is my brother, Malcolm, and his friend."

The man looks them up and down, then turns back to Kyla. "I didn't even know you had a brother."

"Yeah, he's a freshman at Clarion. They're just home for the weekend."

"Sure they are," Clyde says, half-smiling. "They got their college ID's?"

Malcolm straightens up, pulls out his wallet, and rifles through. After a while, he slaps it shut. "Fuck," he says. "I think I left it in the dorm."

The man takes a sip from a plastic cup. "You know the rules, Kyla," he says. Tulsi can feel the stares of the people in line behind them. He pulls closer to Malcolm, tries to will himself invisible.

"Please, Clyde. Just this once?" Kyla says.

The man sets his cup on the table beside him and rubs a thick hand over his buzz cut. "All right, fuck it. Ten a piece for baby brother and his friend." Kyla leans in and plants a kiss on the man's cheek.

Malcolm produces a twenty-dollar bill and hands it over to the man, who then stamps their hands. Tulsi watches him slip the money into his jeans pocket as they follow Kyla into the club.

•

Once inside, Kyla disappears almost immediately, leaving Tulsi and Malcolm on their own. The club is dark and crowded with throngs of warm bodies: dancing, screaming above the music, weaving in and out of each other like some giant pulsing amoeba. Adding to the confusion are the flashing strobe lights that puncture the darkness like lightning. Tulsi keeps close to Malcolm as he maneuvers his way toward a railing. They stand at its edge and look down. Below is a gigantic dance floor filled with couples rubbing against each other hungrily. A circle has formed in one corner and people take turns dancing through it. A DJ yells into a microphone, his words unintelligible above the music.

"What is this place?" Tulsi asks, nearly screaming to be heard.

"I told you, man. It's a club."

"Yes, but what do you do here?"

Malcolm throws an arm over Tulsi's shoulder and pulls him close. He lets loose an exaggerated laugh, artificial and too loud, even for this place.

"Look around, T. You dance, you talk to people. We're in. That's all that matters."

The upstairs of the club is quieter. A bar lines one wall and perpendicular to it is an abandoned yellow school bus positioned between wooden pillars. Its back doors are swung open like a gate and painted along one side in black lettering is *Boogie on the Bus with Us*. The seats have been ripped out so that the entire interior is hulled, leaving nothing but a steering wheel and the corrugated steel floor. Tulsi peeks in and sees couples making out against the sliding glass windows. At the far end, where the driver's seat should be, two girls kiss intensely, the taller of them pressing the other up onto the dash. A blue strobe flashes, and Tulsi sees that both have their hands down the other's pants.

When he turns around, Malcolm has vanished. A rush of panic fills him. He scans the room. Everywhere gyrating figures grind each other into any object stable enough to hold them. Bodies pulse in time to the electronic beat; glow sticks waving from outstretched hands trace their movements in fading neon arcs. The scene appears nightmarish, a subterranean world full of dangers unseen. Tulsi regrets agreeing to come, regrets standing idly by as Malcolm lied to Rachel and told her he'd be staying at Tulsi's house. He is complicit in this deception of Rachel, who has been nothing but kind to him, who cooks meals and allows him to sit at her table as if he was another son. Tulsi heads toward the stairwell and is halfway there when he spots Kyla talking with a group of girls. He walks over and waits until one of the girls looks at him with annoyance. Kyla turns and faces him.

"What's up?" she says in a matter-of-fact tone. Her eyes are glazed and she sways where she stands, as though fighting a strong wind. Her purple dress is hiked up on one side. Tulsi pretends not to notice.

"Have you seen Malcolm?"

"He flake on you?" she says. "Typical."

"Who's this?" one of the other girls asks, pointing a drink at Tulsi. Big silver hoops swivel from her ears. "He's kinda cute." She takes a step in Tulsi's direction and lays an open hand on his chest, pulling the fabric of his T-shirt taut before pushing him back slightly. The other girls laugh and Tulsi's palms grow slick. He senses that he is the object of a joke, something to be laughed at. He wishes he could vanish, just close his eyes and reopen them in his grandfather's apartment. The club is only a few miles from his home on Eleventh Street but suddenly the distance feels much farther, as if he is in a different world altogether.

"Tanya, you slut," Kyla says smiling. "You think anything with a dick is 'kinda cute.'" The others laugh. They go back to their conversation and to ignoring him outright. Tulsi turns and walks away.

Back downstairs Tulsi makes his way to the railing and circles it, scanning both the room around him and the dance floor below. When he's nearly completed a full rotation, he spots Malcolm standing at the edge of the dance floor talking to an older boy. His anger vanishes at the sight of him. All he feels is relief. Relief to not be alone in this place. Relief to have a friend to go to. He makes his way down the stairs just as Malcolm and the boy finish talking.

"Where'd you go?" Tulsi asks, trying to sound nonchalant. "I thought you left."

"Left? We're just getting started, T."

"Who was that?"

Malcolm smiles widely. "Just follow me." He cuts across a corner of the dance floor, negotiating his way past the grinding couples. Tulsi trails behind.

●

Upstairs Malcolm pushes through the bathroom door and Tulsi follows. A man in an oversized Lakers jersey holds his hands beneath a hot air dryer, its roar filling the narrow room. Malcolm disappears into one of the stalls and Tulsi, unsure what to do, begins to wash his hands. The dryer clicks off and the man leaves. A moment later Malcolm emerges from the stall.

"Okay, good," he says, seeing that the man has left. "Look." He holds out his right hand. Two purple pills sit in his open palm, the outline of a leaping dolphin etched into each.

"What is it?" Tulsi asks.

"Drugs, motherfucker!" Malcolm is beside himself with glee. "It's fucking Ecstasy, man. I scored it from that guy. One for you, one for me. It's our ticket to an epic night." The door swings open and Malcolm buries his hand in his pocket. A man rushes past them and into the first stall. There's the sound of gagging and then the sickening splatter of vomit on the tiled floor. "Come on, let's get out of here."

In the hallway outside the bathroom, Malcolm slides one of the pills into Tulsi's hand. "I've never done it before, but Kyla has. Plenty of times. It's supposed to be awesome."

Tulsi doesn't say anything, just stands there, the pill as solid as a pebble in his palm. "I think I might go," he says suddenly, almost without meaning to. It's as if the words come from somewhere else, somewhere outside of him.

"What?" Malcolm says. People glide past the hallway laughing and screaming over the music. Those with wristbands carry drinks, some of them cradling three or four against their chests. Tulsi stands there looking out, watching as the flashing lights paint their faces in ghoulish reds and greens. Malcolm's expression changes gradually, as though he is beginning to understand something important for the first time.

"Fine," he says, "fucking go if you want to. But I'm staying. I just wanted us to have a good time."

Tulsi leans one shoulder against the wall. "I know," he says. There is a lull in the music filled by the DJ screaming out to the crowd.

"Listen, T. It's not a big deal. Trust me." Malcolm pulls his hand from his pocket and pops the pill into his mouth. Tulsi watches his

Adam's apple rise and fall. The DJ quiets as a new beat starts up. Tulsi thinks of all the weekends he's spent alone since coming to the States, all the times he's fallen asleep watching late-night TV while his grandfather is at work, the fuzzy images of the Sanyo working their way into his dreams. He understands he is not in the position to lose a friend. Not when one is all he has. He pinches the pill between his thumb and forefinger and places it onto his tongue.

•

An hour later Tulsi stands near the center of the dance floor. Lights flash at the edges of his vision like scenery streaming by the windshield of a fast-moving car. He no longer simply hears the music; he feels it working inside him, tugging at his bones, his blood, the densest parts of his body, pulling every piece of himself inward until he feels he could explode if he needed to, if that's what he desired. He is unsure when, exactly, this transition took place, when he went from being the old Tulsi to suddenly inhabiting this new and better version of himself. He cannot think about it for too long. It is a trivial concern.

Malcolm dances around him, his body a liquid thing. He is smiling, and Tulsi realizes that so is he. Everyone, it seems, is smiling. Tulsi lets the music move him and he understands, with a clarity he has never known, that that is exactly what is happening. It is not him moving, dancing, circling the same square of laminated flooring over and over. It is something that is being done *to* him, and he is watching it happen, utterly transparent and untroubled. He is floating. He is light. He senses more than he ever has that he is completely himself.

Across the room a girl with jet-black hair dances in and out of the shifting columns of light. Glow sticks dangle from her neck. When she twirls they twirl with her, swinging out like a living shadow of her rotations. She moves perfectly, twirling faster and faster, arms outstretched like wings, dark hair a revolving record, and then she stops suddenly, as though she were a spinning coin and an outstretched finger has been laid upon her. When she stops, it is as though Tulsi knew she would, was aware of it before it even happened. She is left facing his exact direction. Tulsi understands without a doubt that there was no other way. She looks up, the dark curtain of her hair concealing her face. She brushes it away, and Tulsi is not at all surprised to see that the girl is his sister.

Those are her eyes.

That is her smile.

It is Susmita, lost to him no more.

Brother,

I write in haste. Three nights past I awoke to what I took for fever. A burning in my lungs, my eyes stinging. When I rose from bed I found Purna collapsed beside it. Smoke rolled through the slats of our hut, choking us. A great conflagration was alive in our camp. I remember I screamed. In little time neighbors arrived and helped Purna and I to safety. His mother had been in the care of the clinic. She too is safe.

Three nights and still the ashes smolder, two thirds of the camp gone. The official word has not arrived, but those in charge believe the fire's source to be a cookstove. You recall how we crowded around them at meals. Such a small, comforting thing. So much ruin.

Brother, I have faith this letter will find you. It is only to say that my husband and I are well. Again, we are without a home but it is a trial we have known before. They have moved us to Camp Beldangi Extension. We are welcome here though there is no room for us. Do not worry, brother. God will make a way. I must go, as there are many preparations ahead. Have peace in your new life and assure our hajurba that his granddaughter lives and breathes.

When I awoke and stood, a thought came to me. A thought of you among the flames. Such time has passed and still, as I retreated from our home, I reached down where you once had laid. I held the terror of you being left behind. Know that my only solace was finding the space you once occupied vacant, and understanding that your absence meant you were safe.

Your Sister

Before he can reach his sister she is gone, replaced by air. A fog machine pumps billowing clouds that descend upon the dance pit. Tulsi scans the faces of the other dancers, all of them still smiling, still moving. She is not among them, but rather than be worried, Tulsi feels at ease. He has seen her. That is what was expected of him and he has done it. How can he worry when a gift was offered and received?

He turns to look for Malcolm and sees him standing near the wall, drinking from a bottle of water. At the sight of the water he's struck by the dryness of his own mouth. When he runs his tongue over his teeth, the sensation is one of scraping. He walks toward Malcolm but before he can reach him he feels a hand on his shoulder, every cell alerting him of its touch. He turns, fully expecting to see Susmita. Instead, he finds a girl with bright pink hair. It is the color of the lipstick worn by women in cigarette ads, vibrant and glossy. He wants to reach forward and touch it. He wants to know how that color feels.

"Do you know him?" the girl asks. At first Tulsi is certain she is asking about someone they have already alluded to, as though he's awoken in this conversation midstream and *him* is a person they've been talking about for some time. Tulsi is trying to recall who this *him* might be when he notices the girl motioning over his shoulder with her chin. Tulsi turns and sees she's referring to Malcolm. He is still by the wall, rolling the water bottle back and forth across his forehead, his dark skin slick with sweat.

Tulsi looks at the girl and nods. She lets her hand fall from his shoulder.

"Man," she says. "It's too bad how that shit went down last year at Central." Tulsi is confusedm then remembers that Central is the high school Malcolm went to before coming to East.

"Him?" he asks.

"Yeah, him," the girl says. "My younger sister knew him. Said shit turned south for him real quick and your boy caught an epic beatdown. An ass whooping to end all ass whoopings. He transferred to East, right?" The girl doesn't wait for an answer but turns to her friends and nods, as if to confirm that Malcolm is who they thought. "Yo, how'd he get in here anyway? Isn't he only like a junior?"

Tulsi shrugs. He is confused. He is not sure what this girl means, what it is she is telling him. The music is still pounding. It seems to originate underground, sending shock waves of energy rippling up through his legs. He remembers what Malcolm said about his previous school, that he was not welcome back. That some people there had chosen to fuck with the wrong guy. He senses that these stories do not match up, that there are more questions than answers. But these questions seem unimportant to him right now.

"What about you?" the girl asks. She smiles as though just now seeing Tulsi for the first time. Her teeth reflect the pulsating red lights so that her mouth appears filled with blood. "What are *you* into?" She bites her bottom lip, then steps closer. Tulsi remembers what his friends told him before he left, that Pennsylvania was ruled by vampires. He wonders if this girl is one of them. He can feel the heat coming from her body, and though there is space between them it is like they are fused together.

"I'm looking for my sister," he says. "I think she's here." It is the first time he has mentioned Susmita to anyone since Abigail. He is not surprised he does so. Something tells him it is part of the plan. The girl puts a hand on Tulsi's waist. He can feel each fingertip, even the whirling patterns of their prints.

"She look like you, your sister? She cute like you?" The girl leans close, presses her lips to Tulsi's neck. Their dry imprint sizzles against his skin. "Where you from?"

"Camp Goldhap," Tulsi says, the name out loud conjuring a wave of images, faces he has not thought of in a long time.

"Goldhap," the girl repeats. "Sounds exotic." She lifts herself up on her tiptoes and before Tulsi knows it she is kissing him, her lips parting his own, her tongue prodding his mouth. His eyes are open and what shocks him most is the proximity they share, the way their bodies are connected. It is the first kiss on the lips Tulsi has had since childhood, when the girls in camp would surprise the boys with innocent pecks meant to tease. The pink-haired girl runs her hands through Tulsi's hair, digs her nails into the flesh of his scalp. She leans back. "Exotic," she says, "like you." She is about to kiss him again when her friends appear and pull her back playfully by the shoulders.

"Come on, Lindsay," a tall girl says, laughing. "That counts already."

"Just making sure," the pink-haired girl says. "Better safe than sorry."

"It's her birthday," says another. "She's crossing off her checklist. Where are you from?"

"He's from Camp Goldhap." The pink-haired girl lays her hand on Tulsi's chest. "I think it's in India or something." She turns to her friends. "How am I doing?"

"You're crushing it. Now we just need to find you an Asian guy to make out with." The tall girl holds up a tattered napkin. "There's no way you're gonna finish all this tonight."

"Watch me."

Before Tulsi can ask what they're talking about, they are gone. He watches them disappear into the crowd, the sensation of intimate contact already vanishing. He places a finger to his lips and is immediately reminded of his thirst, a thirst that has gone from unnoticed to all-consuming. He turns and rushes up the stairs to the bathroom. Inside, he opens the faucet completely and scoops handfuls of water to his waiting mouth. He gulps them down, splashing his pants, and the basin, and the floor. He is still drinking when Malcolm bursts through the door.

"What the fuck, T! I've been looking all over for you. We gotta get out of here." The expression on his face is pure fear. For him, the release of the Ecstasy is gone. Tulsi straightens, his T-shirt soaked below his waist.

"What's happening?"

"It's the police," Malcolm says, grabbing Tulsi's hand and dragging him toward the door. "They're raiding the club."

•

Outside the bathroom, the scene has turned to panic. Some of the clubgoers stand around idly, while others rush past. Near the entrance, a crowd of bodies surge, all trying to get out. The music has stopped, and a uniformed policeman stands in the DJ booth speaking over the address system. He tells the crowd that only patrons with a valid ID will be able to leave. The club is under investigation for admitting under-agers.

"We're fucked," Malcolm says. Tulsi sees the tattooed bouncer who let them in shoved against a wall near the entrance and flanked by two policemen. Even in the confusion he senses his own satisfaction at the sight.

"Come on," Malcolm says, heading toward the stairway that leads to the uppermost part of the club. They fight through the mass of people clogging the stairs. Once they reach the top floor, they head back toward the hollowed-out school bus.

"What about Kyla?" Tulsi asks. "Where is she?" His euphoria has vanished. In the midst of the raid, the already dwindling effects of the Ecstasy are like a light switch that has been shut off.

"Fuck Kyla," Malcolm says. "You think she'd wait for us? She's probably already gone."

At the far end of the room is a busser's station overflowing in dirty dishes and half-empty glasses and bottles. Next to it is a hinged door. Malcolm bursts through and Tulsi follows. Inside, stainless-steel counters are awash in fluorescent track lighting. An aproned man stands at an industrial-sized sink rinsing plates.

"*Hey,*" he says when he spots them, "you can't be back here." At the other end of the room, a glowing red EXIT sign hangs above a door. Malcolm sprints toward it with Tulsi right behind. The man continues to yell as they rush past. Through it is a fire escape, and below that an alley.

They bound down the iron-grated stairs, using the handrails to turn themselves quickly. Flashing police lights are visible at one end of the alley and so they run the other way, weaving through dumpsters and piles of trash. From the far end of the alley someone yells for them to stop. Tulsi's breath burns in his chest. His heart feels as if it might explode. At the end of the alley they turn right, following a set of train tracks that run through a thin cut of trees. Undergrowth and trash litter the bottom of the track bed where they creep, their hands steadying them against the ballast-covered grade. To their left, the lights of downtown Erie burn brightly through the turning leaves. In the distance they can still hear the police sirens, high-pitched wails piercing the night.

•

They travel steadily for nearly half an hour. They've been heading east, toward Tulsi's neighborhood, crouching low and hugging the train tracks the whole way. They finally stop at an overpass where the tracks cross Parade Street. It is late and only the occasional car moves below them, headlights swallowed up for an instant before reappearing on the other side. They find a discarded wooden pallet near the edge of the overpass to rest on.

When they have caught their breath, Malcolm points to a large concrete structure on the south side of the tracks. "You know what that is?" he asks.

Tulsi shakes his head. He feels too exhausted even to speak.

"Erie County Prison," Malcolm says.

In the scant moonlight, Tulsi makes out the high razor-wire fence enclosing the building and its adjacent yard. Only a few of the windows are still lit, but he sees that they are barred. Tulsi's T-shirt is soaked through with sweat. A rising breeze sweeps up from the street and sets him shivering. Malcolm lets out a laugh.

"We could've ended up in there," he says, motioning toward the jail. "What a crazy fucking night, huh? I mean, can you believe it? I didn't even think we'd get in. And then the E, and us running from the cops." He turns to Tulsi with a wide smile. "Did you see that guy's face when we busted into the kitchen?"

Tulsi remembers the way the man's eyes looked, as though they might pop out of his head, and begins to laugh. "I thought we were going to spend the night playing video games again," he says.

And then, out of fear or relief or simple joy, they are both cracking up, leaning forward on the wooden pallet, their sneakers sending gravel skidding down the slope. They laugh until Tulsi's stomach hurts, until the pain in his aching legs disappears and all he feels is lightness. He cannot remember the last time he has laughed so hard.

"How late is it?" Tulsi asks. Malcolm checks his cell.

"Quarter after two."

High above them, the tallest buildings of downtown Erie stand silhouetted against the night sky. Right now his grandfather is probably taking his first of two breaks at the juice plant, pouring soup into his thermos cap or stepping outside for a cigarette. By now, he expects that Tulsi will be at home, asleep on the pullout sofa, the old Sanyo casting its calming underwater glow on the whitewashed walls. There is a beat of guilt and then it is gone.

Tulsi is about to stand when, with a clarity that scares him, he remembers seeing Susmita, the way she stopped twirling in exactly his direction, the hair swept away to reveal her face. "There was a girl back there…" Tulsi says.

"Who?" Malcolm asks, but the impossibility of it being his sister strikes Tulsi wordless. Of course it was not Susmita, only a girl with dark hair. He stands.

"No one."

"What were you gonna say?"

"Just that there was a girl back there who reminded me of my sister," Tulsi says. "Who looked like her kind of."

For a moment the only noise is the wind pushing past the leaves, the occasional hum of distant cars.

"I didn't know you had a sister," Malcolm says. A plastic bag clings to the brush near Tulsi's feet, its ghostly form filling and emptying in the breeze. He thinks of the girl who kissed him, the way she walked away laughing before he could even ask her name.

"Yeah," he says, the wind catching him flush across the chest. He wishes the Ecstasy were still working, wonders what the wind would feel like then. Maybe it would cut right through him, flowing over his insides and out his back. "Come on," Tulsi says, moving toward the slope that leads to the street below. "We've still got a long way to go."

•

Tulsi lets Malcolm sleep on the foldout. He stays in his grandfather's room where the bed is smaller, a narrow twin. His grandfather is shorter than he is, and Tulsi discovers that his heels jut over the edge. He sets the bedside alarm for seven so he'll be up before his grandfather arrives home. In the morning he walks into the living room and finds the foldout empty, the sheet and blanket folded neatly on top.

•

A week later East plays its first soccer match of the season against McDowell, a super-sized high school from Millcreek Township. East does not have their own field and so they share Veterans Stadium with several other city schools. It is a huge concrete bowl built into the side of a hill. The playing surface is bright green artificial turf and staggered sections of blue and red seats rise up in rows from the field. Tulsi stretches beside Malcolm while scanning the stadium. A light mist falls, glazing the field and the players. Rachel sits in the third row, a red vinyl rain jacket pulled tightly around her. She waves at them but only Tulsi waves back.

"I wish she didn't come," Malcolm says. "I probably won't even play. Besides, she makes me nervous."

In front of them, a senior captain leads the warmup. "Time to stretch those twigs and berries, boys," he calls out. The players sit up and pull their heels in toward their crotches.

"Did you tell your grandfather to come?" Malcolm asks.

Tulsi's grandfather had wanted to attend, but at the last minute had been offered an extra shift at the juice plant. Tulsi knew he could not turn it down, but rather than be disappointed, he was secretly relieved. He'd watched knowingly for the past few weeks as the other players' mothers and fathers picked them up from practice, ushering them into the passenger seats of sedans or the backs of minivans packed with screaming children. It seemed he was the only player who lived alone with a grandparent, and he was also the only one with a guardian not from here, his closest family member so obviously a stranger to this place. He hated to admit it, but when he thought of his grandfather sitting at the games in his worn leather sandals and secondhand button-downs, or worse, a traditional kurta, he shuddered. He felt guilty and ungrateful, but he was happy his grandfather had not been able to come.

"He's working," Tulsi says, leaning his elbows into his knees, pushing until the stretch burns up his thighs and into his groin. Like the others he wears a gray jersey with scarlet trim. The East High logo, a stone-faced Indian warrior complete with headdress, is silkscreened onto the right side of the chest. Raising himself up from the ground, Tulsi contemplates this as he continues to stretch. The coach has worked him in with the midfielders and told him he might see time at sweeper as well.

He is a midfielder for the East High Warriors.

He is a member of the team.

His number is 17.

•

At the end of the first half they are already losing by three goals. McDowell plays a disciplined game, whereas East is all over the field. Coach Davies screams constantly: barking out instructions, reprimanding sloppy play, even berating one of their forwards for dogging it. A thick vein pulses in his neck when he yells and Tulsi is afraid it may explode, blasting through his skin like a burst water pipe.

They are down five goals to one with twenty minutes left to play when Tulsi is called in. At first he doesn't realize it's him being beckoned, Coach Davies's accent and urgent tone making his own name unrecognizable. But then the boy next to him taps his shoulder and points down the sideline and there is their coach, waving him over.

"Go in at right midfield," he says once Tulsi reaches him. "It's already pissed away so just play smart and try to get the ball to the strikers. Or at least onto their goddamn half of the pitch."

At the first stoppage of play Coach Davies waves off Simmons, the midfielder Tulsi is replacing. A lanky senior, Simmons is also co-captain. He jogs to the sideline, making sure to bump into Tulsi.

"Fucking ridiculous," he mutters as he moves past. Tulsi ignores him and runs onto the field where he awaits the throw-in.

The game has slowed down but Tulsi's legs are fresh and he tries to maintain position, darting to the ball whenever it is near. The opposing midfielder is a muscular boy of medium height, quick but obviously tired. His jet-black hair is long and held back with a plastic band. Down the field, the ball rolls out of play across the end line and as the players shift for the corner kick the boy approaches Tulsi.

"Where's your towel, Haji?" he hears the boy say, though he is not facing him. Tulsi remains silent.

"You hear me, Haji? Where's your fucking towel? Gotta wrap that head up nice and tight."

Tulsi keeps his eyes on the ball, its movements. He has been called this name before, and others. Too many to keep track of. This one, like many he has heard, assumes he's Middle Eastern. To explain the boy's mistake would only grant it merit and so instead Tulsi monitors the ball, tries to shadow its progress and maintain position. This is what he tells himself as the boy continues to chatter across from him. He repeats it like a mantra. *Maintain position and strike. Maintain position and strike.*

The boy is still talking when the ball shifts to their side of the field.

"Better get that camel gassed up, Haji. This shit is over." Tulsi tries his best to ignore him, but the boy is relentless. He stays within earshot no matter where Tulsi moves.

"Why don't you go back to your own country?" the boy says. "Nobody wants you here."

From the corner of his eye Tulsi sees Rachel clapping in the stands. He remembers the feeling of relief at learning his grandfather could not come, the embarrassment he'd feared. He wonders what this boy would say if his grandfather was here cheering for him, what names he'd call him.

At the far end of the field East's striker battles the sweeper for position. McDowell's player gets control and punts the ball downfield, right toward Tulsi and the other boy. Tulsi sprints to where the ball will land just as the opposing midfielder arrives. They jostle for position and both jump at the same time. Tulsi ends up in front and heads the ball back downfield. There's a shove in his lower back as he lands. "Goddamn you reek," the boy says. "You fucking stink like shit, Haji."

Tulsi turns and before he knows what he's doing, he tackles the boy to the ground. He straddles him and grips his jersey, pulling the boy toward him. He slams him into the turf once, then again. He does not even think to punch the boy. His hands will not let him release. He keeps slamming him into the ground, over and over. He wants the boy's back to break, his ribs to split, he wants him to die where he lies. The boy yells below him, squirms to get away, but Tulsi's knees are vises holding him in place. The boy throws punches but Tulsi cannot feel them. They are nothing-punches with no momentum. This is a nothing-boy and Tulsi wants him to know it. More than anything, Tulsi wants the boy to understand what he is.

After what seems like the briefest of moments Tulsi is ripped away by his jersey, a linesman standing above him. He lands sprawled on his side, and the boy rolls over and struggles to stand. The linesman is yelling though Tulsi cannot decipher the words. Other players gather. The referee runs over and holds a red card in Tulsi's direction, orders him off the field immediately. The other boy has made it to his feet and is doubled over, winded, hands on his knees. As Tulsi is escorted from the field he sees the boy is smiling.

•

Coach Davies meets him on the sideline, an inch from his face. "What the fuck was that, Tulsi?! What the fuck was that?"

Tulsi stands there, still out of breath; his head bent slightly, eyes on the ground. He can feel the others on the sideline staring at him. Play has not resumed and those on the field stare too, along with everyone in the stands. All the spectators and family members. Rachel, he thinks. Rachel, who has treated him so kindly, like a second son; Rachel is watching this happen.

A thought, to tell Coach Davies what the other midfielder said, passes quickly. In it there is nothing but shame. To admit to this man that he was provoked to anger by a stranger is to lay his weakness bare. That he was ridiculed as a person of a completely different culture only confounds that shame. He is not even worth insulting correctly.

Tulsi's arms lie limp at his sides. He clenches his hands, digs his nails into his palms. He hopes to draw blood, anything to keep from crying, from exposing his weakness further. He is certain the boy is staring at him from across the field, still smiling, boasting to his friends. In front of him Coach Davies continues to yell. Tulsi feels the vibrations of each word on his face. He clenches his fists tighter.

"That's not the way we do things around here," Coach Davies says.

"You better get your goddamn act together, or I'll cut your ass from this team."

Play resumes and Coach Davies walks away, leaving Tulsi standing there alone. The other players turn their attention back to the game, and Tulsi pretends to watch.

Goddamn you reek, the boy said. *You fucking stink like shit, Haji.*

Tulsi cannot help but think of his grandfather. This is why he did not want him there. It is hard enough simply being himself. Tulsi replays the boy's insults, and more so how he said them, with pure disgust. He remembers the disdain that laced each word, is certain he will remember it for a long time.

•

After the game, Malcolm finds Tulsi in the tunnel that leads from the stadium.

"What the hell happened out there, T? What did he say to you?"

Tulsi does not want to talk about it. All he wants is to be home, his grandfather gone at the juice plant and the apartment empty. He wants to lie on the pullout with the lights shut off, think of nothing, be alone. He turns toward the tunnel's exit, a blurry square of light in the distance. From the stadium he can walk home through Erie's Lower East Side, anonymous among the cracked sidewalks and tree-lined streets. The light mist that fell earlier has let up. Tulsi wishes it were still raining, fat drops pounding the Earth. He wishes the fog that hung that morning still hovered like a dark cloud above the ground, a portal for him to disappear through.

"Tulsi," Malcolm keeps on, "what was it?"

"Nothing," Tulsi says. "All right? He just pushed me and I got angry."

Malcolm's face shows his disbelief, his dark eyebrows arched dramatically. "Come on," he says. "Don't give me that. I saw him talking shit."

Tulsi's pulse quickens as the anger that surged through him on the field returns. He wants to get home. He wants today to never have happened. Malcolm will not let him go, will not stop talking about it.

"Tell me what he said, T. Don't be a pussy. I know some people at McDowell. Maybe we can find out who he is, go over there and beat his ass."

"Like you got your ass beat at Central?" Tulsi hears himself saying. For a moment Malcolm does not seem to understand and then his expression changes, eyes narrowed, the smooth skin of his forehead tightening.

"What are you talking about?" he says. Tulsi sees he has upset him, but he cannot stop. It is the same feeling he had holding the other boy's jersey. He cannot let go.

"An epic beatdown. That's what I heard."

"Who were you talking to? *Kyla?*" When he speaks his sister's name, his voice cracks, shattering beneath the weight of it.

"I thought some people there chose to fuck with the wrong guy. Isn't that what you told me?"

"Fuck you, Tulsi. Who said what? Tell me." Malcolm is screaming, tiny flecks of spit flying from his mouth.

Tulsi turns to go and Malcolm grabs his shoulder, tries to spin him around. Tulsi tears his hand away and runs.

•

Outside the stadium a line of traffic waits by the stoplight at Twenty-Sixth and State. Tulsi darts between two cars and heads east through the Kwik Fill parking lot. He jogs past a man walking a pit bull. The dog issues a single, weak bark. He is still wearing his East High Warriors jersey, its damp fabric sticking to his skin. Coach Davies supplies the jerseys at each game and they are to be left there after. He wishes he had remembered to leave it but keeps on moving.

People sit on their porches talking and drinking beer, happy to be outside after the rain. The clouds that covered the city earlier have rolled out over the lake. There is the smell of wet grass and charcoal doused in lighter fluid. Across the street, neighborhood kids pick sides for a football game.

Tulsi walks quickly down Parade Street past the people enjoying the warm fall night and break in the weather. There is something artificial about it all that Tulsi cannot name: the cars gliding slowly past, the couples laughing on their porch swings, the children moving to opposite sides of the yard to await the start of their game. It feels fake to him, made up, like something from one of his television sitcoms. A version of things that can only exist when viewed from the other side of a screen.

•

He turns on Elevenh Street and right away sees the police cruiser. It sits idly next to the curb in front of his grandfather's apartment. Inside are two policemen, the backs of their heads visible through the rear windshield. Tulsi has seen police vehicles on his street before, but he senses suddenly, and without any doubt, that this is different. They are here for him.

Before he can turn to run, the passenger door swings open. He stands frozen in place, his feet rooted to the splintered asphalt. A volley of thoughts bursts through his mind. They are there because of the altercation at the stadium. He will be taken to jail for a fight he did not provoke. He has brought shame on himself and his team, and worse yet, he has brought shame on his grandfather. But then another thought occurs. He remembers the Ecstasy, his flight with Malcolm from the King's Rook. They were able to escape at the time, but his punishment has caught up with him. One way or the other, he knows he is in trouble, knows he will be found guilty of whatever they choose to accuse him of.

The policeman is tall with a barrel chest and thick arms. His legs, however, are skinny and bowed, as though he has spent his life on a horse. He moves toward Tulsi with a wobbling gait, the heavy black baton that hangs from his belt swinging with every step. He stops a few feet away. "Tulsi Gurung?" he asks.

Tulsi can only stare back at him. Coming from this man, his name does not sound like his own. He wishes it were not. He wishes this man was here for another boy.

"You hear me, son?" the man says, his voice stern. "I asked you a question." He takes a step forward and stares down at Tulsi. "I asked you your name."

Tulsi's legs feel weak. His side hurts from where he landed on it when the linesman threw him. All he wants is to be inside his grandfather's apartment. He wishes he had never left that morning, that this day had never taken place. He nods wordlessly.

"I'm going to need you to come with us," the policeman says. He walks abreast of Tulsi to the rear of the cruiser and opens the back door. Tulsi lowers himself in. The officer behind the wheel is a woman. Tulsi hadn't been able to tell before, but now sees the long dark ponytail bound tightly and hanging down her back. Her face is visible in the rearview mirror, though she does not look back at him. She says nothing when Tulsi enters the vehicle or when the other officer gets in. She simply switches on the ignition and puts the car in drive, the three of them pulling onto the street in silence.

•

After a few minutes they turn onto Twelfth Street and head west. The front driver-side window is rolled down slightly and a steady stream of wind whistles past. Dividing the front and back seats is a metal grate consisting of a diamond-shaped pattern that repeats itself over and over, each opening smaller than the width of a finger. There is something delicate about the grate's design, something oddly reassuring in its repetitive structure. Tulsi focuses as hard as he can on it. He stares at the diamonds until his vision goes blurry. He tries to ignore the fear bleeding through his mind.

A radio crackles to life on the center dash, muffled voices speaking from far away. The policeman who led Tulsi to the car lifts the receiver and presses a button. "We just picked him up," he says. "Headed there now."

Tulsi does not know what is happening. He realizes with alarm that his bladder is full. He drank water for the entirety of the game before he was substituted in and has not yet had a chance to use the bathroom. The sweat that cooled and dried on the walk home has returned, trickling along his scalp, blooming his jersey with stains. He senses it would be best to remain silent but cannot any longer. His heart is racing and he feels a desperation that is uncontainable. A picture appears clearly in his mind, his grandfather arriving home to an empty apartment, expecting to find Tulsi but discovering him gone.

"What is happening?" he asks, his voice a quivering reed. "Where are we going?"

The female officer makes eye contact with him in the rearview, then glances at the other policeman. They are stopped at a red light. A man walking his bicycle crosses the street slowly.

"We're headed to the hospital, honey," she says.

•

They pull up to the emergency room entrance off Parade Street. The female officer lets Tulsi out and escorts him through the sliding-glass doors while her partner remains in the car. The waiting room is large, with both a nurse's station and check-in counter. At the far end is another set of sliding-glass doors and across from that a seating area with several rows of plastic chairs. The officer walks to the nurse's station while Tulsi waits behind her, still unsure. The waiting room is half full: a wailing toddler sits perched on her mother's lap, an elderly couple hold hands, a thick wad of gauze taped to a cut on the man's cheek.

Tulsi stares at the policewoman as she speaks with a nurse. He is relieved it was she who came in with him and not the other officer. She is taller than he would have imagined, and there is something about her that reminds him of Abigail, her walk perhaps, or the tone of her voice when she called him honey. Still, it is little comfort standing in the waiting room, the biting ammoniac smell making it hard even to breathe. He lifts a hand to wipe his brow and finds it shaking. He can barely control it to slick away the sweat.

After a few minutes, the policewoman turns around. She beckons Tulsi to follow and he does, the nurse leading both of them through the second set of sliding doors and down a long white corridor where gurneys and medical equipment line the walls. They pass rooms and more nurse's stations and waiting areas, making a series of turns until Tulsi is certain he could not find his way back if he had to. A doctor in scrubs and white clogs rushes past them in the opposite direction. They reach an elevator and take it to the third floor. After some more walking they arrive at a door with a small rectangular window. The nurse walks right in, but the policewoman lays a hand on Tulsi's shoulder as they enter the room.

Straight ahead a window overlooks the hospital's massive garage, a thin sliver of Presque Isle Bay just visible above it. To Tulsi's right is an IV stand and monitor, a series of tubes and wires trailing downward, each one attached to the old man lying in the narrow bed, his grandfather.

Another man waits in the corner. He wears a dark blue suit and polished wingtips. As he approaches, his jacket parts and Tulsi catches a glimpse of the silver badge affixed to his belt. Tulsi tries to see his grandfather but he is angled away from him so that only a small portion of his face is visible. He steps closer, and the suited man stops him with an outstretched hand.

"You're the grandson?"

"Yes," Tulsi says, trying to get past. The man sidesteps him, cutting him off.

"Please," Tulsi says. He has begun to cry without realizing it, the sound desperate and broken, a child begging. He tastes the salt on his tongue from when he spread his lips. Had he not uttered the single word he would not have known. "Please," he says again, and then, "*Hajurba,*" his name for his grandfather. This last word he says louder, speaking not to the man in front of him but to his grandfather who will understand. His grandfather, all he has in the world.

"He's going to be okay, son," the man says. His right hand presses against Tulsi's chest, holding him back. "But he got worked over pretty good. I just want you to be prepared." The man steps aside and allows Tulsi by.

Tulsi moves quickly to the far side of the bed, taking care to avoid the network of wires and tubes attached to his grandfather. The room is dark, but Tulsi sees that the right side of his grandfather's face is completely swollen, his eye sealed shut. A line of stitches stretches horizontally above his upper lip. Another holds together a cut on his forehead.

"He's resting," the nurse says. "We gave him something for the pain."

Tulsi wants to grip his grandfather's hand, stroke his graying hair, he wants to lean over the bedrail and embrace him. But the wires and tubes make him nervous. It occurs to him that these are the avenues by which his grandfather is receiving help, perhaps even being kept alive. He does not know and so instead hovers above him, swaying back and forth slowly, shifting his weight from one foot to the other. He understands that to remain still would be to signal the world of his resignation, a helplessness he's unwilling to admit.

The policeman walks over and stands across the hospital bed from him. He places both hands on the railing and stares at Tulsi.

"Son," he says. Tulsi does not respond, but keeps swaying, a prayer he refuses to cease.

"Son," the man repeats. "A doctor is going to come speak to you and then a social worker, someone to help you out while your grandfather gets better." The man opens his suit jacket and pulls a small leather-bound notebook from the inside pocket. He flips through, the rustling pages like the chatter of insects.

Tulsi tries to listen as the man explains what happened but has trouble following. His grandfather leaving the plant after the first of his two shifts, walking to a nearby gas station to buy a sandwich before heading back. A group of teenagers driving past, pulling over to harass him. Cornering him then beating him up and taking his wallet. His grandfather bleeding alone on the sidewalk. There were some witnesses. A storeowner called 911. But no suspects yet. No arrests made.

"Unfortunately, this isn't the first time something like this has happened," the policeman says, putting away his notebook and buttoning his jacket. He turns to address the nurse who stands nearby. "There's been a number of attacks targeting Erie's immigrant population." At this, Tulsi looks up, stops swaying.

"*No*," he says sternly. He cannot help it, the word coming from somewhere deep within. The man is confused, his head tilted slightly to the side.

"Come again?"

"No," Tulsi repeats, "not 'immigrant population.'" He lowers his gaze to his grandfather's sleeping form. His breaths are deep and ragged, but evenly spaced. A hospital bed sheet, so thin as to be nearly transparent, rises and falls with each one. "*He* is my *grandfather*," Tulsi says.

He has stopped crying.

That, at least, is over.

•

After a series of questions, both officers leave, the policewoman casting a final sympathetic glance at Tulsi before exiting. The nurse follows them out, and not long after a young doctor appears, the same one who rushed by them earlier. Most of what he says Tulsi does not understand. He speaks quickly, using acronyms and medical jargon Tulsi is unfamiliar with. He reads from a clipboard without looking up.

"Insurance?" he says at one point. "Is your grandfather insured?" When Tulsi does not answer he goes on.

"Either way we're going to have to keep him a couple days for observation. Just to make sure. Somebody from OCY will be by to talk to you." He walks out and closes the door behind him, leaving the lights shut off.

Tulsi sits in a chair beside the hospital bed watching his grandfather. Occasionally, his breaths sound more ragged, or he jerks in his sleep. When this occurs, Tulsi jumps to his feet, ready to run for the nurse in case something is wrong, but each time, his grandfather settles back into an even slumber. The rhythmic beeping of the monitors and his grandfather's breathing combine to form an eerie melody that Tulsi memorizes instinctively. He tries to focus all his energy on his grandfather, on what he can do to help in this moment.

Sit here, he thinks.

Be right here should he awake.

But his mind keeps wandering back to the game. He hadn't wanted his grandfather there. Tulsi had felt relief when he picked up the extra shift and announced he couldn't come. He'd been happy. And now this. If his grandfather had only worked the overnight shift, he would have been safe at the stadium, sitting with the other spectators enjoying the game. He would have never been hurt.

And then there is the fight, Tulsi losing control on the field in front of everyone. It is possible, he understands, that as he pinned the other boy to the turf, as he slammed him over and over into the ground, his own grandfather was being attacked, knocked down, beaten and robbed. If Tulsi knows anything, he knows this. In more ways than one, he is responsible for what has happened.

•

"Do you have any other family here?" the woman asks. "Anyone you can stay with for a while?"

They are in a small office down the hall from his grandfather's room. The woman, a caseworker from the Office of Children and Youth, sits across from him. She is young, right out of college Tulsi guesses, with short dark hair cut at an angle above her shoulders.

"I want to stay here," Tulsi says.

The woman shifts uncomfortably in her swivel chair, lets out a sigh. "So you've said, but, as I've already explained, that's not possible." She uncaps her water bottle and takes a drink. "It's against hospital policy. And besides, you've got school." She points to the soccer jersey Tulsi still has on. "And practice."

"I want to stay here," Tulsi repeats, "with my grandfather." The woman puts her water bottle down and leans back, stares at the ceiling. She lowers her gaze.

"You're not doing your grandfather any favors here," she says, shaking her head. "He needs to focus on getting better, and that will be a whole lot easier if he knows you're being properly taken care of." Tulsi does not respond. He does not know what to do. He understands what the woman is implying but he feels responsible for what has happened. To leave means abandoning his grandfather a second time.

"Look," the woman says, "there's a saying we have here. You can do something the easy way, or you can do it the hard way. And right now you are *definitely* choosing the hard way." She taps her fingernails against the laminated tabletop. "Now you can decide to give me a name, an address, a phone number, something, and I can look into it. Or I can call my superior and we can get you fixed up with a foster family. I'll have the two officers who brought you down here come back and they'll personally escort you to your temporary residence. What's it going to be, Tulsi?" She continues to tap her fingernails, long manicured nails painted a deep shade of violet, the clicking like steps coming down a hallway.

"I have someone who can watch me," Tulsi says.

•

A half hour later, Rachel pulls the blue LeSabre into the hospital's circular driveway. She leaves the car running as she steps out. The moment she spots Tulsi standing beside the OCY worker, she rushes to embrace him. Her arms envelop him and all at once he smells the familiar scent of her: incense and wintergreen gum underscored by the faintest trace of heated canola oil. She holds him tightly, pulls him into the fold of her large chest.

"It's gonna be all right, baby," she says, rocking him in place. "Everything's gonna be all right."

•

Hamot Hospital, where his grandfather is staying, is the same one where Rachel works. She assures him she will take care of everything. She leaves him in the waiting area while she goes to talk to the nurses on his grandfather's floor. When she returns, she tells him she's asked them to take special care of his grandfather, to keep a close eye on him and call her should anything come up.

For the first time, Tulsi sits beside Rachel in the front seat. She leaves the radio on, a gospel station playing an old-sounding hymn. Tulsi doesn't know if Malcolm has told her about their argument, but he is certain she saw the fight on the field, watched as he was berated by Coach Davies. Either way he feels ashamed, responsible for everything. First he let the other midfielder expose his weakness, then he insulted Malcolm, his only friend. Worst of all, he's imposing on Rachel, taking advantage of her kindness. He wishes the OCY worker had let him stay with his grandfather. He assured her over and over he was willing to sleep on the floor, told her how he wanted to be there when his grandfather awoke.

Rachel drives across Eighth Street, the bay below them a dark reflection of the night sky. The Bicentennial Tower at the foot of State Street is lit at the top like a giant torch.

"We can pick up some of your things tomorrow," Rachel says after they've been driving for a few minutes. "Tonight I think it'll just be good for you to rest."

"Thank you," Tulsi says, and then, "I'm sorry." Rachel slows the car, reaches forward and turns off the radio.

"Tulsi, you've got nothing to apologize for. Why are you saying you're sorry? For what?" Tulsi lifts his hands from his lap, motions at the interior of the car.

"For this. For everything. Coming to get me, letting me stay with you." He drops his arms and crosses them, rubs the insides of his elbows. "It is a lot to ask." He pauses, trying to find the words for what he wants to say next. "Especially after today," he adds.

Rachel is quiet. The car ahead of them turns into the lit parking lot of a bar.

"Malcolm wouldn't tell me what all happened between the two of you, just that you were going to find your own way home from the game. But I'm sure whatever it is you'll work it out. He's just a sensitive boy, you know? He's been through a lot." Rachel takes a hand off the steering wheel and pats Tulsi's knee. "You two have that in common."

Tulsi nods. He is relieved she does not know what he said, embarrassed still that he said it. The street they are on is poorly lit and Tulsi cannot make out the expression on Rachel's face. He is sure she is disappointed in him, that she is just being kind, but then, as they pull onto the block where she lives, Rachel lets out a stifled laugh, barely audible over the hum of the engine.

"As for that fiasco during the game," she says, "well, I don't condone violence but I saw that boy chirping at you. Something tells me he got exactly what he deserved."

•

Tulsi finds Malcolm in his room, sitting on the bed with his laptop open before him. He has on his gaming headset and doesn't look up when Tulsi enters. His iPod rests in its console, a rap song streaming through the speakers. Tulsi stands near the open door.

"I'm sorry about your grandpa," Malcolm says without looking up.

"Thanks." Tulsi takes a step closer, shuts the door behind him. He stares at Malcolm, who is clearly not playing the video game, his fingers idle above the keyboard. He has not moved since Tulsi came in, though he refuses to look away from the screen.

"Is he going to be okay?"

"Yes," Tulsi says without hesitation. "That's what the doctor said."

"That's good." Malcolm reaches up and removes the headset, lays it on the bed beside him. "I'm glad."

Tulsi is about to apologize, about to tell him he didn't mean what he said, when Malcolm shuts his laptop.

"It's true, you know? What you heard. I don't know who told you, but it's true." With his index finger, Malcolm traces figure eights over his right thigh.

"It was some girl at the King's Rook. I don't even know her name," Tulsi says, remembering the shock of her kiss, the way she walked away laughing with her friends. "I didn't believe her," he adds. He's not sure what he believes. In truth he doesn't care. It doesn't matter to him. He wants Malcolm to know this.

"Well, you *should have*, 'cause it's true. That's why I transferred to East. Daryl Montgomery. Jim Williamson. A couple other guys. They jumped me after school." Malcolm watches him, gauging his reaction.

Tulsi stands perfectly still. He wants to say something to reassure Malcolm, something like *Fuck them*, or *Payback's a bitch*, but none of it feels honest to him anymore. Even in his mind it sounds like a lie. He is tired, he realizes suddenly, exhausted. He walks to Malcolm's desk, pulls out the swivel chair and sits. Neither of them says anything for a while. Across the hall, they hear Rachel turn on the shower.

"Why?" Tulsi asks. He asks as much for Malcolm as for his grandfather. He cannot understand it. Even his fight on the field earlier confuses him. Thinking of it now, he cannot picture himself as the aggressor, cannot for the life of him remember what it felt like to tackle that boy, grip his jersey, slam his warm body down. In his memory it seems like someone else, like something he watched happening from the sidelines.

"Daryl and Kyla used to date. Daryl used to be over here all the time." Malcolm shrugs. "I guess when Kyla dumped his ass he was just looking for a way to get back at her." Malcolm stops talking but Tulsi senses there is more, something he is still not telling him.

"I don't know what it was like for you and your sister," Malcolm says, "but Kyla and I used to be close, used to talk about stuff. This was a long time after our dad died. Mom would be working and it would just be the two of us. I guess there was a point I felt like I could tell her anything."

Tulsi is surprised to hear Malcolm reference Susmita. He had almost forgotten he told him about her. That night at The King's Rook feels so long ago. The release of the Ecstasy, the pink-haired girl, the raid and their maddening dash through the kitchen and down the fire escape. He remembers the train tracks near the prison, the way the lights of the buildings downtown shone in the distance like low-flung stars. It occurs to Tulsi now that he has never been inside those buildings and perhaps never will. That even to imagine their interiors, marbled bank lobbies and cubicle-lined offices, is an exercise in make believe. For an instant he is happy his sister is not here with him, to share in his alienation, in the pain of watching their grandfather suffer.

"We used to talk," Tulsi tells Malcolm. "But not for a long time."

"Yeah, well, I guess it's the same for us then." Malcolm pauses, kicks his legs over the side of his bed. "Before they jumped me, Daryl kept telling everyone I was a queer. That I liked guys. After that I couldn't go back to Central." He stops, his face somehow smaller, compressing as he tries to hold back tears. "Kyla," he says. "It was something we had talked about. I said I wasn't sure, that I thought maybe... She must have told Daryl before they broke up." Malcolm grips both knees, his knuckles dark knots. "Now I never tell her *anything*. I'll never tell her *anything* ever again." He stares at the wall over Tulsi's shoulder, toward his sister's room, the expression on his face more sad than angry.

Across the hall they can hear the shower shutting off, the pipes squeaking to a halt. Tulsi thinks of Rachel, losing her husband, working to raise two children, enemies beneath the same roof. He imagines Kyla betraying Malcolm, Malcolm hating her in return. Maybe if he and Susmita had not been separated, if they'd both remained in camp, they too would have grown to resent one another. Maybe, if given enough time, that's how all things ended, in pain.

"My sister sent me here to live with my grandfather," Tulsi says. "When he dies, I'll be alone."

Malcolm nods, loosens the grip on his knees. "It's not fair," he says, "none of it."

Tulsi looks at his own hands, the slender fingers braced in his lap. "I shouldn't have said those things to you after the game. We're friends." There's the sound of the bathroom door opening, then Rachel's humming as she walks to her room.

"You're still wearing your jersey," Malcolm says.

Tulsi looks down, the face of the East High Warrior wrinkled against his chest. "Coach Davies is going to be pissed."

Malcolm stands, runs a hand over his buzzed head. "Man, fuck Coach Davies," he says. Tulsi tugs at the front of the jersey, trying to smooth the mascot, then gives up.

"Yes," he says in agreement. "Fuck Coach Davies."

Then they are both smiling, then laughing, filling the space between them with laughter. They laugh like they did the night they ran away from the Rook, when they still had so far to go, laughing to spite themselves, ignoring completely all the danger they so narrowly avoided, all the hardship yet to come.

•

Rachel has fixed Tulsi a bed on the living room couch. He lies awake as the headlights of passing cars illuminate the curtains. In the dark he can just make out the slow revolutions of the ceiling fan, the faint outline of the TV. He is exhausted but unable to sleep. He feels how badly his body needs rest, but it will not come. He is like a starving man standing before a feast he is forbidden to touch.

No matter how hard he tries to calm himself, his mind will not stop racing. He keeps picturing his grandfather's swollen face, the line of stitches above his lip. He checks the time on the DVD player across the room, the digital numbers never seeming to change. It is as though everything has slowed down, as though he's entered a night that will go on forever.

After a while he stands and walks to the kitchen for a glass of water, tracing the hallway wall with outstretched fingers. Malcolm's laptop is charging on the kitchen table. Tulsi takes a seat and opens it. He logs onto Facebook the way Malcolm taught him. He has twenty-three friends. Malcolm, some soccer teammates, even a few of the more tech-savvy residents of Eleventh Street. He scrolls to the top of his News Feed and types his sister's name into the search function.

Susmita Gurung.

Not her married name but her given one. Not the name of Purna's wife but the name of his sister. He has tried both ways, but neither has yielded what he hopes for. He hits enter and the familiar *NO RESULTS FOUND* pops up. He erases the last name, tapping the delete key until that part of his sister vanishes. He hits enter again and this time a whole list of Susmitas appears, a catalogue of young girls and women who bear this name. They are all smiling, all of them happy to be having their photo taken and added to this online community, this record to the world that not only do they exist but they have family and friends. There are people willing to search for them, eager to find and connect with them, keep tabs on their comings and goings. Tulsi scans the list, studies each name, each picture as he has so many times before. His sister is not among them.

•

Tulsi spends the next three days at the hospital. He sits beside his grandfather's bed and talks to him, brings him ice chips in paper cups from the vending area down the hall. He rubs lotion onto his grandfather's chapped hands, accompanies him to the barrage of tests he is subjected to, waits in the hallway when he is not permitted to enter. He answers the doctor's questions when he visits and fills out the paperwork the hospital and police require.

Every morning Rachel drives him to Hamot whether she is working that day or not. She introduces him to all the nurses on his grandfather's floor and he memorizes their names. They take a liking to him and look out for him, checking on his grandfather frequently, making sure they both remain comfortable. After the third day, his grandfather is cleared to return home.

Before Rachel drives them, the detective who handled the case visits the hospital a final time.

"No new leads," he informs them bluntly. None of the witnesses thought to write down a license plate number and other than a generic description of the assailants there is nothing to go on. He delivers the news with a certain amount of ambivalence, as though making no arrests had been a foregone conclusion. "We'll keep the case open," he adds, "but it's not looking good."

•

Though he says nothing, Tulsi notices a change in his grandfather. Since the attack, he speaks less frequently, and when he does it is with little optimism. It is as though his hopes for their new home have been compromised, the sheen of America worn off to reveal rust and decay. More and more lately he speaks only of Bhutan, his life there. Having been born in the camps in Nepal, Bhutan is a country Tulsi has never known. Still, he listens, watches the glint in his grandfather's eyes as he recalls a childhood more idyllic than seems possible, speaks of his wife, his love for her, caring for her as she succumbed to illness in the camps.

He skips over the bad parts, for which Tulsi is grateful. He has already heard these. Bhutan's Citizenship Act, its One Nation One People ideology. The only culture permitted that of the northern Bhutanese, not the southern Lhotshampa like his grandfather. Tulsi has heard him discuss the census and the violence that followed, the imprisonments and forceful carrying out of the Driglam Namzha, Bhutan's national dress and etiquette code. The message so simple: dress like us, speak like us, act like us, or leave. His parents and grandparents, like the other Lhotshampas, were deemed illegal immigrants though they'd lived in Bhutan their whole lives. Their Nepali ethnicity and language, their culture, all of it suddenly considered antinational, a threat to Bhutan's purity.

With a soldier's rifle point pressed between his shoulder blades, his grandfather was forced to sign a Voluntary Migration Form.

Tulsi remembers what his grandfather told him, what the soldiers made him repeat over and over as he gathered his family, as he packed their things to go.

"I am leaving forever," he'd been forced to say. "I am leaving forever of my own free will."

•

Watching his grandfather now as he sits at their tiny kitchen table, Tulsi is filled with sadness. His face has returned to its normal shape, his cuts have healed, but he is changed.

"And the mountains," he is saying. "You've never seen such wonders." At this his grandfather stops and looks across the room, at the windows that face out onto Eleventh Street, a row of identical buildings standing on the other side. He stares as though waiting for something to appear.

"Here there are no mountains," he says. He pushes back his chair and stands slowly, his joints cracking from the effort. As he walks past, his fingertips graze Tulsi's shoulder. He disappears into his bedroom and closes the door softly behind him.

Dear Brother,

I pray this finds you well. I have not heard from you and I fear time will only deepen the divide.

Camp Beldangi Extension is overcrowded, and they have placed us in tents. Though the residents here have little they share what they can. It is something I have found in this life. Those with least often give most.

When the IOM arrived, they informed us the fire had forced them to shift resettlement orders. Those of us who were slated to leave in due time have nowhere to stay. The tents are impermanent and we must abandon them before the rains commence. As Beldangi's residents are resettled, we will take their huts. In short, our futures have been delayed. It is not uncommon but many are disappointed.

Purna has taken construction work outside the camp near Damak. There he has met others who plan to leave of their own accord. They are headed west. They tell us Qatar is rising and hands are needed to lift it. Purna agrees, and we have decided to join them. He believes we make our own fates. Is it so, brother? Do you make yours even now?

I do not know whom we will find in Qatar or how long we will remain, but the others have sworn that jobs are plentiful. Purna is hopeful as always and I try to maintain the same. So many hardships in this world. Why inflict more on ourselves?

For so many years we have breathed uncertainty. What I long for most is steadfastness. A life where the sun rising and setting are not its only constants. This is what I hope you have found.

Pray for us, brother, as I do for you.

Susmita

PART TWO

AUGUST 2012

TULSI WATCHES THE CARDS CLOSELY, tries to keep count in his mind. He has always been good at math, has always carried a fondness for numbers, but what he keeps forgetting is that aces can be either one or eleven, whichever the player prefers. This duality is troubling to him. It seems somehow too good to be true. He cannot help but doubt its validity.

He is seated in an auditorium at the Bayfront Convention Center. Along with three hundred others, he has come to attend Presque Isle Downs and Casino's dealer training school. In front of them a petite woman with a pageboy haircut lectures onstage. A tiny microphone arcs around the side of her face.

"Most of you won't make it," she says. Behind her, a massive projection screen displays a cartoon blackjack table. "I'm not trying to discourage you," she adds. "Those are just the facts." She turns back to the screen and clicks a remote. A cartoon dealer distributes cards to four simulated players.

•

During their lunch break Tulsi sits alone outside. The convention center is situated right on the bay, and so he finds an open bench overlooking the water. It is early August and several sailboats cut across the glassy surface, headed toward the channel that leads to the open expanse of Lake Erie. Across the bay is Presque Isle State Park, a sandy spit that curves seven miles out into the lake. A pair of seagulls glides on the breeze, then dives in unison toward the water. Tulsi opens a bag of chips, tosses a few in, and watches the birds dart to retrieve them.

A week ago, Tulsi celebrated his twentieth birthday. Since graduating from East, he's held a number of jobs: cutting grass for Erie's Parks Department, delivering pizzas for Lucchetti's, even bar-backing at The Plymouth, carrying case upon case of import beer upstairs from the coolers.

All this summer he has worked as a ticket-taker at Jerry Uht Park, standing at the entry gate before games then selling concessions for the remainder. Erie's Double-A baseball team, the SeaWolves, draws a decent crowd, especially on Monday's Buck Night when draft beer, hot dogs, and popcorn go for a dollar each. Slowly, he has been putting money away for college, his savings account growing in modest but steady increments. Malcolm has been gone a year, off studying video game design at Carnegie Mellon.

A friend of Tulsi's from Eleventh Street recommended he look into the casino's dealer training school. Chandra is a few years older and has been in the States longer. He'd started working at Presque Isle Downs as soon as it opened but had since taken a job dealing Texas hold 'em at the Rivers casino in Pittsburgh.

"It's good money and you get a twenty-minute break every hour," he told Tulsi before moving. "You should give it a shot."

Ever since, Tulsi had been waiting for another session of dealer school to begin. If he can survive the four weeks of training and a live audition, he has a chance at getting hired. The base salary, Chandra told him, is only four dollars an hour, but that's not including tips.

"If you get the job," Chandra said, "always be gracious to the gamblers. Always make it seem as though you're on their side. If they like you and think you're rooting for them, they'll tip better."

Now Tulsi is having second thoughts about the casino job. He wonders if it's something his grandfather would have approved of.

The previous November, Tulsi arrived home from bar-backing and found his grandfather's door shut. It was late, almost three in the morning, and his grandfather had been scheduled to work third shift at the juice plant that night. When Tulsi opened the door, he found him sitting on the side of his bed, doubled over in pain, his hands locked beneath his knees. He looked up when Tulsi entered, his face ashen.

"It's nothing, my son," he said, wincing. "Rest." Tulsi ignored him and called an ambulance, kneeling beside his grandfather and holding his hand until he heard the sirens wailing, red lights pulsing in the windows.

The tests revealed pancreatic cancer, too advanced to treat. In so many words, the doctors explained, his grandfather's life was beyond saving. For two months Tulsi did nothing but care for him, quitting both of his part-time jobs and focusing his entire being on his grandfather: feeding him, bathing him, filling his prescriptions, and portioning out the cocktail of pills he secretly hoped would perform some miracle.

Near the end he spoke only of Bhutan, the land of his birth, the home he would never return to. There came a day he believed he was still there. He began to ask Tulsi to part the curtains so he could look out onto the countryside, to open the windows so he could breathe the sweet air sweeping off the Sankosh River. It was a small blessing and Tulsi nurtured the hallucinations.

"Yes, Hajurba," he would say. "We are here. They are celebrating the Winter Solstice."

"Are they dancing?" his grandfather would ask, staring excitedly at the ceiling. "Are they wearing their masks?"

"Yes," Tulsi would say. "The dragon is fighting the demons." His grandfather would close his eyes as the morphine took over.

"The dragon will be victorious," he'd say. "It is always this way."

Tulsi slept on the floor beside his grandfather's bed, layering blankets for a makeshift mattress. In the final days, the International Institute paid for a hospice nurse who stayed every night, a quiet woman who sat vigil in the armchair near the window, reading paperbacks or doing cross-stitch as Tulsi and his grandfather slept. One night she awoke Tulsi with a hand laid gently on his arm. Before she could speak, he was already crying.

For many weeks afterward, Tulsi had trouble sleeping. He moved into his grandfather's room, held his kurta close to his face, left his razor and toothbrush sitting parallel beside the bathroom sink. To change anything, to throw out his grandfather's tobacco or give away his shirts, to move his sandals from where they sat near the door, even to drink his grandfather's tea would be to admit to himself what he'd feared all along.

In this new life, he was now completely alone.

•

Tulsi thought often of Susmita during their grandfather's illness. In the years since their separation, Tulsi learned of a fire in Camp Goldhap, his neighbors circulating the news like a blaze of their own. Hearing it, Tulsi felt for the first time in his life something akin to terror, but all reports claimed that no one was harmed. The fire had left some five thousand without shelter but miraculously had not taken a single life. Tulsi read every article he could find, searched the print for useful details and names, and finding none, was forced to take solace in knowing that had Susmita still been in camp, she'd survived. He'd printed the articles and kept them near his bed. When he awoke trembling in the dark, he switched on his lamp and reached for them, studying the words carefully: *zero casualties*, his own private gospel.

Though it saddened him, Tulsi was relieved Susmita had not had to witness their grandfather's fast decline, the way the disease took hold of him, withering his body like a flower left to dry in the sun. It was a suffering he was happy not to share. Tulsi wondered if Susmita sensed their grandfather's death. He had heard of people aware the moment a loved one passed, even from thousands of miles away; breath catching in their chest, heart racing at the unexplainable certainty. He was not sure he believed in such things. He was not sure he wanted to.

•

The dealer auditions are held in a back gaming area of the casino that has been closed off to the public. Tulsi waits his turn among the dozens of others who've made it through training. They are being kept in the casino's buffet, which has not yet opened for the night. All around them, employees ready for the dinner rush, lowering stainless-steel trays of food into serving stations, turning on heating lamps, arranging silverware and glasses. Behind them the casino's racetrack is visible through floor-to-ceiling windows. Tulsi watches as it's readied for the next race. A tractor pulls the starting gate into position as the jockeys try to calm the skittish thoroughbreds beneath them.

Dealer trainees are ushered out in groups of five. Tulsi goes over the rules again in his mind. He is trying out for blackjack. Roulette and mini-baccarat would be next, then craps, the toughest of the table games to learn, but those are still a long way off. First, he has to prove himself here.

When he's finally called, Tulsi follows the others to the pit. He takes his position behind the blackjack table, where three casino employees sit posing as gamblers, the woman who led the training sessions among them. Two already have chips but the third pushes a stack of twenties across the table.

"Do you have a player's card?" Tulsi asks.

"Not interested," the man says brusquely. The woman with the pageboy haircut jots something down in her pad.

"Check change a hundred," Tulsi calls out after counting the bills. He waits for the pit boss to come over and okay it, then slides the man his chips.

The first couple hands go easily, but on the third he shows an ace and forgets to ask the table if they'd like to buy insurance. He watches the woman write something else. On the next hand, the anchor player asks to split eights, then separates the cards himself.

"Please don't, sir. I'll take care of that. Just go like this," Tulsi says, making an upside-down V with his fingers and tapping the felt. The man acts upset and pulls out a cell phone.

"No phones at the table, please, sir," Tulsi adds. The man puts it away and nods.

After another twenty minutes, his audition is up. He shows the players the tops and bottoms of his hands and walks back to the buffet with the others.

An hour and a half later, the casino posts its list of hires. Tulsi waits patiently as the candidates run over and search for their names, some of them exchanging high fives, others heading dejectedly toward the exit. When the crowd thins, he walks over and scans the names. Midway down, he sees it, misspelled, but there.

Tulsi Guroong. Blackjack.

•

He spends the next several weeks working two jobs, tearing tickets and selling concessions at the ballpark then arriving at Presque Isle Downs by 11:45 for third shift. The casino is open twenty-four hours a day, even on holidays, and so from midnight until eight in the morning, Tulsi deals blackjack. For new hires third shift is a rite of passage. Like the others he is learning the ropes, learning how to handle any situation thrown his way. There is no better time slot to do so. The casino serves alcohol until quarter till two and so for the first few hours after he arrives, he is met with the drunkest gamblers, the most belligerent. Along with the cocktail waitresses, he is responsible for making sure the casino floor is cleared of alcohol by two, a job in itself. Those still with drinks never give them up easily. More than once he has had to signal for security.

Around three in the morning, most of the drunks are gone, but by then many of the tables become deserted and he simply stands there, cards splayed before him. Toward early morning, some of the serious gamblers show up, looking to avoid the crowds. These are the players who sit studying their hands, saying nothing, only speaking to curse him for bad runs. Most of them never tip and refuse even to acknowledge he exists. For them, he is not a man but a machine, a robot that makes dreams come true, or shatters them.

Despite its difficulties, the casino exudes a certain atmosphere that makes him feel less lonely, even late at night. Gamblers shift from one slot to the next, sirens and clinking coins signaling winners. Strangers grouped together at tables become fast friends, cheering when a dealer busts or when a hot shooter comes out on the dice. By the time he arrives home at eight thirty, he is exhausted. He collapses into bed, rising by noon if the SeaWolves have a day game.

By the end of September, baseball season is over and he is only working at the casino. Eventually he's promoted to full time, a move that brings extra hours and some limited benefits. He spends much of his free time at Erie's public library, looking up colleges online, printing applications, researching in-state tuitions and the various scholarships he might be eligible for. He does not know what he would choose to study if he could afford to go, each career enticing him in its own way: businessman, journalist, doctor.

Civil engineering, however, holds a certain appeal, the idea of building things strangely exciting. In Camp Goldhap, all construction was haphazard and hastily executed, the roads that connected living sectors nothing more than a network of packed-dirt paths, most of the buildings thatched huts. Tulsi discovers that the University of Pittsburgh has a good engineering program. Carnegie Mellon is located in Pittsburgh as well, and though he and Malcolm have not spoken for some time, Malcolm having formed a whole new group of friends, the prospect of knowing at least one other person in a strange city provides some comfort.

In a little over a year, since graduating from East, he has put away nearly six thousand dollars, a full term's tuition. By his calculations he'll have enough for an entire academic year by spring. If he does, he's considering applying for early admission. Chandra may be able to get him a job dealing blackjack part time at the Rivers, and he could work nights and weekends while taking classes. He finds the prospect of moving to Pittsburgh both exhilarating and terrifying. Some days, as he lies in bed after work, the early morning light filtering through the curtains, it is all he can think about.

•

Tulsi is scheduled to work Thanksgiving and arrives for his shift twenty minutes early. He'd completely forgotten about the holiday until earlier that week, when the casino put up decorations: tiny gourds at the ends of the bar, cardboard cutouts of Pilgrims and turkeys atop the slot machines, their bases fanned out in orange and brown tissue paper. The casino is busy with out-of-towners visiting family for the holiday, looking for an excuse to get out of the house after a day spent bingeing on food and drink.

For the first part of his shift, Tulsi deals to a continually packed table, its occupants rotating, each empty seat quickly claimed. Every new shoe brings several new players, and by break time he's certain he's paid out and taken away enough money to fund an entire college education. He waits for his relief dealer, then shows the players his hands before leaving.

In the break room, he sits reading a magazine someone left behind. A TV in the corner plays SportsCenter on a loop, showing highlights of the day's football games. At the far end of the table is a woman he has never seen before. He suspects she is a graduate of the most recent round of dealer training school. She is hunched over, talking on her cell phone, visibly upset. Wisps of steam rise from a Styrofoam cup and float past her face. Tulsi looks away. His propensity to stare is still strong. He pretends to read the magazine as the woman's urgent whispering grows louder. She is angry, frustrated. He can tell by her tone. Her words are thick with it.

It is just past three in the morning when he sees the woman again. The casino has emptied out, the festiveness that pervaded it gone. The cleaning crew makes their way through the rows of slots. Their vacuums drown out the music.

The woman deals at the table beside Tulsi's. His is empty, but she has two players: a pair of surly-looking men, both drunk. Lit cigarettes smolder in an ashtray between them. The first of the two, a skinny man in a sleeveless T-shirt, leans forward on his chair and studies the woman's nametag.

"Becky," he says. "Becky, why don't you be a doll and deal us some cards we can actually play?" His friend snickers and draws on his cigarette. The woman tries to ignore them. She is slim with frizzy straw-blond hair, cut short and brushed to the side, a single silver barrette holding it in place. She waits for the men to bet, then deals the next hand. She is showing a jack and once both men stay, she turns over her undercard, a ten. She pulls back their bets and racks the chips.

"What the fuck, Becky?" the other man says, slurring his words. "How are we supposed to win when you're not even giving us a chance?"

"Come on, Becky," the first man says. "It's Thanksgiving for Christ sakes."

Tulsi listens as they repeat her name over and over. It was one of the first lessons he learned working at the casino, the tendency of some gamblers to latch onto a dealer's name and not let go. Some are looking for a way to make the game a little less impersonal, but others, like these men, repeat it only to goad the dealer, to sharpen their insults when they're dealt unfavorable hands.

"Let me ask you something, Becky," the first man says. "How does one end up dealing blackjack in an establishment such as this at three in the morning on Thanksgiving?" He places his bet, then slides forward a five-dollar chip. "Play this one with me," he says. The woman deals the cards.

"I mean, was this your ultimate career goal or did you just luck out?" The other man laughs and wobbles unsteadily on his chair. The skinny man motions for a hit and busts.

"See, you just lost yourself a tip," he says as she pulls back his bet and the five-dollar chip. "Wait," he adds, mocking alarm, "did you even get to celebrate today? Did you get any turkey? Tell you what; I've got some leftovers in the car. Why don't you meet me out there and I'll fix you a plate. We can have ourselves a little party, just the two of us."

"Don't forget about me," the other man says. "You all can't throw a party without me."

"I'm sure Becky here wouldn't mind if you joined us. Would you, Becky?"

Tulsi turns off the neon minimum-maximum bet sign that signals his table is open. In one fluid motion, he gathers the spread cards and places them into the automatic shuffler. He walks over and taps the woman's shoulder, signaling a dealer change. It's not his table to cover and he's sure the pit boss will call him out later, but he doesn't care.

"Take five," he says, when the woman turns around, surprised. He nods, letting her know it's all right. There is relief in her eyes as she shows her hands and walks away.

"Whoa, whoa, whoa," the first man says. "Becky just got here, buddy. We were just getting started."

The second man blows a stream of smoke directly at Tulsi's face. "We're celebrating an American holiday, chief. If it's all the same, we'd prefer an American dealer." Now it's the skinny man's turn to laugh.

"Ah, Rich," he says, smirking. "That ain't right." He shakes loose a cigarette. "This boy's just trying to make a living. You sure you know how to deal blackjack though?" He narrows his eyes at Tulsi's nametag. "Tesla? You sure you shouldn't be running the mahjong table or something? Why don't you go fetch Becky, let her finish this shoe?"

Tulsi slides out the burn card and shows it to them, an ace. He tucks it into the plastic discard holder.

"Rules are rules," he says. "Now, let's play some cards."

•

Walking to his car after work, Tulsi hears a series of quick footsteps behind him. He turns, his lunch pail raised in his left hand, his right hand balled to a fist. It is the woman from earlier, jogging to catch up. An old North Face jacket covers her casino uniform, black with purple trim.

"Hey," she calls out. Tulsi lowers his lunch pail and buries the other hand in his pocket.

She slows and catches her breath. "I just wanted to say thank you. For earlier."

"Not a problem," Tulsi says.

"Those two were following me around all night. Every new table I'd get to, they'd pop up to give me some more shit."

"Unfortunately, guys like them come with the job," Tulsi says. "That and the cigarette smoke. They leave that part out in dealer school."

The woman smiles. "I hate that too. I've only been working here a week and my apartment already smells like an ashtray."

Behind them the sun has just cleared the tops of the trees beyond the racetrack. The sound of traffic from I-90 fills the morning air, shoppers heading to cash in on Black Friday.

"Those guys were right about one thing," she says. "It wasn't much of a Thanksgiving for me. How about you? You been here all night?"

"Since midnight," Tulsi says. "It's the time and a half for the holiday. I couldn't pass it up."

The truth is he would have worked regardless. In the past, he'd sometimes roasted a small turkey breast for him and his grandfather, made Stove Top stuffing and instant mashed potatoes, sliced a can of gelatinous cranberry sauce. After he'd been in the States for a while, he and his grandfather had done their best to embrace the various American holidays, to adopt the culture as a complement to their own. It made them feel a part of something, less alien in their new home. Now, Tulsi has no one to cook for, no one to decorate the apartment for. Work is a good excuse not to bother.

"Listen," the woman says. "I have a little while before I've got to be at my other job, and I was going to get some food. Can I buy you breakfast? Pay you back for helping me out earlier?"

•

They sit across from each other in a corner booth at an all-day diner. Further up Peach Street, the Millcreek Mall and its surrounding superstores teem with deal-seekers, and so the restaurant is mostly empty. Tulsi waits for the woman to order then asks for the same thing, the Hearty Man's Combo: two eggs sunny-side up, bacon, sausage links, wheat toast, hash browns, and three buttermilk pancakes with maple syrup. The waitress brings a plastic carafe of coffee and sets it between them.

The woman's name is Rebecca. When the casino asked her what she'd like on her nametag, she'd asked for Becky so she could maintain some semblance of anonymity. Tulsi studies her whenever she looks away: the smooth skin of her broad forehead, the slightly upturned point of her nose, the shape of her lips. She is unassumingly beautiful, plain at a distance but intricate and lovely up close. Her eyes are green.

"No one I know in real life calls me Becky," she says.

She is twenty-four years old and has a daughter with her ex-husband, an Erie City cop.

"Grace," she tells him, holding her phone across the table for him to see. "I picked her name. She just turned five." On the screen is a small girl with thick glasses and long dark hair. She is standing on the beach at Presque Isle, Lake Erie an expanse of blue behind her, a stone breakwater visible to her right. She has on a pink two-piece bathing suit and holds a plastic shovel above her head triumphantly.

"She's a trip," Rebecca says, beaming. "An absolute trip. Crazy smart too. Wants to be like eight different things when she grows up." She takes back her phone and puts it in her purse. "You have kids?"

"Me?" Tulsi says, shaking his head and smiling. "I'm too young."

Rebecca lowers her eyes, circles her finger around the rim of her coffee mug. He instantly regrets what he's said, cannot believe his own stupidity. The waitress arrives with their food and sets the steaming plates in front of them.

"I'm sorry," Tulsi says once she's left. "I didn't mean...I've just never been married or anything."

"That's all right," she says. "I was really young. And me and Steve weren't married at the time." She reaches for the salt and sprinkles some on her eggs. "I mean, it wasn't exactly planned."

Outside, a line of cars moves by. A man gets off his bicycle and walks it. Tulsi searches for the right words, a way to let Rebecca know he wasn't judging her.

"Sometimes," he says finally, "that is how the best things happen."

●

They eat together two or three times a week. Sometimes in the break room, Tulsi packing extra sandwiches and snacks, and sometimes after work at one of the early-morning diners. Though she protests and snatches at the check when it arrives, Tulsi insists on paying since she first treated him. Rebecca, he finds out, is of Italian heritage. She brings him Tupperware containers of minestrone and sausage and peppers, homemade ravioli and gnocchi in a meat sauce she calls gravy.

He soaks lentils and shops for spices to make his grandfather's famous dal, bringing it to the casino in a pair of thermoses and serving it with fresh roti and a spicy relish she raves over. While they eat, they share their plans for the future. Tulsi tells her about college and the University of Pittsburgh's engineering school. He talks about Malcolm and what he said he was learning at Carnegie Mellon, how exciting it was to be living in Pittsburgh.

Rebecca talks of making enough money to move out west to Colorado. She has an aunt in Steamboat Springs and they've always been close, closer than Rebecca was with her own mother. If she can get the money together, she wants to move, work at her aunt's salon, or open a shop. Her aunt has three children her age, all with families of their own. She wants Grace to be raised alongside her cousins.

"It's a long-term dream," she says. That's what she calls it whenever she talks about moving. Her long-term dream. First she needs to put enough money away and secondly, more importantly, she needs to settle things with her ex, Grace's father.

"He can be so frustrating," she says. Rebecca has told Tulsi how he has partial custody but often cancels last minute or arrives hours late. Tulsi knows it is a touchy subject and avoids it unless Rebecca brings it up.

Sometimes she'll ask about his childhood, about his life before arriving in the States. Growing up in the camps is something he has learned not to talk about. It is a secret history he keeps hidden, the early part of his life so different from other people's. With Rebecca, though, he feels he can share some part of it and so he does, telling her about going to school in Goldhap, learning English, leaving to join his grandfather, the long journey that brought him to Pennsylvania. He does his best to explain the history of his people, the Lhotshampa, the convoluted web of Bhutanese laws and exclusionary tactics that forced them out of their country and into the camps. The more he explains, the less sense any of it seems to make. It is a history he's learned secondhand, living the effect but not the cause. His people were a part of Bhutan, and then they weren't. It's as simple as that.

•

One morning after they've finished their shifts, Rebecca invites Tulsi to come with her. When he asks where they're going, she says it's a surprise. They drive to a small apartment complex off Thirty-Eighth Street. They park on the street and Tulsi follows Rebecca inside and up a stairwell to the third floor. Rebecca knocks at a door, and a moment later a large woman with her hair done up in curlers answers. She smiles and ushers them inside.

"She's just finishing up in the bathroom," the woman says.

"Tulsi, this is Ms. Hammond." Tulsi shakes her hand. She has on a brightly colored housedress and blue plastic sandals.

"Sit, sit," she says, directing them to the couch. She shuffles off to the kitchen and reappears with two mugs of coffee with cream.

"I live one floor down," Rebecca says. "Ms. Hammond watches Grace on nights when I'm working. She's an angel."

"Oh, go on," Ms. Hammond says, beaming, "tell me more." She lets out a high-pitched laugh, her cheeks reddening. When she stops she says, "Your girl is the angel, an absolute joy. She watches me." From the back hallway comes the sound of a door opening and then the girl from Rebecca's phone walks into the living room. She darts to Rebecca and hugs her around the neck.

"You smell like smoke, Mommy," she says, "but it's okay." The girl lets go and looks at Tulsi. She has on purple jeans and a long-sleeved shirt sparkling with glitter. Her pant legs are tucked into pink boots.

"Hello," Tulsi says and extends a hand. The girl shakes it.

"Do you work at the horse track too?" she asks.

"Grace is very interested in the horse track," Rebecca says. "Not so much the actual casino. I promised I'd take her to see them when the season starts next summer."

"I work inside with your mom," Tulsi tells the girl, "but I've seen the horses. They're beautiful. And so fast."

"When we move to Colorado, I'm going to ride one everywhere," the girl says, "even to school." She begins to dance in place.

"That sounds like a great way to get around. Much more fun than a car." The girl nods in agreement, then rushes to the hallway. She reappears wearing a coat and backpack.

"Off we go," she says.

•

The three of them walk along the sidewalk on Thirty-Eighth Street, Grace a few steps in front with Tulsi and Rebecca trailing. Christmas is a week away and the city has readied itself. Red and silver tinsel encircle streetlamps, wreaths hang from doors, nativity scenes and wicker reindeer populate nearby yards. It's been an unusually mild winter so far and only a thin dusting of dry snow covers the ground. It drifts across the sidewalk like sand.

Grace is in kindergarten, Rebecca tells him. At first, she'd been scared to go, but now she loves it.

"Her friends, her teachers, it's become a huge part of her life," Rebecca says. "Not like it was for her mother. I was awful in school. Couldn't wait to get out." Grace skips along the sidewalk ahead of them, her Dora the Explorer lunch pail swinging at her side.

"I'm sure you weren't that bad," Tulsi says.

Rebecca shrugs, the look on her face pensive, as though she's no longer beside him but somewhere far away. She watches her daughter run ahead. "There was always something to deal with at home. It became hard to concentrate on school, to take it seriously." She has never elaborated, but in so many words Rebecca has let Tulsi know that her upbringing was not an easy one. Besides her aunt it seems she doesn't speak to any of her family. She's only mentioned her mother in passing and an older half-brother who lives in Florida. She's never spoken of her father.

"Getting out and getting a job just always felt like a foregone conclusion," she says. "If I could do it all over again, I'd pay more attention. I was always interested in law."

"You're only twenty-four," Tulsi says. "You could go back to school. You have time to do anything you want."

Rebecca smiles and cinches her coat tighter. There is something in the way she looks at him that he has not seen before, her eyes meeting his and lingering until he has to glance away. "You're an eternal optimist, Tulsi," she says. "I wish it were that simple." They arrive at the school's parking lot. "Besides," she adds, "I'll be twenty-five in a week." She points at herself proudly. "Christmas baby."

"You're kidding."

"Nope."

They walk Grace into school, kids of all ages streaming past. Rebecca kneels and hugs her, holds on until she begins to wriggle.

"See you at three," Rebecca says and stands. Grace looks up at Tulsi.

"Thanks for walking me to school," she says. "We can talk more about horses sometime."

"I look forward to it," Tulsi says, smiling as she rushes down the hallway to join her friends.

•

Rebecca invites him for Christmas Eve dinner. Tulsi obsesses over what to bring. He finally settles on a maple-glazed ham the clerk at Urbaniak's recommends. He is still just twenty, not old enough to buy wine, and so he picks up two bottles of sparkling cider instead. He arrives early, just as the sun disappears into the lake, streaking the sky a sherbet orange. Rebecca and Grace greet him dressed in oversized, amazingly tacky Christmas sweaters.

"We got these at Goodwill," Rebecca says, laughing, pointing at the felt reindeer affixed to the front of hers. Grace rushes down the hallway and returns with one they've bought for him, a baggy black crewneck displaying a neon Frosty the Snowman. A new tradition, Rebecca tells him and smiles.

"Do you like it?" Grace asks. Tulsi slips it over his button-down and smooths the front.

"I love it," he says.

He hands them the cider and ham, and they lead him to the living room where *A Christmas Story* plays on TV. In the corner a miniature Christmas tree is wrapped in strands of popcorn. Candles scented like pine trees and cinnamon sit atop a small entertainment center next to pictures of Grace from infancy on.

Grace and Rebecca disappear into the kitchen, where he hears their laughter alongside the clanking of pots and carols playing on the radio. After a while, Grace walks out ceremoniously and leads him into the kitchen, where the table is dressed in a white linen cloth, three place settings arranged elegantly. Serving dishes hold green bean casserole, mashed potatoes, gravy, candied yams covered in melted marshmallows, crescent rolls, and stuffing. A pecan pie sits on the stove for dessert. Rebecca hands Tulsi a long stainless-steel knife.

"If you would do the honors," she says. Tulsi carves slices of turkey and ham for each of them. They drink the sparkling cider from plastic champagne flutes he brought along, a trio of tea candles flickering between them.

Tulsi helps clear the table after dessert, but Rebecca refuses to let him wash dishes. She banishes him to the living room, where he waits with a cup of coffee. Grace and Rebecca appear shortly after. He has brought them each a gift but has been worrying over when to give them, uncertain of the protocol. Finally, he walks over to the bag he brought them in and takes out the wrapped packages. Rebecca shakes her head.

"Tulsi, you didn't have to. Really."

"This," he says, and points to the room around them, the candles and Christmas tree, the kitchen. "You didn't have to do all this, invite me here, cook. But you did." He smiles at her, looks in her eyes for a moment longer than he has all night, then hands her the smaller of the two packages. She unwraps it, splitting the shiny paper at the seams, undoing the tape carefully, her maneuvers so delicate that Tulsi does not notice he's holding his breath.

It is a bottle of perfume. The deeply rouged saleswoman at Macy's had assured him it was the finest they sold, that any woman would love it. Rebecca holds it up for them to see and uncaps it. Two spritzes: one for her, one for Grace. They both tell him it's wonderful.

Grace's present is next and he watches intently as she pulls away the colorful wrapping paper. It is a ceramic horse figurine, painted in bright pinks and purples. He found it in the collectibles section of a boutique toy store across town. Grace studies it admiringly then prances it through the air.

"I'll name her Angel," she says, "because she can fly." She walks over and thanks him with a hug.

•

At the end of the night, Rebecca walks him to the door and follows him into the hallway.

"Thank you," she says. "That was the best Christmas we've had in a long time." She leans forward and embraces him. Her body feels firm against his, her breath warm on his neck. For a while they stand there holding each other.

"It's your birthday in an hour," Tulsi says, and then, "I'm glad I met you." They separate slightly and before he can stop himself, he leans in and kisses her. When she kisses him back something rises within him, elevates a happiness he thought had reached its apex. The kiss is different from any he's experienced; he feels it instantly in a way he cannot explain. Before it ends he opens his eyes, looks at this woman he finds so beautiful, touches the side of her face as softly as he can.

•

On mornings when Rebecca doesn't have to work her second job, they walk Grace to school together. They gather her from Ms. Hammond, who is always kind and inviting them to stay. Then they brave the Erie winter and walk together along Thirty-Eighth Street,

Grace huddled between them, shielded from the wind and snow. It becomes another tradition.

One morning, a couple of weeks after Christmas, Rebecca invites Tulsi up for coffee after they've dropped Grace off. When they reach her apartment, she leads him into the darkened living room and sits beside him on the couch.

They remain there quietly, Tulsi's heart beating a wild rhythm. He swallows, tries to measure his breaths. He is suddenly aware of the position of his hands, crossed awkwardly in his lap. Rebecca reaches over and turns his face toward hers, looks at him in a way that makes him feel every cell of his body.

They sit there kissing, Tulsi's hands still crossed politely in front of him, until Rebecca takes one, rises from the couch, and leads him into the bedroom.

She seats him on the edge of the bed, a narrow twin covered in pillows and a white comforter. Behind him a window dressed in lace curtains filters the soft morning light. Rebecca stands there looking at him wordlessly, then unbuttons the starched white shirt the casino requires them to wear, turns and drapes it over a dresser. She unhooks her bra then slides off her black pants and underwear until she is standing before him naked, her skin incredibly smooth and white, ribbons of light illuminating it. There is a tiny tattoo of a half moon near her hip, a thin scar beneath one rib. Tulsi's breath catches in his chest. She is beautiful.

She steps forward until the hollow of her navel is even with his eyes. He inhales the scent of her, soap and cotton, the smoke they carry with them. He feels a hunger he has never known. She is tender when she unbuttons his shirt, when she pushes him gently back, then takes off his pants and climbs on top.

He lies there motionless, afraid still to touch her, afraid to make some clumsy mistake, cross some unknown, unforgiveable threshold. He watches her lift his hands, which he can see are trembling, and lay them on her collarbones, running them down the swells of her breasts, tracing his fingers over her stomach, across her hips and buttocks, all the way back around to the crease of skin where their bodies meet. She lifts herself, cocks her hips and places him inside of her, rocking back and forth gently, evenly, until all he can feel is warmth, so sweet and sudden and complete it is impossible for him to imagine ever having lived without it.

•

Soon they spend all their time together. Stealing kisses in the break room at the casino, cooking dinner with Grace on shared nights off, making love in the mornings after dropping her at school. Before he knows it, Tulsi is in love. He has seen enough movies, has read enough books to know that is what this is. The sensation of not being able to live without another person, every moment of your day spent thinking about them, obsessing over them, concerned only with their happiness and your role in it, their proximity to you. Dreaming of them and being at once purely happy and incredibly terrified of waking and finding them gone. No other combination of person, place, or circumstance offering any more favorable an alternative than being by their side. Always by their side.

Suddenly things make sense. Why he has ended up in Erie. The reasoning for it, preordained, decided by some omnipotent being, benevolent and just. In a few short weeks he cannot imagine his life without her, cannot remember what it was like before.

Rebecca. The answer to every question he never thought to ask.

•

"I wish you could have met my grandfather," he tells her one morning as they lie in bed. "He would have liked you so much. Grace too."

"What was he like?" Rebecca rests her hand on his chest. She spreads her fingers slowly then pulls them back, the contact comforting.

He can feel it everywhere.

"He was kind," he says. It is the word that most often comes to mind when he thinks of his grandfather. Kind. Simply that. At peace with the world. Gentle. Hopeful. At least until the attack, and then bearing it privately, his disillusionment. Tulsi knows it but does not say it now. The way he has chosen to remember his grandfather is as he was when he arrived, the type of man who would point to a statue of an American hero and suggest that one day his grandson might be honored in such a fashion. The type of man who worked endlessly without complaint, who celebrated Tulsi's soccer victories with pizza and wings on the porch. He misses him. Being with Rebecca has helped, his loneliness reduced exponentially. Still, he thinks of him often.

Sometimes Tulsi wants to tell Rebecca about Susmita. He wants her to know he has a sister. That somewhere in this world is someone who looks like him, remembers him, knew him as a child. What he does not want to talk about is the squalid place they came from, the hopelessness that pervaded the camp. He does not want to mention the friends he has lost, the faces he'll never see again. He does not want to tell her he is unaware of where his sister is, that he might never know. It is a private sadness, an old wound. Rebecca, he senses, has some of her own. It would be selfish to add his, and so he does not.

"What about your aunt?" Tulsi asks. "What's she like?"

"Funny," Rebecca says. He can feel her smiling beside him. "And sweet. When I was little, she still lived in Erie and she doted on me. Took me to the movies, to McDonald's. We had sleepovers at her apartment and stayed up late watching old movies."

"She sounds wonderful," Tulsi says, rolling onto his side to face her.

"She really is," she says. "It's what I want for Grace, a childhood like that. But not just sometimes. All the time. That's why I want to move us out there."

In the past few weeks, since the morning they first made love, they have spoken less and less about their future plans: Tulsi's education,

Rebecca's long-term dream of moving to Colorado. Tulsi has stopped going to the library to research colleges, has stopped printing out applications and working on the personal statement that had so troubled him. To do so would be to acknowledge the temporality of their situation, a future apart from one another.

"She deserves that," he says now. "You both do."

•

One Wednesday evening Tulsi works a table in the back gaming section. It's the only area of the casino where smoking is banned, and he enjoys the change. He'd been called in early and has been on the clock since eight. Quarter past two and the casino is dead around him. His table has been empty for the past twenty minutes. His back aches, and he flexes his knees slightly to keep them from tightening. Some nights, if the action is really slow, the pit boss will send a couple dealers home. Tulsi hopes he might be one of them. Rebecca has given him a key to her apartment. He is imagining climbing into the warm bed beside her and sleeping till morning when a man walks up to his table and takes a seat. Tulsi gathers the fanned-out cards and places them in the shoe.

"How we doing tonight, sir?" he asks, but the man remains silent. Tulsi waits for him to pull out his wallet or take some money from his breast pocket but he doesn't. He simply sits there staring at him. The man has a buzz cut and thin lips set in a ridged line. A small scar stretches along the tan skin beside his left eyebrow. Tulsi smells the alcohol on him; sees the glassy film covering his gray eyes. And there is something else, a familiarity in the man's features he cannot quite place.

"Ready to win some money?" Tulsi asks, but the man keeps staring at him, says nothing. He has on a plain black polo, buttoned all the way to the top, the short sleeves stretched over muscular arms. Tulsi feels his own discomfort growing, senses that something is not right.

He looks around, but the tables beside his are closed. On the other side of the pit, an old man plays mini baccarat, the floor manager making small talk with him and the dealer. A few women sit at a distant cluster of slots.

Just as Tulsi is about to say something else, ask if he'd like to change some money, or if he needs some coffee, the man stands. He's a few inches taller than Tulsi, and wide across the chest.

"You just watch yourself," he says. And the moment he does it is like a light switching on. The stubbed nose, the full arching eyebrows, Grace's features intensified, undiluted. Grace's father. Rebecca's ex. Steve.

The man smiles. It is not a kind smile, his thin lips parting to reveal a row of slightly off-centered teeth. He shakes his head, his face displaying pity, as though he's just heard a dumb joke and is embarrassed for the teller. Then he turns and walks away.

When his shift ends, Tulsi walks out into the employee parking lot to his car, a used Honda Civic he financed after high school and is still paying off. Across the green of the driver's side door is a long metallic scratch where the paint has been keyed, a single sequence of pointed peaks like the jagged readout of a heart monitor.

•

Tulsi doesn't tell Rebecca about the encounter. He goes on spending time with her as if nothing has happened. They take Grace to story time at the library, to interactive exhibits at the Children's Museum, to celebrate her birthday with her friends at Chuck E. Cheese's. If neither of them is working, they go to the movies at the dollar theater, catching matinees while Grace is still in school. Tulsi never lets Grace see him stay over, slipping from the apartment silently before she wakes. He does not want to confuse her. To her he is simply her mother's friend, the man who has promised to take her to see the horses when the weather warms. She is as bright and cheerful as Rebecca claimed, and she always has something to ask him: how he arrived in Erie, if he has any pets, why Ms. Hammond has so many veins in her legs. She is a wellspring of amusement and joy for both Tulsi and Rebecca, a tiny living doll.

•

Grace's father has partial custody, picking her up every other weekend. Tulsi is never there when he comes to get her. Steve objected to the custody agreement after the fact and it is a constant source of worry for Rebecca. She does not want to give him anything he can potentially use against her, anything he could bring up as ammunition. The thought of Grace spending any more time with him terrifies Rebecca. She dreads the weekends Grace is with him, worries constantly over how she's doing. Tulsi has let her believe that Steve does not know about them, that they have never met. He feels guilty not telling her what happened at the casino but does not want to upset her.

One afternoon Tulsi arrives to find her sobbing in the kitchen.

"Steve's petitioning for full custody," she tells him. "And he's going to get it. I know it."

Tulsi tries to calm her, lays a hand on her back.

"He knows everyone because he's a cop," she says. "It isn't fair."

Tulsi kneels before her on the linoleum. He stays like that for a long time, rubbing her legs, telling her it's going to be all right. Inside he feels nothing but pain. He wants to be angry with this man for doing this, for upsetting her so deeply, but right now he cannot. All he can do is suffer with her, endure a helpless sort of grief. He cannot control it. Her sadness is his.

When she finally calms, Tulsi places his fingers gently beneath her chin, lifts her face toward his.

"What can *we* do?" he asks.

•

The lawyer's office is downtown. It's a stately two-story brick building that looks more like a home than a place of business. Inside they wait holding hands in a tiny reception area. Pictures of Erie's historic buildings hang framed on the wall: the Courthouse, Gannon University, Presque Isle Lighthouse. A young secretary stares at her computer screen at the desk across from them. They've given her their names and are waiting to be called back. The fax machine beside the woman's computer jolts to life and Rebecca flinches.

"It's going to be all right," Tulsi says, and squeezes her hand. "These guys are the best."

After Steve filed the petition with his own lawyer, they'd begun asking around for referrals. Almost everyone they asked had mentioned Sandberg and Lakes, the family law practice they're now waiting at. Tulsi did as much research as he could online and discovered in the process just how many lawyers Erie had, an astronomical amount, it seemed, for a city their size. Still, this firm was the one that kept coming up.

Beside him, Rebecca sips habitually from a paper cup of water. He has refilled it for her twice.

Eventually a woman emerges and introduces herself as Patricia Lakes. She is tall and sharply dressed in a sleek gray pantsuit. Tulsi notices her shoes, narrow brown heels with stitched patterning; so new and solid-looking they appear to be made of polished wood. She asks if they need anything and when they say no, leads them to her office, closing the door behind them.

"From what you told me on the phone, I think you're in fairly good shape," she says. "Mothers typically receive the benefit of the doubt in custody agreements. That being said, it's almost certain to drag on for a while. Your ex-husband is an Erie City police officer, correct?" Rebecca nods. Patricia reads notes from a yellow pad. "And you were granted primary custody during the divorce?"

"Yes," Rebecca says. The attorney looks up, sets down the pen she's been tapping.

"Any idea why he's doing this now? Any changes in your relationship with your ex, new developments he might not be happy about?" The woman glances at Tulsi, who looks down. He can feel the sweat slicking his palms.

"I'm dating," Rebecca says, "but I don't think he knows about my relationship with Tulsi."

"And really, it's none of his business," Patricia adds. "That's important to remember." She swivels her chair slowly from side to side. "But," she says, "there's got to be a reason he's chosen to do this now." At this Tulsi looks up, turns toward Rebecca, who is already facing him.

"He came into the casino," he says. His cheeks flush with the shame of having kept this from her, with the realization that in a way he has lied to the woman he loves. "About three weeks ago. At first, I didn't know who he was, but then he told me to be careful. I'm pretty sure it was him."

"Why didn't you tell me?"

"I thought you'd worry. I didn't want you to. I'm sorry."

The lawyer stops swiveling and jots something down. "Is there anything else?" she asks. "Did he say anything else that could be considered threatening?"

"No," Tulsi says, staring at his lap, "but I think he may have keyed my car. It was scratched along the door when I left work that morning." He looks up. Rebecca watches him, a trace of disappointment in her eyes.

"I'm sorry," Tulsi says again. "I should have told you."

"What's done is done," Patricia says. "It's good we know. It could be that or any number of reasons he's doing this now. What's important is that we have all the facts. So, you're both employed at Presque Isle Downs?"

"Yes," Rebecca says turning toward her. "And I temp part time at Schuyler, Meeks, and Associates."

The lawyer asks Rebecca more questions, writes down what she says. Tulsi wants the meeting to be over, wants to be alone with Rebecca so he can explain. It feels like they've been there forever.

"Any history of drug or alcohol abuse?" the woman asks.

Rebecca is silent. Tulsi thinks that perhaps she has not heard the lawyer's question and so he glances over. She stares absently out the window on the other side of the room. The sky beyond is a slab of solid gray. It is the beginning of March and snowflakes swirl past.

"Ms. Rossi?"

Rebecca turns to her, surprised, as though just woken from a dream.

"Any drug or alcohol issues?"

"Yes," Rebecca says, "in high school. I got in some trouble then. Some drug charges, two DUIs. I was in outpatient rehab." She falls silent as the lawyer scribbles something in her pad.

"That could complicate things," Patricia says. "Not necessarily, but potentially."

Tulsi tries to make sense of what Rebecca has said, this new part of her history. It dawns on him that his not being twenty-one has never presented a problem precisely because he has never seen Rebecca have a drink. Not a glass of wine at dinner or a beer after work. She's never gone to the bar with her friends. She keeps no alcohol in her apartment. Nothing.

Rebecca turns to him as though remembering he is there. "I guess there's a lot of things you don't know about me," she says. "A lot we don't know about each other."

•

The ride home is silent. It is only ten, still five hours until they have to pick up Grace from school. Tulsi drives while Rebecca stares out her window. The snow comes down harder, powder accumulating on the sidewalks and road, drifting like a low-hanging fog. He drives slowly with both hands on the wheel. He's had the same set of tires on the Civic since he bought it and they're balding badly, the treads grown completely slick in spots.

They drive past a string of dive bars, then Sigsbee Reservoir and the Erie Cemetery. Tulsi has the urge to pull over, shut off the car and explain to Rebecca that he's sorry to have lied to her. And that he doesn't care about her past, the drugs and drinking, the trouble she's known. What he cares about is helping her now. Making all of the sadness in her life disappear. He sees the faint outline of her face reflected in the window. When they turn onto her block and come to a stop in front of her building, she says, "Do you think less of me?" She is still not facing him.

"No," he says.

"It sounds worse now. Now that I have Grace. But at the time it felt so normal, to be with my friends, to stay away from home for days. It felt like it was all of us doing it, like it was something everyone went through. Anything to be away from home. Then I started getting in trouble."

"What happened then?"

"I met Steve. He was in college. I was already working." She laughs quietly. "He was going to *save* me," she says, shaking her head. "He was going to be a cop, and he was going to *save* me." Tulsi hears the bitterness in her words, knows she is angry not just with Steve but with herself. "There was to be no more drinking and no more drugs. For me, anyway. He could do whatever he wanted. And he did. And for a little while I thought I had been saved. Even when I got pregnant, I thought, this is a life. This is what other people have. This is the kind of life other people live every day."

She inhales deeply, lays her head back against the seat. Her eyes are closed, the lids fluttering. She rocks her head from side to side.

"I told myself 'other people's husbands sleep around,' 'other people's husbands tell them what to wear and how to act and when they can or can't leave the house. This is your perfectly normal life.'"

Her voice catches in her throat. It sounds like a gasp for air. Tulsi sees he's clutching his knees, the dark skin of his knuckles paling from the effort.

"And then one morning I was ironing his uniform and Gracie started to cry in the other room. I went to check on her. When I brought her out, I saw I left the iron flat, that it burned a hole right through his shirt, all the way to the board." She stops, but she is not crying. Her face hardens, lips drawn in a solid line.

"And then?"

"And then," she says, "then he let me know how much that shirt meant to him."

Tulsi feels the pulse pounding in his neck, the sweat dampening his collar. Hatred rises from somewhere deep within, hardens beneath his breastplate.

"It was the first time he slapped me in front of her," Rebecca says. "The only time. I packed our things that day." She opens her eyes and turns to him.

"I'm sorry," he says, leaving unspoken the other things he wants to say. That if he could, he would punish this man, vanish him from the face of the earth. That he wishes there was some way he could spare her the pain she's already endured. Impossible wishes, he thinks. Faithless words. Still, there is the shame at having lied. "I should have told you about him coming to the casino. I should have said something."

Rebecca shakes her head. She grazes his cheek with her fingertips, leans across and kisses his trembling jaw. "I know why you did it," she says. "You have a good heart."

•

Inside they lie atop the covers and hold each other. A watery blue light fills the room. Outside snow continues to fall, tiny flakes flaring like sparks. A single candle sits on the nightstand, unlit but fragrant. Its scent is what Tulsi imagines the beach smells like, sand and saltwater.

He's never been to the ocean, only seen it from a plane. Twenty years old, he thinks. Twenty years old and so much lost. Even things he never had.

•

Back at the office, when she finished with her questions, Patricia told them her retainer fee. Three thousand dollars to take the case and an hourly rate of two hundred.

"There are cheaper attorneys in town," she'd said, "but I'm good at what I do and I can get us in front of the right judge. That's what matters most. A sympathetic judge."

Tulsi had seen the shock on Rebecca's face when she heard the price, knew immediately that she did not have the money.

"Three thousand just to start?" she said.

"I know it's a lot." The lawyer flipped through the pages of her notepad. "But these cases are highly involved." Tulsi reached over and laid his hand on Rebecca's arm, rested it there for a moment before turning to Patricia.

"I can pay," he said. "No matter the cost."

•

Saint Patrick's Day and the casino is a madhouse. Tulsi has been moved to second shift, prime time for today's celebration. Irish drinking songs play nonstop and an ever-revolving cast of drunken gamblers cycles through the casino. There are several fights, including one in the parking lot. Tulsi watches as security guards rush toward the exit. People complain even more vindictively than usual when dealt losing hands, and early on in Tulsi's shift a man throws up at a roulette table across the pit. Rebecca has quit working at the casino since her ex filed the custody suit.

"I understand you earn a higher wage there than you do temping," Patricia said, "but the judge is going to be making a custody decision between a police officer and a blackjack dealer. Your ex-husband can argue that he provides a more stable living environment. Also, with your record, employment at a casino that serves alcohol just doesn't sound good."

It made perfect sense but had been hard on them both. Not only was she losing the better pay, but having Rebecca at work had been the high point of Tulsi's time there. Now he was alone again, eating his meals in the break room or out by the empty track.

Tulsi operates on autopilot for most of the day, his normal banter reduced to near silence. He does his best to ignore the drunken insults, but misdeals twice over the course of his shift and must wait for the pit boss to come over and clear it. Midnight finally arrives and he is free. He gathers his coat and gloves from his locker and slips out the employee entrance. Exhausted, he plans to head straight to his apartment and collapse in bed. He can call Rebecca in the morning, see if she'd like him to bring over coffee and donuts before they walk Grace to school. The weather has been getting steadily better, but the holiday has brought with it freezing rain and a sudden drop in temperature. The parking lot sparkles beneath the fluorescent lights of the lampposts. Tulsi starts his car, then scrapes the ice from his windshield with the back of his snowbrush. He waits for the insides of the windows to thaw before pulling out.

For a holiday, Perry Highway is surprisingly empty. Tulsi navigates the dark road, staying well clear of the yellow centerline while watching for any late-night pedestrians on the shoulder. He drives beneath the I-90 overpass and waits at the stoplight beyond. Motels and gas stations crowd the road on both sides. There is the glowing neon sign of a country bar, its parking lot filled. The freezing rain has started back up and Tulsi flicks on his wipers. As he descends the hill toward Old French Road, he sees a line of cars being diverted one at a time into a wide parking lot at the intersection. The flashing police lights atop three cruisers strobe the darkness. A DUI checkpoint for Saint Patrick's. A failsafe against the day's drunken drivers.

A police officer directs him to pull in. Tulsi does so, then rolls down his window. The officer, a hefty man in raingear, stoops to eye level.

"Evening," he says, resting his arm on the hood of the Civic. A thin stream of rain drips from his hat liner, splashing the interior.

"Good evening," Tulsi says.

"You coming from work?" he asks, motioning toward the nametag still pinned to Tulsi's shirt. In his haste to leave the casino he'd forgotten to remove it.

"Yes," Tulsi says.

"Where?"

"Presque Isle Downs," Tulsi says. "I'm a dealer. Blackjack." He is suddenly nervous and feels the urge to be exact. The officer squints.

"Where you headed?"

"Home. I just finished."

In front of them, a female officer watches as a man attempts to walk a straight line between two cones. Across the lot another man leans against the side of a cruiser, his wrists cuffed behind him.

"I haven't had anything to drink," Tulsi says. "I was working, and besides, I'm not old enough."

The officer studies him. "Old enough?" he says. "You think that stops anybody? Besides, I didn't ask." He stands and studies the exterior of the car, then bends back down. "License and registration."

•

Tulsi waits for a long time while the officer sits in the cruiser behind him. He wants to call Rebecca, tell her what is happening, but his cell phone is in his book bag on the passenger seat. He's afraid to retrieve it, afraid of what the policeman might think he's reaching for. He's shut off his ignition as the officer directed. The inside of the car is dark and growing cold. Finally he sees the cruiser's door swing open, watches in the sideview mirror as the man walks back to his car.

"Looks like you've got some unpaid parking tickets." The man looks down at the leather-bound pad in his hands. "Mr. Gaeroong," he says, mangling Tulsi's last name. "Several in fact."

Tulsi shakes his head. "No," he says. "That's not possible. I have an employee permit for work and the parking on my street is free." He is amazed to hear himself speak, surprised he finds the courage to defend himself. He knows what is happening, knows how he's being ambushed. It is not right.

"And I suppose those are the only two places you ever go," the policeman says.

"No, but I have not received a parking ticket. Not *several*. Not even one."

The officer smiles, shakes his head. "Oh, well then," he says. "My fault. Guess my computer's got it wrong, and the parking authority and city clerk just messed up." He remains still for a moment, smiling at Tulsi through the open window, and then his smile fades and he pushes his face closer. Tulsi smells the coffee and cigarettes on his breath. "I could boot you right now," he says. "Let you walk your ass home."

Tulsi stares at him, doesn't flinch. He is in his own car, he tells himself. He has done nothing wrong. He repeats it in his mind over and over as the policeman stares him down. After what seems a long time, the officer reaches to his pad and tears off a pink sheet of wet paper, thrusts it through the window, lets it drop to Tulsi's lap.

"That's a summons to appear before a district justice," he says. "You can take it up with him. Next time, I'll haul your ass to the precinct." He straightens, pounds Tulsi's roof twice, and walks away.

•

Tulsi drives toward home in a fury, accelerating through yellow lights and turning sharply down the mostly empty streets.

"*Fuck you*," he says into the space around him. He has left his window open. Rain pours in, soaking the sleeve of his jacket. "*Fuck you*."

He repeats the words block after block until they lose all meaning. If he was to be pulled over now, he would be in the wrong, would have broken some law, but he doesn't care. Rage has evaporated the exhaustion that plagued him earlier. He decides against going home. He couldn't sleep now if he tried. He knows the summons is either an empty threat, or an invented one meant to punish him. Tulsi can still see the officer's face, the smugness. Can still smell his stale breath, hear the disgust in his tone.

It is always the same, Tulsi thinks. Those who can, will.

•

Tulsi drives through the darkened streets of Erie's lower east side, past sagging front porches and littered yards. It is too late to go to Rebecca's and he wants to be alone. He passes an Irish pub, green-clad revelers spilling onto the sidewalk. A little farther on, Tulsi turns onto the Bayfront Connector. He follows it past industrial lots and then the library where he spent so many hours researching colleges and careers. It seems like forever ago, a different person sitting at those computers, printing out applications, keeping meticulous notes.

At the Port Access Road, Tulsi takes a left. The giant white tanks of the wastewater treatment facility glow dimly in the moonlight. Tulsi parks at Lampe Marina and walks to the edge of the channel that connects the bay to the lake. The rain has quit but a strong wind blows, cutting through the thin fabric of his jacket. Bare branches make strange shadows on the concrete pier. Below him the water is choppy and dark. He wonders how deep it is, how cold.

He walks out along the channel until he reaches the farthest point, below him the exact spot where Lake Erie begins. Across the water is Ontario, close enough that he has heard their radio stations broadcast over the airwaves late at night. Beyond that are Lakes Huron and Superior, cities like Winnipeg and Calgary, distant British Columbia and then the Yukon Territories, all the way to Alaska. He could have ended up anywhere; he could have been sent to the ends of the earth. Staring out over the dark water it is almost too much to fathom.

He cannot tell where the lake ends and the night sky begins. In the darkness they are the same. He inches forward until the black toes of his work shoes jut over the edge. In Nepal he was landlocked, a term he only learned upon arriving in the States. The Himalayas to his north, India to his south. Barriers, not pathways. He spreads his arms, feels the wind pushing him forward. From here, he thinks, he could be blown into the water, disappear into its darkness and be carried off forever.

•

June arrives, and with it good news. Rebecca's case is looking up. After months of continuances and postponements, delayed hearings and court dates, the custody trial is set to begin. Rebecca's lawyer is optimistic about the judge. To celebrate they take Grace to Waldameer Amusement Park. It is a pristine early summer day: blue skies and warm temperatures, few bugs to speak of yet.

They ride the bumper cars and Tilt-a-Whirl, toss rings at clustered bottles, and shoot squirt guns into the gaping mouths of ceramic clowns. For lunch there are corn dogs and boardwalk fries dowsed in vinegar and ketchup, slushies and funnel cakes snowed over with powdered sugar.

Tulsi and Rebecca stand by the old-fashioned carousel and watch Grace glide by on the saddled back of a glimmering white horse. Her feet sit atop the steel stirrups, and she beams. She clutches the golden-colored pole that juts from the horse's back, her right side reflected in the paneled mirroring at the carousel's center. Tulsi drapes his arm across Rebecca's shoulders. She kisses his cheek, then leans back and raises both hands. In front of her face she forms a square by connecting her thumbs and middle fingers. She snaps the imaginary camera with a flick of her pointer finger.

"There," she says. "Perfect." Tulsi smiles, pulls her back to his side.

"What's that for?" he asks. Around them, the park buzzes. Teenage couples holding hands stroll down the clustered midway, kids run laughing and screaming ahead of their parents, somewhere a baby cries.

"For whenever I need it," she says. She taps her temple twice just as Grace calls out to them. They turn in time to see her soaring past, laughing, one of the red ribbons Rebecca tied in her hair coming loose, floating through the air like a string of confetti. Tulsi stares, tries to take it all in.

This is the moment he will think about months later, when the trial has ended, when all is said and done and the court has made its decision. Not the fireworks over the lake later that night, or the very first time he saw Rebecca, distraught and clutching her phone in the break room. Not the breakfast they shared that morning, or their Christmas Eve together, or any of the countless times they walked Grace to school, just the three of them, a makeshift family. Not any of the nights he spent in Rebecca's arms, the two of them moving together as one. Holding her after. Being held.

It will be this. Rebecca beside him, his arm resting easily across her shoulders. A single red ribbon whisked one way then another. And Grace before them, waving with one hand as she circles past.

It will be a picture arrested in his mind, ingrained there, sharp at first then gradually blurring at its edges, fading in focus as he taps the source time after time. Until finally it is gone, and he is alone again.

Dear Brother,

Today in the market I thought I saw you. A young man passed me, head bent low the way you sometimes held yours. He had your frame, brother, he moved with your exact gait. He disappeared around a row of stalls and I followed, trying to overtake him so that I might turn and see my brother's face. He walked quickly as though late for an appointment. It was the busiest hour, when the merchants lower their prices and try to sell the last of their goods. Soon the crowd swallowed him and I lost sight.

Would you think me foolish, brother, if I told you I stood and wept right there? In full view of the vendors selling their fruits and spices, the mothers shopping for their family's meals. Would you chastise me for such an open display of pain? More foolish things are done every day.

I wonder sometimes, had our road been easier, if I would miss you how I do. If our mother had lived. If our father had stayed. Senseless questions, I know. An alternate history. Still, brother, steel forged in the hottest fire is the hardest to break.

Your Sister

LABOR DAY WEEKEND, TULSI RETURNS to Lampe Marina. He has taken up fishing. It is a simple thing and one he enjoys. For his birthday he bought himself a sturdy two-piece rod and reel from the Erie Sport Store along with a tackle box, bobbers, sinkers, hooks, and a foldable nylon chair. Now he sits at the edge of the pier, his reel wedged carefully between the chair's seat and arm. In front of him the water is a blue sheet of glass. It is hot for early September, but a breeze works in from across the lake.

Rebecca and Grace have been gone since July. In the end Patricia Lakes had been worth every penny. Not only had she gotten Rebecca's old arrests and drug use deemed inadmissible, but she pushed for relocation rights as well. Tulsi supported the decision, Rebecca's long-term dream: Colorado, family, cousins for Grace. Her aunt had even flown in to testify. Tulsi paid for her ticket. She spoke of stability and the support her family could provide, the job that was waiting for Rebecca at her salon in Steamboat Springs. Steve fought it tooth and nail, but in the end told Rebecca he would agree if he could have Grace for one week at Christmas and four in the summer.

There was, of course, one other thing. Steve's final caveat before conceding.

Tulsi was not to go with them. It was not a demand he could bring to court, but he made it understood. He had the ability to make

Rebecca's life hell. In truth, Tulsi had known he could not go. When he imagined Rebecca and Grace's life in Colorado, he could not picture himself in it.

When they first left, Tulsi had entered a darkness so complete he thought it might envelope him forever. He picked up extra shifts, worked maniacally. Anything to be away from the solitude of his apartment and to occupy his thoughts. Still, he understood. There was so much that had happened in Erie that Rebecca wanted to put behind her. A whole lifetime. He was a part of that now.

And somewhere, beneath it all, there was fear. Pennsylvania was where the IOM had chosen to resettle him, the location he had set out for when he parted from Susmita. It was where he had reunited with his grandfather, the place where his grandfather's remains now rested. Outside of the camps, it was the only place Tulsi had ever lived.

Tulsi reels in his line and finds the nightcrawler gone. Some slick rock bass or sunny has picked his pocket. He baits the hook and casts, watches as the bobber disappears over the side of the concrete and listens for the splash below. A couple of old timers sit at the end of the pier smoking, lines over the edge. A bucket of water rests between them. Tulsi never brings one, never keeps what he catches. He always throws the fish back, even walleye. It's too late in the season for perch and they're mostly farther out anyway. Tulsi's caught a few, their shimmering sides striped like some delicately scaled tiger.

In a few hours he'll drive to the casino for an extra shift, but he tries not to think of that. Instead he watches a sleek blue sailboat navigate the channel, a couple in matching windbreakers side by side on deck. Far out on the lake he can just make out the Brig Niagara, a wooden-hulled flagship from the War of 1812. In high school they'd taken a field trip to Erie's Maritime Museum and watched its crew ready it for sail.

He thinks he feels a bite but when he checks his bobber, finds it's only a rogue wave from the sailboat's wake. Out on the horizon the sun sets, bleeding burnt oranges and reds across the water, setting the whole lake ablaze. Every month like clockwork he receives an envelope with a note and a check from Rebecca, her sworn promise to pay him back. By the time the trial ended his college fund was nearly gone. He has told Rebecca not to send them, that it was not a loan to repay. Each time he receives an envelope he saves the note, tears up the check.

Across the water the sun is too bright to look at. He'd heard somewhere that once its circumference meets the horizon it disappears completely in exactly two minutes. A hundred and twenty seconds on the dot.

He feels what might be another bite but ignores it. He thinks again of that day at Waldameer, the picture he returns to. He wonders if Grace has ridden a real horse yet, hopes that she has. Already the image he carries with him is vanishing, fading as though left too long in the sun. Tulsi forces himself to stare out at the horizon, suddenly diligent for the burning edge to meet the Earth. He is waiting to begin his count.

PART THREE

MARCH 2015

TULSI LIVES ON PITTSBURGH'S NORTH Side, not far from the Mexican War Streets, a network of narrow, tree-lined roads flanked by restored row houses. He walks them daily, to classes at the Community College of Allegheny County and to his job dealing blackjack at the Rivers Casino behind Heinz Field. In this new life, Tulsi walks everywhere. To school, to work, along the paved pathway that runs beside the glittering Allegheny, the pair of them turning and twisting together like train tracks. In Pittsburgh there are bridges everywhere. The city is full of them. They connect it to itself like tendon and bone.

After working another year and a half at Presque Isle Downs and moonlighting at the Plymouth, Tulsi sold the Civic and had just enough money for the move. The community college's in-state tuition is half the University of Pittsburgh's and now that he is officially a resident of Allegheny County it is halved again. He is taking eighteen credits, the maximum allowed before extra tuition is charged. Freshman English, Statistics, Intro to Sociology, Computer Science, Biology 1 and a lab. Sometimes he cannot keep his days straight but it is a good problem to have. At twenty-two he is older than many of the other students, but not all. There are several like him, even older than him, in each of his classes. "Non-traditionals" they are called. At first he didn't know what to make of the name, wasn't sure if he wanted such a moniker, but now he takes pride in it. There is a traditional way of doing things and there is not. He understands there is nothing traditional about his life thus far, nothing that would be considered normal by his peers.

He thinks of Rebecca often. He wrote her a long letter when he first arrived. Told her he missed her and hoped the best for her. He said he was sure Grace was turning into an incredible young woman, just as beautiful as her mother. He told her it was difficult to think about, but he hoped she'd meet someone who would treat them right, that maybe she already had. He wrote that he'd moved to Pittsburgh, that he was back in school like he planned. He mailed the letter with no return address, got a new cell phone with a Pittsburgh number. Rebecca had never stopped sending the checks, which he never cashed. She'd never stopped writing him. Now she could inhabit her new life fully, free from guilt. It's what he wanted for her.

He pictures her and Grace living in a cabin just outside some sleepy ski town, white-capped mountains the canvas they paint their days upon. At night, a star-filled sky. He imagines appearing on their doorstep with a duffel slung over his shoulder. Knows he never will.

•

Malcolm is gone, completing his senior internship with a video game design company in Silicon Valley. He calls occasionally to tell Tulsi how it's going. He was still living in Pittsburgh when Tulsi first arrived and had been the one to show him the city: the masses of black and gold clad fans swarming the Roberto Clemente Bridge on Steeler Sundays, the glimmering glass towers of PPG Place downtown. It was December, and weather-beaten wreaths and tinsel decorated the city's lampposts and stoplights. Tulsi had enrolled for the upcoming spring semester, a first-time college student. Malcolm was preparing to move. A week before he left, they met for lunch at Primanti Brothers in the Strip District.

"You're gonna love it here, T. This city has heart." They sat at the counter eating capicola and cheese sandwiches with fries and coleslaw on them. Malcolm ordered his with a fried egg on top.

"I like it already," Tulsi said.

They doused their sandwiches in hot sauce and washed them down with Iron City beer, the restaurant filling up around them.

"I really found myself here," Malcolm said, looking outside at the shoppers bustling along Penn Avenue. "I know that sounds corny as hell, but I don't care." Malcolm told him about a man he was currently seeing, a junior at Pitt, and how the man wanted to stay together despite Malcolm's move.

"I just don't think it's gonna work out," Malcolm said, sipping his beer. "If the internship goes well, I might land a job out there. It's like a fresh start, you know? How many of those do you get in a lifetime?"

Tulsi thought of Rebecca, though he hadn't mentioned her. "I guess not many," he said.

Malcolm raised his plastic cup of beer and touched it to Tulsi's. "To fresh starts," he said. "May we make the most of them."

•

Tulsi is trying to do just that. If his grades remain where they're at and he continues to work at the casino, he believes he'll have enough saved up to enroll at Pitt in another year. Not all his credits will transfer over, but some will. He can start next spring's term like any other student, several prerequisites already taken care of and an open choice of studies before him. Lying in bed at night he imagines the possibilities, tries to narrow them down. He still likes the thought of engineering, of building things. It is impossibly far away, but he tries to picture himself standing at jobsites, hunched over blueprints, returning again and again as something substantial materializes before his eyes. A bridge or a highway slowly coming into existence where before there was only empty space.

Faint and ringing, like an echo in his heart, there is still the hope of finding his sister. In his new city, he looks for her. He cannot help it. In the crowded aisles of Wholey's Fish Market, walking past the storefronts and bars on Forbes Avenue, in Schenley Park. Sometimes, he thinks he's seen her. A flash of dark hair, the graceful stride of a woman with her exact height and frame, but each time, when the woman turns, he finds he's mistaken. Not his sister, the last person on this earth who shares his blood, his story, but a stranger. His new life is full of them.

•

Chandra had gotten Tulsi the job at the Rivers. Chandra is not in school but works full time dealing Hold 'em in the casino's poker room. He rents a condominium in one of the expensive new complexes on Mount Washington, a sleek two-bedroom with shiny marble countertops and gleaming appliances. Floor-to-ceiling windows provide a view of the city below, the dark Monongahela and Allegheny Rivers merging like lovers to form the wide Ohio. When the Pirates play weekend home games at PNC Park, Chandra tells Tulsi, the fireworks display goes off at eye level, illuminating the downtown skyscrapers.

"You'll have to come over," he says. "It's incredible."

Chandra leases a new Ford Mustang, which he keeps parked in the complex's security-monitored garage. Tulsi does not know where Chandra has gotten the money to pay for these things and does not ask, does not want to know. On weekends when they're not working, he tries to convince Tulsi to come with him to the dozens of bars that line East Carson Street on the city's South Side. Normally Tulsi declines, citing an upcoming test or essay assignment, but sometimes Chandra insists and Tulsi feels guilty. Had it not been for him, Tulsi would have no job, no prospects in a city that is still largely a mystery to him.

On a Saturday night in late March, Chandra picks him up at his place. Tulsi rents a room on the top floor of a century-old row house. He shares a bathroom with an elderly Polish man across the hall, and the landlord lets Tulsi keep a desk in the attic, where he studies. The room itself is not much, a long narrow space with warped bay windows and flaking paint. Still, it is warm in the winter and a family of magpies has returned to the maple tree outside, singing in the late afternoons. He has a dresser and nightstand beside his bed, and a table opposite the door on which he keeps a hotplate and coffee maker. The coffee maker was one of the more expensive models at Sears, the lone luxury he allowed himself. He sets the timer every night and wakes every morning to the smell of dark roast filling the close room. His books are stacked on the wooden alcove along the windows and he reads there in the mornings. It is a modest space but it is his.

He hears Chandra blow his horn from the street below and is happy he does not come upstairs. Once, when Tulsi first moved in, he invited Chandra for tea. Chandra took in the room with one brief revolution, a look of pity on his face, then suggested they go out instead.

Outside, the air is crisp. Gray snow and puddles of slush line the street. Tulsi pulls his coat close and gets into the car.

"About time," Chandra says and hits the gas. They drive through the city's darkened neighborhoods toward the South Side. "The Mad Monk is finally ready to paint the town red."

Chandra gave him that nickname after the first few times Tulsi turned him down. Ahead of them, the massive silhouette of PNC Park is just visible, a mountain against the blue night sky. They merge onto Fort Duquesne Bridge.

"When are you gonna move in with me so I don't have to drive all the way to the North Shore to pick your ass up?" Chandra asks. He wears a black leather jacket over a denim button-down. He keeps his hair shorter than he did in Erie, his sideburns shaved to points like upside-down arrows.

"I could never afford what you must pay," Tulsi says.

"You'd be surprised," Chandra says, and turns up the stereo. A rap song streams from the speakers.

"Even if I could," Tulsi adds, "I'm trying to save money." Chandra laughs and shakes his head. A gold chain with a crucifix hangs around his neck.

"Tulsi Gurung. Always counting his pennies." He switches to the right lane, cutting off a rusting Bronco. "Money's made to be spent," he says, the sound of the horn blaring behind them.

●

They get lucky and find a spot on Carson, then walk down the block to Jack's, a popular college bar. It's early but already filling up. A table of girls near the entrance yell something at the bartender while a man feeds dollar bills into the digital jukebox. Colorful bras hang from a moose head mounted above the rows of bottles.

Tulsi is not opposed to drinking. He likes the taste of beer and sometimes joins the other dealers for a drink after work, but bars like Jack's make him uneasy. The proximity of strangers in such close quarters fills him with dread. Overcrowded tables and a mass of people, four or five deep, waiting for a drink at the bar, screaming over the music, every available space taken, even along the walls. There is something of the camps in it, something eerily similar to the days when he and his grandfather and Susmita would wait their turn in line to receive rations, those behind them urging them on, shoving them forward though there was no space to move. He tries not to think of that now. Instead he follows Chandra through the smoky room, watching as he waves to the bartender, who acknowledges him with a nod. He knew the bouncer as well, a large bearded Black man who allowed them in without checking their IDs. It seems to Tulsi that Chandra knows people wherever they go. Bartenders and bouncers, the cocktail waitresses and valets at the casino. Even the limo drivers and cabbies dropping off the gamblers. He leads Tulsi through a hallway and into a back room, even larger than the first. There is another bar here, less crowded. Chandra orders them a pitcher of Yuengling and pours two glass mugs to the brim.

"Come on," he says. "There's someone I want you to meet."

Past the pool tables and up a set of narrow, turning stairs at the back of the room is a wood-paneled door. A long, jagged crack runs down its left side. Tulsi waits several steps below, holding the mug and pitcher. Chandra knocks twice. Inside is the sound of voices and then footsteps. The door opens slightly and a round face appears in the void, a set of dark eyes studying Chandra. The door is shut and then reopened a moment later. A squat man in a track jacket and black jeans stands in the threshold, his face expressionless. He moves aside and Chandra walks in with Tulsi close behind.

The space is larger than Tulsi would have imagined, a dank low-ceilinged room with a circle of couches at its center. On one wall is a large flatscreen TV tuned to the Penguins game, the muted roars of the arena leaking from a pair of mounted speakers. A mini fridge hums beside the entrance. The squat man shuts the door behind them and walks toward the couches, where a woman types on a laptop. Another man sits alone at a poker table in the corner, a newspaper spread open before him.

"Chandra," the woman says. "What brings you out tonight? A dollar to be made somehow, I suppose." Her words are slightly accented and pronounced with purpose. When Tulsi lived on Eleventh Street, he became proficient at guessing where others had emigrated from based on how they spoke. Russia or Poland, he thinks now, somewhere in Eastern Europe.

Chandra bows slightly in the woman's direction. "Just dropping in to say hello and introduce an old friend. Not all my motives involve money, V."

The woman rolls her eyes and shuts the computer. She looks to be in her late twenties, her dark hair set in a bun. She has high-ridged cheekbones and a thin nose, her appearance beautiful and somehow severe at the same time. The man at the poker table turns the pages of his newspaper but says nothing.

"Lucky me," she says, "I was just headed out." She slips the laptop into a leather satchel and stands. "See you in the morning," she calls to the man at the table. He raises his right hand in acknowledgment. There are the dark stains of tattoos on his knuckles.

"Chandra, always a pleasure," the woman says. She puts on a puffy black coat and as she passes, nods to Tulsi. "Be careful with this one," she says, motioning toward Chandra. She walks out the door and is gone.

An uneasy silence fills the room. Tulsi is still holding his mug and the pitcher of beer. An irrational fear of losing his grip on one or the other enters his mind. He hears the shattered glass, sees the mess. Sometimes his nerves do this to him, make him imagine an uncomfortable situation getting worse.

The man at the table turns a page. "Did you see what the drunken fools did to my door?" he asks without looking up. His words carry the same accent as the woman's but are heavier, undiluted. "They believed it was a bathroom and tried to break it down."

Tulsi remembers the crack in the wood paneling, jagged as a lightning bolt.

The man closes his paper and stands. Chandra takes it as a signal and moves to the table. Tulsi follows closely, glass handles sweating in each hand.

The man is barrel chested with a slight paunch beneath his black polo. His hair is buzzed, the ridges of his skull visible below a thin down of gray. He turns toward the TV and when he does Tulsi sees his skin. In several places it is taut and plastic-looking, as though sections of his face and neck had been dipped in paraffin and left to set. They appear to be burns, healed over but still disfigured. Tulsi forces himself to look away.

The man points to a player churning down the ice. "I had tickets to this game. Then that asshole Brooks called and said he could play. Now he cannot play and we are short."

"I could find you another," Chandra says, but the man waves him off.

"The night is dead. Another time." When the man sits, Chandra turns to Tulsi and points to the couches. Tulsi walks away as Chandra joins the man at the poker table.

Tulsi sits as Chandra and the man speak. He cannot hear what they are saying and tries not to look as though he's paying attention. Instead he turns to the hockey game, feigns interest as he waits. The stout man who let them in remains standing, never once speaking or moving from behind the couch. After about five minutes Chandra gets up. The burned man reopens his newspaper without ever acknowledging Tulsi's presence. Chandra never introduces him to the man and the man never asks about him. They leave without another word and shut the door after them.

•

"Who was that?" Tulsi asks when they're downstairs. The bar has filled up and they sit across from each other at a small table along the wall.

"He owns the bar," Chandra says. "I met him in the poker room at the Rivers. He's a regular."

"And the girl?" Tulsi asks. "She doesn't seem too fond of you."

"V? That's his daughter. She's harmless. Just likes to razz me." Chandra pours the last of the beer into his glass. "Relax, I just wanted you to meet him."

"I didn't meet him," Tulsi says. Chandra lifts the empty pitcher and signals the waitress.

"Yes, you did."

•

On the ride home, Chandra explains how it works. Twice a week, sometimes more, the man holds a cash game in the upper room at the bar. Chandra is one of several dealers who work these games. The players come by invitation only, most of them friends or business associates of the Owner. This is how Chandra always refers to the man:

the Owner. Chandra occasionally recommends new players from the casino's poker room: wealthy guys in town on business, high-stakes players looking for extra action, even professional athletes visiting Pittsburgh for sporting events. He also keeps an eye out for fish, weak players with money to lose, and more importantly, whales, weak players with lots of money to lose.

"I'll throw in a degenerate every once in a while too, but only if they're staked," Chandra says. "The Owner doesn't front players unless they're already at the table. And you've gotta have something to get to the table."

"So he owns Jack's and he runs the games?" Tulsi asks.

"He owns more than just Jack's," Chandra says. "He has a few other bars and properties around town, and they hold games too." They sit at a stoplight and Chandra turns up the radio. A group of drunken coeds stumble across the street. The light turns, and they take a left onto the Birmingham Bridge. The Monongahela is a black strip of tar beneath them. "I just wanted you to meet him," Chandra says again. "You know, in case you were ever looking to make a little extra money." They speed across the bridge, the wind off the river whipping through the open window.

"I don't know how to deal poker," Tulsi says. "I've only ever dealt blackjack." Chandra is quiet as they turn toward downtown. Ahead of them they can see the traffic leaving the Pens game, a line of headlights streaming away from the arena.

"The Owner runs other businesses besides card games," Chandra says.

•

At home, Tulsi changes into a pair of sweatpants and a waffled long-sleeve shirt. They'd finished another pitcher at Jack's before heading over to Casey's Draft House for a few more. The beers have left him feeling flushed but awake. He'd climbed the stairs to his room silently with liquid legs. Now he lies in bed, trying not to think about what Chandra meant when he said the Owner had other businesses. He hopes his friend has not gotten in over his head. In high school at East, Chandra had been two grades ahead of him, and while they both wanted to fit in, to make friends and adapt, Chandra seemed to take it more to heart. He'd always been interested in designer clothes, in nice cars, in making money as quickly as he could. Tulsi thinks of Chandra's gold crucifix, the way it seemed to glow in the car's dark interior.

"Tulsi Gurung," he'd said, "always counting his pennies."

Tulsi tried not to let it bother him. On the few occasions he and Chandra had gone out since Tulsi moved to Pittsburgh, he always made sure to buy rounds. He never told Chandra about the money he'd saved for school, how he used it instead to pay Rebecca's attorney. He was doing all right now, was again heading in a direction, approaching a goal, but sometimes the teasing got to him.

Tulsi rises to go to the bathroom. He opens his door and steps out into the dim hallway. His neighbor, the old Polish man he shares the bathroom with, has just left it and is returning to his room. He turns and smiles. He's dressed in blue long johns and heavy wool socks. A wisp of his thin white hair stands up in back like a feather.

"Hello," he says. He does not know much English and so Tulsi's conversations with him have always been brief. The woman who owns the house brings the man a single sack of groceries twice a month. On weekends, Tulsi has seen him walking alone through the neighborhood, sitting in a nearby park feeding the returning birds from a plastic sleeve of bread. Other than that, he rarely leaves the house.

"Cold," the man says, crossing his arms over his chest and hugging himself.

"Yes," Tulsi agrees. "Soon, spring will be here." The man lifts his eyes and leans his head to the side as though this fact is debatable. Then he smiles again, his lips parting to reveal toothless gums. Deep wrinkles crease his face, partition the skin into sagging folds that hang limply along his jaw.

"You are studying?" he says, clapping his hands in front of him, then opening them like a book. The man has seen Tulsi on his way to and from class, a swollen backpack strapped to him.

Tulsi nods.

The man smiles. Wiry black hairs protrude from his nostrils. "Good," he says. He lifts one bony finger into the air and taps his temple. A faint indigo light frames him in the dark hallway. He steps backward into his room as though assured enough for slumber. "Goodnight, child," he says, and gently shuts the door.

•

While in Erie, Tulsi had exhausted every avenue he could think of for locating Susmita. When he first arrived, he visited the offices of the International Institute weekly. He'd walk to the small brick building on Twenty-Sixth Street after school and inquire about the situation at Camp Goldhap, information regarding Purna's family and their resettlement orders, the names of new families trickling into Pennsylvania and other states, and later, the fallout from the fire. He asked the same questions over and over until the caseworkers began to regard his visits with thinly disguised dread, pawning him off on the newest employee as a sort of occupational hazard. There were never any new leads. All he knew for certain was that neither his sister nor Purna currently resided in the rebuilt Camp Goldhap. There was also no record of them at any of the other six refugee camps in southeastern Nepal. Either they had been resettled and the paperwork lost, or they had left the camp of their own accord and not informed the UN High Commission for Refugees. Whichever was the case, their whereabouts were unknown.

Tulsi had written to the US Committee for Refugees and Immigrants himself and the response he received was the same he heard in the local field office. He'd even sent off letters to the High Commission in Geneva. None of it had mattered. The answer was always the same. His sister and Purna were missing from all files and records. To anyone who bothered to look, they'd simply vanished.

●

The day after Easter, Tulsi takes the number one bus to Sharpsburg. The night before, he'd dealt blackjack at the Rivers. For dinner he ate the lukewarm scalloped potatoes and ham the casino set up in the break room. It wasn't much, but had he been home, he'd have boiled ramen. The holidays meant little to him anymore, the way they had before Rebecca. If anything, they now held the temptation of excuse, a day to idle away in loneliness and self-pity. He'd been happy to get the Easter shift. The casino was fairly empty and he still made time and a half holiday pay.

Traveling along the Allegheny Valley Expressway, Tulsi watches the river reflect the late morning light, glints of silver on slow-rolling waves. The sky is clear with only a few shreds of cloud wisping in the distance. It is the kind of day the whole city has been waiting for. A single barge glides down the river, its sloping mounds of coal heaped before it like an offering.

When they stop on Main, Tulsi climbs off. A cool wind blows across the river and feels good against his skin after the staleness of the bus. He follows the directions he copied in the college's computer lab and walks to Thirteenth Street.

The building that houses the Northern Area Services Center is an old stone church. An arched entryway sits beneath a three-story tower. Inside, the directory lists the office on the second floor. Tulsi climbs the wide, dark stairwell and wanders down the hallway until he finds it. He has not made an appointment. The waiting area is empty, and there is no one at the receptionist's desk. He finds the logbook and jots down his name and the time he arrived, then takes a seat. Ten minutes later, a young man walks in holding a to-go cup of coffee and a pastry box. He looks at Tulsi, then at the empty desk, then back to Tulsi.

"Been waiting long?" he asks.

"Just a few minutes," Tulsi says, standing.

"Good. We're sort of on unofficial holiday, so I'm handling things alone. Just ran out for a coffee. You hungry?" He lifts the pink box tied neatly with brown twine.

"I'm fine."

The man nods and motions for Tulsi to follow.

•

They sit in front of one another in the man's tiny cubicle, their knees nearly touching. They are the only two in the office, and so it seems doubly strange to be restricted to such a tight space. Fluorescent lights hum along the ceiling. The man wears a faded blue dress shirt tucked into jeans. He has close-set eyes and blond, slicked-back hair. He sips his coffee and eats a cheese Danish while Tulsi explains the situation as best he can.

He is twenty-two and has been in the States since he was sixteen. Until then he lived in Refugee Camp Goldhap in southeastern Nepal. He has recently moved to Pittsburgh from Erie, for work and in hopes of attending the university. He joined his grandfather in the States, who has since passed away. His only other family is his sister, Susmita. He has not heard from her in nearly seven years.

Listening to himself explain things in these terms, he cannot help but be overcome by sadness. There is a reduction to it that leaves him hollowed out, as though his whole life has been nothing more than a timeline of losses with empty spaces in between. The man nods along to his story, though Tulsi senses some indifference. He tries to imagine what this man might be thinking, that yes, Tulsi may have lost people who were important to him, but still he is here. There are tens of thousands yet in the camps: some of them waiting patiently to be resettled, others, especially the elderly, refusing to leave. Those who won't go are unwilling to do anything but wait out a repatriation agreement that will permit them to return to their homes in Bhutan. It is an agreement, Tulsi knows, that will never come. To this man, Tulsi is one of the lucky ones. He may be alone, but he has still made it.

The man turns to his computer and types the information Tulsi provides. His sister's name, both married and given, her appearance, profession, and age. He records Tulsi's name and contact information, his place of employment. When he finishes, he pushes his chair back from the desk and crosses his legs.

"Look," he says, "if I'm being honest here, there's not much I can do that you haven't already tried. I mean, if there's any new information I'll contact you, but chances are I'm gonna hear back the same thing from the UN and USCRI that you did." The man pauses, stares into his lap. "I hate putting it that way, but it's true. Most of what we do is secure housing and medical appointments, perform job training, stuff like that. The family tracing thing is a bit outside our wheelhouse, you know?"

It's exactly what Tulsi expected to hear. Another letdown anticipated and received. On the man's computer the desktop switches off and his screensaver appears, a tropical beach: white sand sinking into turquoise water, the red speck of a sailboat far out on the horizon. Tulsi takes in the scene.

"You know," the man says, "there are other avenues you could explore. Have you ever tried an investigative service?"

"Like a detective?"

"Kind of," the man says. "That's not exactly it, but close. Unfortunately, your situation isn't that uncommon. Wars, natural disasters; people go missing. Families are constantly being separated. There are private organizations that help reunite them. Businesses."

"My friend Malcolm helped me search the Refugees United database online," Tulsi says. "Nothing came up."

The man shakes his head, leans back and crosses his legs. He bounces his foot until his right heel slips free from its Docksider. "That's not what I'm talking about. Refugees United is a nonprofit like us. They'll help if they can, but if your sister or her husband never registered with them, it won't do any good." Gripping his desk, the man pulls himself back to his computer. One swipe of his mouse and the beach scene vanishes, replaced by the service's homepage. He types into a search engine and clicks a few links until he arrives at a screen displaying a 3D globe, different countries lighting up sporadically. Tulsi searches for Bhutan or Nepal to flash but they are too small. Only the jagged arrowhead of India is recognizable.

The man jots down the website address and a phone number. "Here," he says, tearing the sheet of paper from his notepad and handing it to Tulsi. "This is the contact information for American Investigative Services. They do a little bit of everything: background checks, legal and corporate investigations, but they also have an international division. They handle missing children, runaways, stuff like that. They might be able to help."

Tulsi takes the paper and stares at the 1-800 number. "But my sister is not a runaway."

"It doesn't matter," the man says. He stands, signaling to Tulsi that their meeting has ended. "It all comes down to finding people. For the right price, they'll track your sister to the ends of the earth."

•

Tulsi finds an empty bench along the flagstone river trail. Aside from the occasional afternoon jogger, it is mostly deserted. He stares out over the rippling water, the motion of it soothing. He did not bring his fishing gear with him to Pittsburgh. Instead he gave it to one of the new occupants of Eleventh Street, a young Bhutanese refugee named Ram, resettled with his parents from Camp Timai. At thirteen, he was younger even than Tulsi had been when he arrived.

Tulsi had taken the boy to Lampe Marina and shown him how to cast and reel, how to rig his hook so the minnows and nightcrawlers would not fall off. He taught him to use a set of needle-nose pliers to crimp the lead sinker that kept the hook submerged at the proper depth and where to affix the bobber in relation. They fished till dusk. When they returned to the neighborhood, Tulsi told Ram the equipment was his.

Now he sometimes sees the old men lined up along the railing beside the Allegheny on his way to work. If he's not in a hurry, he'll watch them casting their lines, reeling their rigs in leisurely. If he watches long enough he can nearly recall the sudden excitement of a strike, the taut line gone live, or the satisfaction he felt in a perfect arcing cast. It is like a shadow passing over him, the pleasure he himself once took in the act.

He studies the number the man wrote down for him, then takes out his phone. He dials and follows a series of automated prompts until he reaches the department of International Location and Recovery. The line goes straight to voicemail and a recording informs him of the information he is to include: name, contact number, and a brief explanation of inquiry. This last part seems impossible, the circumstances of Susmita's absence more than he can possibly explain in a brief message. He hesitates, unsure how to put things. Finally he says, "I'm calling in regards to my sister. She is missing. She has been missing for a long time." He flips the phone shut and slips it back in his pocket, considering what he's just said. He watches the cars move across the Sixty-Second Street Bridge, then stands and heads in the direction of the bus stop.

•

Two days later, Tulsi is walking to a biology lab when his phone rings.

"Tulsi Gurung?" a woman's voice asks.

"Yes."

"This is Candice from American Investigative Services returning your call." Beyond the sidewalk where he stands is a playground, abandoned on this misting Wednesday morning. Tulsi walks over and takes a seat on the edge of a tunneled slide, digs the heels of his sneakers into the damp mulch. He answers the woman's questions and begins to recap the story when she cuts him off.

"That won't be necessary," she says. "I'm just calling to place you. We'd like to get you set up with one of our professional associates, someone nearby." Tulsi tries to imagine where this woman is calling from, what her office looks like. If he could just explain the situation, maybe she'd be sure to connect him with their best investigator, someone with a perfect success rate.

"I have an investigative service in Pittsburgh that's a member of our council. Do you have a pen?"

Tulsi writes the phone number on his palm and thanks her before she hangs up. He slides the pen in his pocket and surveys the playground: rusting monkey bars and merry-go-round, an old steel swing set, sagging in the middle like the abandoned frame of some long-forgotten house. The mist has strengthened into a light rain. He has the sudden desire to skip his lab, a three-hour affair held in the community college's science wing. He wants to be back in bed, covers pulled tight to his chin, curtains shut. He wants someone else to call the investigator for him, arrange an appointment in his name, take his lab, ace his practical. Someone else to cover his shift at the casino later that night, deal hand after hand of blackjack to faceless gamblers blowing smoke at him, spilling drinks, cursing him for poor cards as if he himself has ordained their demise. He wants someone else to take the abuse of strangers whose opinion of him rests solely on how much he can give. He wants to lie back on the slide and hide there, metal pressing cool against his back, the tunnel shielding him from the rain.

•

The investigative office is not what he expects. He's watched enough late-night detective movies to have a picture in his mind before he arrives: upstairs room, dimly lit with a desk, wooden blinds forming bands of light in the smoky air. Instead he finds himself in a mall off of Steubenville Pike, in a tiny storefront between a Baskin-Robbins and a shop that carries nothing but baseball caps. He gives his name to the receptionist and waits. Centered in the mall's wide corridor is a kiosk selling calendars displaying puppies and kittens, and beyond that, a travel agency. He watches groups of teenagers pass by, some of them holding hands, others jostling each other playfully. The receptionist calls his name and leads him to the back room, where a middle-aged woman in a charcoal pantsuit greets him. She shakes his hand and he takes a seat across from her at a long conference table. Her name is Marsha. Tulsi has given her a brief explanation over the phone.

"We've done missing persons before," she says now, "but not of this nature. Typically we handle parent-child reunifications. With those there's a separation or divorce, usually a custody battle. Someone's always left unhappy. Then one parent takes off with the kids, sometimes even internationally."

Tulsi nods along, thinks of Rebecca, the pains she'd gone through to go about things the right way. All the chances she must have had to skip town and risk it.

"We have a very high success rate with those cases," Marsha says. She is built wide across the shoulders, with short jet-black hair and a broad forehead. She seems capable and intense, someone you would want on your side in a dispute, everything about her strong and unflinching, save her eyes. Dark hazel and somehow soft, they are the least intimidating thing about her. Tulsi focuses on them as she speaks. "And those are situations where the parent doesn't *want* to be found," she goes on. "I would think that your sister would be happy to have you looking for her. You never know," she says, "she may even be searching for you."

The thought momentarily fills Tulsi with hope, Susmita looking for him the way he has for her. Is it possible that, wherever she is, she has sought help in searching him out? That she too has written letters and made phone calls and met with caseworkers and investigators in hopes of finding him? Then another thought occurs: Susmita saving her money and leaving her new home, traveling a great distance to arrive in Erie, knocking at their grandfather's old apartment only to be greeted by its new tenants. Asking about Tulsi and finding no one with any knowledge of where he's gone. Despair settles in his stomach. The clock above Marsha ticks noisily like the steady drip of rain on hard-packed dirt. Tulsi closes his eyes, sees rivulets forming. He has an overwhelming urge to know the truth of his chances, how likely it is that he will ever see his sister again. He opens his eyes. Marsha looks at him concernedly.

"How probable is it?" he asks, not sure he's put this the right way. But Marsha understands. He can tell immediately. He is not the first person to have asked this question.

"We don't offer percentages," she says, "but as long as we're in your employ, we'll never *stop* looking."

•

That night, Tulsi reviews the materials Marsha gave him before he left: anonymous testimonials from reunified families, a listing of Marsha's qualifications and professional associations, a breakdown of investigative procedure. He sits in bed studying the papers beneath a reading lamp clipped to his headboard. It's a lot to take in, but he knows this is the right step, the only real chance he has left of finding his sister. Before he'd gone, he discussed price with Marsha. He has enough saved to get the investigation rolling, but not enough to sustain it unless Susmita is found almost immediately. He knows what he must do. In the morning, he will call Chandra.

Dear Brother,

I write with the understanding that these words will not reach you. And yet still I put them down. For what? Why trouble myself with messages that will not be received? It does not matter. I will not cease. It may be delusion, but writing these sentences, I feel as though I am speaking to you. Maybe that is more important than you holding this letter. Maybe it is just as good. Brother, sometimes hope is a small thing.

Presently we are in Qatar. Our journey was successful only in that we arrived at the place we set out for. The men we followed were right. Qatar indeed is rising. But it is not hands that are needed to lift it. Rather, it demands backs broken to rest upon. Brother, we have suffered. To come here we took loans I fear we will never repay. Once we arrived our papers were confiscated, the terms of our payment altered unfavorably. Purna works endless hours, the midday temperatures sometimes nearing 50 degrees Celsius. He lives with the other men in a cramped dormitory on the outskirts of Doha. They sleep twelve to a room, share a single toilet among a hundred. I know now what I did not before. Even in our leanest days at Goldhap, I had never seen true squalor.

Each month they stack the coffins of those who have died working in the heat. Children, Tulsi. Boys younger than you when we parted.

Shortly after our arrival I found employment as a domestic worker, but the conditions are no better. Brother, forgive me. I do not write to sadden you, only to share our truth. We are not free to leave. The Kafala System is custom here and forbids us from changing positions or emigrating without our employer's permission. They will never grant it.

There are many like us, some of whom have endured far worse. Pray *for us, Tulsi. The skyline of Doha glimmers above the Gulf, but it is only a mirage. I fear if we stay longer, we too will disappear.*

   Susmita

As AGREED UPON, TULSI MEETS Chandra at Gooski's, a bar located in Pittsburgh's Polish Hill. Like the rest of the neighborhood, Gooski's is built into the side of a steep slope overlooking the Strip District. Beyond that is the Allegheny, the early evening sun glinting off it like gunmetal.

Inside, the bar is dark. A string of red Christmas lights tacked above the liquor bottles washes everything in a burgundy hue. Chandra sits in a red swivel-back chair near the server's station. Tulsi takes the open seat beside him. An early warm spell has settled over the city and he is wearing shorts, the vinyl cool against the backs of his legs. A young couple sits side by side at the front of the room, sharing a cigarette and punching buttons on an electronic slot. Otherwise, the bar is empty.

"Tulsi Gurung," Chandra says without looking over. "Always saving his pennies and now in need of a few more." He laughs, takes a sip of beer from his pint glass. He motions for the bartender, a big, bearded man in a sleeveless T-shirt, and orders a round for Tulsi. "What changed your mind?"

Tulsi is hesitant to tell him, unsure how Chandra might react. Still, since his meeting with Marsha he's been filled with a sense of possibility, a feeling he's not had in some time. Until he met with her, he thought all avenues had been explored, that the search for his sister had come to a standstill. Now he can feel it starting anew. He is doing his best to temper his expectations, reminding himself of the dozens of dead ends he's hit over the years, but there is optimism alive inside him, as tiny and promising as a seed.

"It's Susmita," he says. "I think I've found someone who can help me."

Chandra shakes his head. "That again?"

Tulsi had told him about the search for his sister when they were both living in Erie, his repeated trips to the International Institute, his letters. Every time a new refugee arrived from the camps, Tulsi made a point to ask them about Susmita. All of Elevenh Street had known he was searching for his sister.

Chandra shakes a cigarette loose and lights it. "Jesus, Tulsi," he says, "you've got to forget that. I'm sure she's fine. Isn't she married to that teacher?"

"Purna," Tulsi says.

"Right, so they probably relocated with his family. You haven't been able to find them either?"

"No," Tulsi says, "and there's no record of them leaving Goldhap. I just want to make sure she's okay, wherever she is."

Chandra takes a drag, taps the cigarette against a plastic ashtray. "They probably got out of there as soon as they could. That place was hell. You remember." Chandra's tone has grown impatient, his words laced with reproach. "That's your problem, Tulsi. You cling to the past. Would you even recognize Susmita? How many years has it been? You need to forget about Nepal, forget about the camp."

"Like you did?" Tulsi says, surprised at his own boldness. He has come here to ask a favor and instead is arguing.

"Fucking right like I did," Chandra says. "Does that make me an asshole?" He tamps his cigarette out in the ashtray and swivels until he's facing Tulsi. "I wake up every day and thank God I'm here and not there. I go where I want, eat what I want, wear what I want." He shakes his head disbelievingly. "There, you take what they give you. Here, you take what you can. That's the difference."

A ceiling fan squeaks noisily overhead. Chandra turns back to the bar. Tulsi stares at his reflection in the reddened mirror.

"You think you're the only one who lost someone," Chandra says, "but you're not. The best thing you can do is hope they left too and forget about them. Forget they ever existed." He rests his hand on his glass. "Either that, or you can go back to Goldhap, see if they're willing to take you." He sips his beer, then smiles. "Hey, fuck it. A difference of opinion. That's all." He reaches over and pats Tulsi's hand. "I thought we came here to talk business."

•

Chandra drives them along Herron Avenue, the city sprawled in miniature below like a child's toy kingdom. The road winds downward toward the Strip District and Chandra takes the curves and switchbacks quickly, the Mustang's bumper hugging the curb. They cross the tracks near Thirty-Third Street and make a series of turns until Tulsi is unsure where they are. Chandra pulls into an empty parking lot, its asphalt scalloped and crumbling. A stationary chain of railroad tankers sits behind the lot. Beyond that is a series of tree-lined hills dotted with modest homes. Abandoned industrial complexes decay nearby: burnt-out smokestacks and exposed steel girders, broken windows and rusted bridges. Before them is the Allegheny, wide and rippling in the last light of day. Chandra has not divulged much, only that some steps must be taken before Tulsi can begin to work for the Owner.

"What kind of steps?" he'd asked at Gooski's.

"You'll see," Chandra said.

Chandra shuts off the Mustang's engine and the ceiling lights automatically switch on. In front of them, the river's movement is nearly imperceptible, only obvious when a branch or bit of debris floats past.

"Is it difficult?" Tulsi asks.

"What?"

"What I'll be doing for the Owner." He is nervous, second-guessing his decision already.

Chandra shakes his head, the gold crucifix swinging free from beneath his shirt. "Shit no, man. Easiest money you'll ever make."

"Is it dangerous?"

"No," Chandra says though not as emphatically, the look on his face pensive. He taps his fingers against the steering wheel. "Really, it's not," he adds when he sees Tulsi's uncertainty. "You've just got to be smart." He leans forward until his head touches the wheel, reaches under his seat, and draws out a small pistol. It is all black and plastic-looking in the dim light, its handle textured with a series of grooves. Tulsi senses his own unease as Chandra turns it over in his hands. After a moment, he slides it back beneath the seat. "A little added insurance," he says. "But don't worry, you won't need it." He steps out and Tulsi follows.

"What do we do now?" Tulsi asks.

"We hang out," Chandra says. "For as long as we have to."

•

Half an hour later a black BMW pulls into the far end of the lot. It is growing dark but the car's headlights are switched off. It drives toward the Mustang and pulls up behind it, blocking it in. The windows are tinted, preventing any view of the inside. The passenger door opens and a woman steps out wearing a knee-length dress, sequins shimmering in the last light of day. It's the woman who'd been sitting in the office that night at Jack's. The Owner's daughter.

"Chandra," she says. Whoever is behind the wheel has left the car running, the engine idling like a constant whisper.

"V," Chandra replies, "you look stunning."

The woman brushes a strand of dark hair from her forehead. In the dusk her face seems to glow, the skin unblemished and exceptionally fair. "Cut it out," she says, annoyed. "I'm already late." She eyes Tulsi closely. "So this is him?" Her tone is completely neutral so that Tulsi cannot tell whether she approves or is disappointed.

"Tulsi Gurung," Chandra says. "We've known each other since Erie. Lived in the same neighborhood."

"And he drives?"

Chandra nods. "We work together at the Rivers. He deals blackjack."

"You people really do stick together," she says. She moves closer to Tulsi until she is standing a few inches away. He smells her perfume, floral and slightly acidic, like some sweet alcoholic concoction. She studies him up close; he can feel her eyes tracing his features. He is suddenly aware of his shorts, the briskness of the night air dimpling his skin. A stale cigarette smell wafts from his clothing, a result of Chandra's smoking. He is embarrassed and he does not even know this woman. Still, Chandra claims she is the daughter of the Owner. Her station is above his, and he requires her approval. Like so many times before, Tulsi understands he's found himself in a position to be judged.

"Let me ask you something, Tulsi Gurung," the woman says, her breath smelling of wine. "Are you trustworthy?"

Tulsi flattens his hands against his thighs. "I believe that I am."

"Good, then I only have one more question." She glances at Chandra. "What do you think of *him*?"

Tulsi is confused, unsure whether she's speaking to him or Chandra, but when she turns back expectantly, he understands. She wants his opinion of his friend. Tulsi's mind races, a thousand potential answers stacking one atop the other. He hears Chandra snickering beside him.

"He's my friend," Tulsi says, "a good man." A look of subtle amusement crosses the woman's face. She turns and walks toward the passenger door.

"What?" Chandra asks. "Will he work?"

"Not for us," she says, about to get in.

"Wait," Tulsi calls out. "I wasn't finished." She stops and looks back. "He's my friend and a good man, but he's also full of himself and overly ambitious. He thinks money and things are what make people matter." Tulsi does not look at Chandra, does not want to see the anger or hurt that must be splayed across his face.

The woman rests her arm on the roof. "Aren't they?" she asks, smiling crookedly. "Aren't those the things that make people matter?"

"No," Tulsi says without hesitation.

The woman laughs and shakes her head. She lowers herself into the car and shuts the door. Tulsi's stomach drops. His one chance to get the money he needs to find Susmita and he failed. He looks up when he hears the mechanical whir of the passenger window, the woman's face barely visible in the dark space inside. She turns to Chandra.

"He'll do," she says.

•

Chandra is silent on the way home, his expression veiled in darkness.

"I'm sorry for what I told her," Tulsi says. "I don't believe that."

"Yes, you do," Chandra replies instantly. The radio plays low, quickened whispers against the whir of the tires. "You think I care, but I don't. Not one bit. I *am* ambitious and I know what matters to people *here*." Chandra motions at the lights of the city around them. A soft rain falls, the pavement glistening beneath the streetlamps.

"It's good you're ambitious," Tulsi says. He turns toward his window, hiding his face from Chandra. He remembers the night years before when Abigail, the pastor's wife, took him to Walmart to buy sneakers and then gave him a ride home. Back then all he wanted was to fit in, to somehow belong to the world he'd found himself in. Being in the States was like awakening inside a dream, looking around and recognizing nothing. It filled him with terror. It still does.

That night he'd sat beside Abigail, oblivious to anything but himself while she was probably thinking of the child she'd lost. It strikes him that perhaps Chandra is right; perhaps he does not consider the losses of others.

Chandra drops him off in front of his house and tells him to wait for his call, that he'll let him know what's expected. Before he goes inside, Tulsi bends to the open window. He wants to apologize again, say something to smooth the terrain between them. All he can manage is, "Thank you." Chandra nods slightly.

"You're welcome," he says, before pulling away down the empty street.

•

That night Tulsi cannot fall asleep for a long while. Once he does he's tormented by dreams. He sees Rebecca and Grace standing at the edge of a prairie, out of focus but undoubtedly them. Snowcapped peaks rise in the distance, white tips serrated against an endless blue sky. Tulsi moves into the field and with every step he takes, Rebecca and Grace shrink, not farther away, but down, into the ground. His very presence opening the earth to swallow them.

When he turns he is back in Camp Goldhap among the endless rows of thatch-roofed huts. The dirt paths are empty, as he's never seen them. He walks from one hut to the next, peering inside. Each is vacant, abandoned. He finds Susmita's hut and it is empty too. He stands near a communal water tap, scanning the streets. Empty. Not even a stray dog searching for scraps. Smoke appears above the huts, great bulbous clouds. Flames jolt the sky. He runs but the fire overtakes him.

He springs upright in bed, hears himself gasp. His blanket has fallen to the floor; a sheet is twisted around his legs like a rope. He reaches out in the dark and switches on his reading lamp, checks the corners of the room for faces. He thinks about calling someone, Malcolm in California, or Chandra. Just to hear a voice. Outside, the city is dark, only a streetlight glowing dimly down the block. He remembers a movie he once watched that ended with the rapture, body upon body being swept into Heaven. Husbands waking without wives, graves opening and relinquishing their occupants, so many millions ascending into the sky. Tulsi lifts the blanket from the floor and pulls it to his chin, switches off the lamp. If it happened now, how would he know?

•

On Thursday night he has recitation for his statistics class. He fills his book bag and is pouring tea into a thermos when his phone rings.

"Meet me in the employee lot at the Rivers in twenty," Chandra says. "And leave your cell at home."

"I have class."

Chandra exhales dramatically. "We don't pick our hours. This isn't like working for the casino. We're not on shift; we're on call. You want this or not?"

Tulsi hugs the phone close to his ear. If he says no, that will be the end of it. He won't have done anything wrong, but he also knows he'll never get another chance.

"I'll be there," he says.

•

Chandra is waiting in his car, smoking.

"You made it," he says when Tulsi gets in, his voice ripe with sarcasm. Tulsi wonders whether he is still upset over what he said to the Owner's daughter.

"I jogged over," Tulsi says. "Didn't want to be late."

"Good," Chandra says. "That's good." He unlatches the glove box, takes out a single key. "I'm working tonight," he says, then nods toward the casino, "for them. My shift starts in half an hour so I've gotta make this quick." He hands Tulsi the key and puts the car in drive. They cross a few side streets and then travel over Brighton Road until they arrive at a tree-lined avenue, then a darkened lot where Chandra parks beside a black compact car. A wide lawn slopes upward in front of them. On its crest sits a structure crowned with three separate white domes, like a grouping of giant mushrooms.

"Allegheny Conservatory," Chandra says when he sees Tulsi staring. "It's nice. I took a date here once." He looks at the building intently as though remembering that night. "Anyway, there's your ride," he says, motioning to the black car. "And I already gave you the key." He opens the center console and pulls out a sheet of paper. "These are your directions to the spot. Now this is pretty simple, so pay attention."

•

Before leaving the city, Tulsi stops at a Citgo and uses cash to prepay for twenty dollars' worth of gas. He throws out the directions as Chandra instructed and gets back on the road. In Monroeville he merges onto the turnpike, taking a ticket at the toll plaza and pulling through when the gate rises. He drives east, tries not to think about what he's doing. Instead he recites the instructions over and over until they become a kind of song he cannot forget. *First rest stop after mile marker 219. Five miles over the speed limit and no more. Steady driving, not a race. Wait till the restroom is empty.*

An hour into his drive he reaches Allegheny Mountain, the tunnel running through it lit ominously like fire in a cave. It swallows him whole. With windows sealed and radio off, the sound is like being underwater, an ambient all-consuming hum. He feels trapped, imagines the mountain above collapsing, burying him alive. He tries to maintain speed but feels his foot heavy on the gas, pushing him through. Emerging on the other side feels like surfacing for air.

He drives the rest of the way in a trance, the mile markers ticking off beside him. Finally he reaches the rest stop. He parks a few spots away from center as he was told, only one other car in the lot at this hour. He walks the paved path to the cement block building. Inside, harsh fluorescent lighting reflects off the tiled floor and ancient vending machines. The astringent smell of disinfectant burns his nostrils.

Tulsi pushes open the men's room door. An older man in jeans and suspenders pumps a soap dispenser then turns on the faucet. Tulsi stands at a urinal while the man washes his hands then holds them beneath the roar of the air drier. Once he's walked out, Tulsi checks each stall to make sure it's empty. He enters the last stall and locks it, steps onto the toilet while ducking his head to keep hidden.

The ceiling consists of fiberglass panels resting in white aluminum partitions. Tulsi rises to his full height and punches the corner panel loose with the flat of his palm. He pushes it aside and reaches in. Glancing at the door, he searches blindly until he feels it, a package the size of a shoebox. He pulls it out, replaces the tile, and steps back down. The package is dense and wrapped in crisp brown butcher paper, cool to the touch. He removes his jacket, lays it overtop, and tucks the bundle beneath his arm, the entire process taking less than a few minutes.

•

The drive home is worse than the drive down. He's placed the package in the false bottom of the trunk that Chandra showed him, covering the compartment with folded blankets. Imagining worst-case scenarios, Tulsi asked Chandra what to do if he got pulled over. Chandra's answer was simple. *Don't.*

The road is mostly empty, the occasional tractor-trailer roaring past, the compact car shuddering in its wake. The sky above the mountains is blue-black. Bright stars glint in the dark like flashing cameras. Tulsi tries to place himself elsewhere, clear his mind. He is walking Grace to school, Rebecca leaning against him. He is dealing a golden shoe, gamblers cheering his generous misfortune. He is sitting on the stoop at the old apartment, eating pizza with his grandfather. None of it works. Fear weighs him down, fills every thought, heavy as wet sand. Each car that passes is a policeman ready to arrest him. Every rut in the road a flat tire leaving him stranded. His hands are locked around the wheel, fingernails digging creases into the skin of his palms.

After an hour, he reaches the toll plaza. He pays the attendant in exact change, his hand trembling as he passes the money to her window. She says nothing about it, only asks if he'd like a receipt, to which he shakes his head, driving on when she raises the gate.

•

He leaves the car where Chandra instructed, in the parking garage of the Byham Theater. He takes the key as he was told and thinks about catching a bus, but decides instead to walk home. The night is cold, wind gusting off the river as he crosses the Roberto Clemente Bridge. Halfway he stops and stares down at the black water, the lights of both downtown and the North Side glinting in its surface. Waves lap the support columns, hungry mouths devouring in the dark. In the distance is the fountain at Point State Park, its white spray rising like a plume of smoke against the night sky.

"There," Malcolm had shown him when he first arrived in Pittsburgh. "Right there." They were standing atop the observation deck on Mount Washington, Malcolm pointing at the confluence below. "The fountain marks the spot where the Allegheny meets the Monongahela to form the Ohio." Three Rivers, he explained, two rivers forming a third. This is the way everyone described it to him. Three Rivers. The namesake for Pittsburgh's old sports stadium, a moniker distributed across its city's businesses ubiquitously. Three Rivers Pizza. Three Rivers Salon. Three Rivers Everything.

Standing there, the thought occurs to Tulsi that in reverse it is also the place where one river is split into two. Each branching off on its own path. Like arms outstretched, pulled in separate directions. A body torn in half.

•

Over the next several weeks Tulsi falls into a routine. Work, school, field trips. This is what Chandra calls it when Tulsi is sent to retrieve a package. Field trips. As in, "We've got a field trip planned this Tuesday," or, "How was that field trip last week?" The term intentionally innocuous, juvenile, as though all Tulsi were doing was visiting a factory or taking in a museum exhibit.

His field trips always send him either east toward Philadelphia or south into West Virginia. Most are within an hour's drive, which pays two hundred round trip. Anything over three hours is good for another hundred. Tulsi never opens the packages. He simply retrieves, leaving the vehicle—sometimes the black compact car, sometimes not—wherever he is told. Chandra slips him his envelopes in the Rivers' parking lot when they pass each other between shifts.

Tulsi deposits every dime into his checking account. Already he has exhausted his down payment to the investigative service, most of what he had saved. At first, small updates trickled in from Marsha. She was aware of the fire that ravaged Camp Goldhap but reassured him there were no deaths. She explained how another fire nearly razed a separate camp the same day. In short, the disaster was more widespread than anticipated. The displaced were sent to the remaining camps or to makeshift shelters, the ensuing resettlement a sort of disaster of its own. Records had been lost or destroyed; survivors moved fluidly from one place to another seeking aid. Still, she was optimistic. "It's pure pandemonium," she had said, "but it's a place to start."

Since then the updates have slowed but Tulsi is determined not to lose what he sees as momentum. He makes sure to let Chandra know that he is always available for the field trips, that he is desperate for the money. He has withdrawn his application as a transfer student to the University of Pittsburgh. Most likely he will not be able to afford the Community College's tuition in the fall semester. One of the first expressions he learned upon arriving in the States was "Having your cake and eating it too." Continuing school or continuing the search for Susmita. He cannot afford both.

When he is not working and not finishing the semester's classes and not driving to rest stops or abandoned warehouses or storage units all over the state, he calls Marsha.

"Nothing more yet," she tells him, the refrain becoming all too familiar.

•

By the middle of June, the city has grown swampy. Trash steams in the alleyways and layers of heat rise from the asphalt like fog. Tulsi's third-floor apartment is a sauna. He leaves his windows open day and night, an oscillating fan doing its best to circulate the air. He showers two or three times a day and keeps a hand towel soaked in cold water on the back of his neck. School has ended and Tulsi has picked up as many extra shifts as the casino will give him. In the past few weeks, his field trips have dwindled. It's money he cannot do without. For the first time since moving to Pittsburgh he's behind on rent. The money he's saved is gone, all of it bled out slowly to the investigative service.

On a Saturday, Chandra arrives at Tulsi's place unannounced. He calls from the street and tells Tulsi to get dressed.

"For what?" Tulsi asks.

"Business," Chandra says.

Tulsi peeks out the window. Chandra sits on the hood of his car. It's too hot to smoke, but Tulsi watches as Chandra looses a cigarette from his pack and lights it anyway. He wears linen pants and a crisp white shirt.

Tulsi dresses quickly, khakis and a blue polo. The heat assaults him the moment he steps outside. Chandra flicks his cigarette away and turns to greet him.

"You working at the Rivers tonight?" he asks.

Tulsi shakes his head. He thinks about asking where they're going but knows Chandra won't tell. He derives pleasure from acting mysterious, from knowing what Tulsi does not. It is one more way for him to feel powerful.

"Good," Chandra says, rapping the hood. "I've got a fun day planned for us."

•

They drive to a marina located at the edge of the Strip District, hidden from view by a thicket of trees. Chandra parks near the only structure, a trailer resting on a platform, one set of wooden stairs leading to a bathroom. A dozen or so boats sit moored, rocking gently on the river. Most are small crafts or pontoons, with a pair of monstrous houseboats docked parallel to shore. Chandra leads Tulsi past the concrete launch ramp and down to the last dock, set at a distance from the others. They walk out over weatherworn boards, Tulsi feeling the flow of the river. Algae grow thick as moss on the pilings. It is not like the concrete walls of the channel where Tulsi used to fish. Here the current seems to tug at the entire structure. Clusters of zebra mussels poke above the water like jagged outcroppings. Chandra climbs onto the larger of the two houseboats, hops down and stretches his hand out to Tulsi to help him aboard. He lifts one of the bench covers, revealing a cooler. Hands a beer to Tulsi and takes one for himself.

"What are we doing here?"

"Fishing," Chandra says. He smirks and sips his beer. "We're just waiting on our captain."

They sit on the edge of the boat drinking and watching the river. A ribbon of clouds stretches like a suspension cable over one of the city's bridges. Chandra smokes a cigarette then drops the butt into his empty can, where it lands with a hiss. He retrieves two more beers. Fifteen minutes later, the boat's lower cabin door opens. A young woman emerges. She has on black stretch pants and a halter top edged with glitter that shimmers in the afternoon sunlight. Dark hair streaked with red is fixed in a stiff ponytail. She walks past Tulsi and Chandra and disappears around the side of the boat without a word. A moment later, the Owner emerges from the cabin's dark interior. He stretches in the open air and lets loose a long gaping yawn like a lion roused from its nap.

"Chandra," he says. "Happy you are here." He steps forward and pats Chandra on the shoulder. He's taller than Tulsi remembers, broader across the chest, as though the daylight has revealed his true proportions.

"And you," he says, turning to Tulsi, "our new associate." Tulsi stands, suddenly conscious of the beer in his hand. Whether or not it was Chandra's to give. The Owner takes a step forward and looks him directly in the eyes, the expression on his face revealing nothing. Tulsi feels compelled to speak.

"Your boat," he says, "it's beautiful."

The Owner looks around as though just noticing his surroundings. "Not a yacht," he says, "but also not a canoe."

"A floating palace," Chandra says. The Owner turns to him, the edges of his eyes wrinkling momentarily with a smile.

"Maybe for some," he says.

Chandra motions at Tulsi with his beer. "Your new associate has been taking a lot of field trips lately."

"Ah, and how are you liking it?"

"It's good," Tulsi says.

"It is boring," the Owner corrects him. "Boring and mindless." He extends a single finger in Tulsi's direction. "But necessary."

"He's interested in becoming more involved," Chandra says. "He needs the money." The Owner watches Tulsi while Chandra speaks. There is a clinical quality to his stare that sends ice down Tulsi's spine. His eyes are small and dark, pinholes in a sheet of black silk. In the sunlight his plasticky skin looks almost translucent.

"Needs or wants," the Owner says, though it is not a question. "Between lies a huge difference." He walks to the side of the boat and looks upriver toward a wooded island in the middle of the Allegheny, a lush floating forest. "More involved," he repeats.

"I told him it's asking a lot," Chandra says. The Owner leans farther out over the water, his hands gripping the side.

"Unto whom much is given, of him much shall be required."

"Luke," Tulsi says. Chandra glances at him, confused. Somehow Tulsi remembers it: the Bible he'd been given at the language class in Erie, the way he pored over it nights when his grandfather was at work, the stories keeping him company.

"Luke was a physician," the Owner says as though impressed, "a healer." When he turns around, the sun glints off his pale forehead, shining like a sheet of tin refracting light. "And what," he asks, "has been required of you?"

•

The Owner instructs Tulsi to follow him to the upstairs level of the houseboat. A narrow hallway, the swaying here more noticeable. Yellow bulbs beneath plastic globes line one wall at uneven intervals. There are several doors on either side. Tulsi is surprised by the number, the houseboat much larger than he thought. From the deck he would never have been able to tell. A skinny man with shirttails hanging out walks past them. From behind one of the doors comes music; others are silent. The Owner opens the last door on the left and waits as Tulsi passes through. He follows and shuts the door behind them.

The room is small and low ceilinged like the hallway. A circular window facing the river is partly covered by a makeshift curtain, a strip of ragged burgundy fabric tacked to the wall. Light spills through at its edges. A narrow bed lies beneath. The Owner lights a cigarette with a sleek torch lighter, butane hissing into flame. Fear masses in Tulsi's belly and sways with the boat. The Owner watches a door at the side of the room. As though sensing his anticipation, the door creaks open and a girl walks through. She is dark-haired and pale, her thin body and awkward movements fawnlike. She steps past both men without acknowledging either and sits on the edge of the bed. Tulsi feels the flattened palm of the Owner on his shoulder.

"Go on," he says, pushing him forward. The girl holds the side of the mattress with both hands as though to keep from falling off. Her head lolls sickeningly on her neck, a spinning top ready to collapse. When she looks up her eyes are glazed, dilated pupils drowning out gray irises.

"No," Tulsi says.

"No?" The Owner walks past Tulsi and sits beside the girl. "No?" He raises his hands as though perplexed. "How are you ever finding your sister?" He smiles knowingly, thin lips parting. Tulsi's stomach sinks. There is confusion, then anger, Chandra's smug face filling his thoughts.

"You think I do not know these things? I know them, Tulsi. All I want is to help. To pay you. But if you say no to *me* how am I ever to trust *you*?" He takes a drag on his cigarette, its end glows red as a stoplight. He leans over and presses his mouth to the girl's neck, releases the smoke against her skin. Tulsi is watching it billow from the corners of his mouth like steam from a sewer cover when he hears the brief sizzle, like meat dropped onto a hot grill. He looks down and sees the Owner holding the lit end to the girl's thigh. She does not move, does not look away from Tulsi whose gaze she now holds steadily.

"Please," Tulsi says.

"If I am not to trust you, you are worthless here." The Owner stands, drops the spent cigarette on a dresser near the foot of the bed. He takes the lighter from his pocket and sparks it, the flame sharp and blue. He returns to the girl's side, lowers the flame toward her cheek. She sits unmoving.

"*Please*," Tulsi yells. The Owner stops and looks at him. Tulsi realizes he is shaking but cannot stop.

"If you are not having fun with her, I am having fun with her." A series of small circular burns dot the girl's left thigh like the points of a constellation. "Are you having fun?"

Tulsi pins his hands to his legs to steady himself. "Yes," he says.

The Owner moves back to Tulsi and this time, when he urges him forward, Tulsi goes.

The girl's arms are outstretched as though awaiting an embrace. She wraps them around Tulsi's waist, a buoy to cling to. The girl steadies herself and begins to undo his belt. He cannot look. He turns to the window instead, the dark fabric of the curtain so threadbare he can see through. Below, the river moves past, silt and trash churning underneath. Crescents of sunlight hug the curtain's edges.

He could stop this right now. Smash the window glass with his bare hands, dive through, fingers and palms shredded. He sees the blood floating off like clouds underwater, envisions himself staying submerged, not coming up for air until he's far downstream, arms arcing out in slow graceful strokes. He shuts his eyes tight, tries to picture the world he will exist in when he finally breaks the surface.

•

When it is finished the girl sits looking straight ahead, her gaze vacant as an empty glass. Tulsi fixes his pants and turns to see the Owner watching from the doorway, nodding approvingly.

"See," he says before leaving the room. "Now *you* are the one who is owing *me* something."

•

For two days Tulsi does not leave his apartment. When he closes his eyes, he sees the girl staring through him. He tries to turn away but cannot. Her gaze follows his, though now, when she looks at him, her pupils and irises have vanished and there is only white, her eyes blank as eggshells. When he tries to sleep her silence wakes him, louder than any scream. It is everywhere.

He doesn't eat. When thirst overtakes him, he walks to the bathroom and holds his mouth beneath the open faucet. Late on the second night, he passes his neighbor. The old man tries to speak with him but Tulsi ignores his words and disappears back into his room. He thinks of the girl again, the sound of her skin burning. Awful things had happened to her and he is a part of that now, as culpable as the men who go there willingly. Lying in bed staring at the ceiling, he watches the shadows shift like smoke. In the patterns he sees his grandfather's face, gaunt and compressed in anguish. The way it looked in the final days at the hospital when the cancer achieved full dominion. He sees Rebecca and Grace standing at the edge of a shoreline with their backs toward him. He watches as they walk hand in hand into the water, their dresses floating on the surface like seaweed, before disappearing beneath the waves.

Other faces, unrecognizable and hideous, appear in the swirling shadows and scowl. They open their awful mouths as though ready to devour him.

On the third day he makes tea but does not touch it. That afternoon his landlord knocks at his door. When he doesn't answer she cracks the door and asks him if he's all right, if he needs a doctor.

At first he doesn't respond, just sits on the edge of the bed, his head in his hands. She begins to ask again when he cuts her off. "I'm fine," he tells her.

"Good," she says, but does not leave, just stands there, one eye peeking through the crack. And then, "Your rent?" hesitantly, as though embarrassed to even bring it up.

"I know," Tulsi says.

She shuts the door and leaves.

•

When he returns to the casino he has to beg the pit boss not to fire him. He's missed two shifts without so much as a phone call, his cell shut off the entire time. The pit boss is a preppy-looking guy not much older than Tulsi. He has straight white teeth with tiny gaps in between like close-set fence posts. His hair is spiky and gelled. He's recently been transferred from the Mountaineer Casino in Morgantown and wants to make a name for himself. He looks at Tulsi like he's a vagrant.

"I was very ill," Tulsi tells him. "I haven't left home except now, to come here." It's as close to the truth as anything he can think to say.

The pit boss shakes his head in disgust. "Last chance, Gurung," he says before walking away.

•

For a few days things nearly return to normal. When not working at the casino, he spends his time walking the riverfront, watching the Gateway Clipper ferry spectators from Station Square across the Allegheny to the baseball park. In the distance tourists ride the incline up Mount Washington, the wooden cable car rising steadily as its counterweight descends. When thoughts of the houseboat come into his mind, he focuses on something outside himself, something he can watch. Things are worst when alone in his room. He spends as little time there as he can manage.

The Tuesday after he returns to work, Tulsi finds Chandra waiting for him in the casino's employee lounge. He has not seen him for almost two weeks, since the day he took him to meet with the Owner. On the way back to Tulsi's apartment that day, Chandra had asked him over and over what happened in the houseboat, but Tulsi refused to speak. He could not bring himself to look at Chandra.

Now he sees him sitting alone at a table near the back of the room, his face ashen. He stands when Tulsi enters, approaches him hesitantly.

"T," he says. Tulsi walks past him to his locker. His shift is over and all he wants is to leave.

"T," Chandra repeats. He reaches out and touches Tulsi's shoulder, but Tulsi shakes himself free.

"I'm in trouble," Chandra says. "Big trouble." Tulsi takes his book bag and water bottle from the locker and shuts it, walks toward the exit. Chandra catches up to him outside.

"Listen," he says, moving in front of Tulsi, blocking his path. "I don't know what happened in that boat, but I swear to God I had no part in it. I told the Owner you wanted to get more involved, that you were looking to make some real money. He said to bring you by to make sure he could trust you." Tulsi watches him speak, sees the desperate look in his eyes.

"And Susmita," Tulsi says. "How did he know I was looking for her?" His hands ball at his sides, fingernails cutting into his palms.

"He wanted to know what you needed the money for. I told him what you told me, that you'd hired someone to look, that it was expensive. I thought I was helping."

Tulsi moves past him in the direction of the river. The sun dips behind Mount Washington, a crescent of blinding orange atop the buildings and trees.

"I had nothing to do with it," Chandra says again. "I swear it on our friendship."

"What friendship?" Tulsi asks and continues to walk.

"Tulsi," Chandra says, his voice softer, unclenched. "They're going to kill me."

Tulsi slows and turns. Chandra's face is hidden by the sun's glare reflected off the blacktop, but it doesn't matter. By his voice Tulsi can tell that he means it.

"I made a mistake. Skimmed some of the private games I was working. The Owner found out and now they're going to kill me." His shoulders are hunched, head bent as though in prayer. When he steps forward the glare lifts and his face is exposed, drained of color, blank as a wall.

Tulsi remembers a TV special he watched about the survivors of near-death experiences. One man had come close to drowning before being rescued. Recounting his story, he told how he'd fought to stay afloat. There'd been a moment, he said, when he realized without question that he was going to die, that there was nothing he could do. A sense of surrender had come over him and he had simply stopped struggling. Seeing Chandra now, this is what Tulsi thinks of.

"How much?" Tulsi asks. Chandra looks away, ashamed.

"Over the past year, ten, maybe fifteen grand."

"Sell your car," Tulsi says, turning away. "That'll be more than enough."

"I don't own it. I don't own anything."

"And you think *I* have it? I can barely pay my rent."

"No," Chandra says, stepping closer. "It's not just the money, it's that I took it, that I cheated him. I have to go talk to him, see if there's any way…" Chandra looks down at the fissured pavement. His black hair is oily and unkempt, his clothes wrinkled. It looks as though he has not slept in days. "I can't go alone," he says.

Tulsi understands what he is asking and shakes his head. He glances out over the river and remembers that day: broken sunlight heating his skin through the threadbare curtain, the room's mustiness mixing with the smell of the spent cigarette, the girl's vacant stare fixed upon him.

"I'm not going back there," he says.

"Not there," Chandra says. "He'll be at Jack's." He moves closer, palms upturned in supplication. "There's no one else I can go to."

Somewhere in the distance a car backfires. A group of pigeons at the lot's edge explodes into the sky. Tulsi watches them disappear in the darkening dusk. He remembers walking Grace to school with Rebecca in the early morning chill, swinging her through the air between them like a pendulum. In that moment, their breath billowing out, he could never have guessed where his life would take him, could never have imagined he would not always be that happy.

•

Jack's is nearly empty when they arrive. A pair of college-aged men in Pirates T-shirts sit watching highlights from that afternoon's game, bottles of Iron City sweating on the bar. The smell of stale beer and burnt popcorn turns Tulsi's stomach. He follows Chandra into the back room. No one is working the bar there, the space completely empty. They climb the rear stairs to the Owner's office. The crack that had splintered the door when they first visited has been duct taped over, three silver strips concealing the damage. Tulsi watches from a step below as Chandra raises a palsied fist and knocks.

•

Inside, they stand near the door. The Owner sits at the card table across the room, flanked by two men. They appear to be around the same age as him, both slim and dressed alike in dark slacks and sport coats. One of the men shuffles a deck of cards over and over, the rhythmic slapping the only sound. The other holds a thin cigarette, a continuous stream of smoke curling upward. Tulsi looks away. The Owner has yet to acknowledge them other than his muffled order to come in. A newspaper sits spread before him, a can of Diet Coke resting on one corner.

He looks up at the man shuffling the cards. "Is this bravery or stupidity?" he asks. The man cuts the deck, leaves the two stacks separate.

"A little of both."

"Yes," the Owner says, "and cowardice."

The man smoking rests his cigarette in an ashtray. He slides a gold ring off his finger and spins it slowly on the felt like a coin.

"Why bring *him* except for cowardice?" The Owner turns to face them. Chandra keeps his head bent—a child being reprimanded. From below come the sounds of the back room filling up: a song on the jukebox, the clack of pool balls being racked. Chandra says something too low to make out.

"What?" the Owner demands. Chandra raises his head a fraction of an inch, as though afraid to look. "*Speak* if you want to be heard," the Owner says.

"I'll do anything." The words scant and small, the crackle of kindling ready to be snuffed out.

The Owner looks to the man spinning his ring, begins speaking to him in another language. The words fire in rapid bursts as though chained one to the next. At first his tone is flat and composed, but as he goes on it grows in fervor. He pats the felt with an open palm, beating an invisible drum. It sounds like Russian, though Tulsi can't be sure. All he knows is that hidden in the translation lies the fate of his friend and possibly himself. There is the sensation in his legs of blood draining, flowing into his feet and then somehow evaporating, leaving him empty, weakened. He watches the Owner speak. The other man keeps spinning his ring. Every time it topples he rights it and spins again. A flick of his thumb and pointer finger and the gold band spins. Despite the Owner's insistent tone, his slapping the table, at some point it becomes clear that he is not telling the other man anything. He is asking.

The other man never speaks. He listens to the Owner until he is finished, then lifts his cigarette with its gray column of ash. He taps it against the ashtray and the column collapses. From the inside of his sport coat, he pulls a silver Zippo and sets it beside his ring. The man across from him picks up the two halves of the deck and resumes shuffling.

Chandra is trembling, his fear so palpable it's contagious. Tulsi's underarms are soaked. The Owner watches the smoking man intently. The man reaches out toward the lighter and ring. When he lifts the ring and slides it back onto his finger, the Owner shakes his head.

"Today," he says, turning toward them, "is a very lucky day for you."

•

The conditions are simple. Chandra is now in debt for what he has done. Since Tulsi has come with him, he assumes the debt as well. They will work, without compensation, until the debt is settled. Afterward, barring any setbacks, Chandra's penance will have been served. All told Chandra owes fourteen grand, plus a five grand penalty, plus the vig, which will keep running until the full amount has been met.

Tulsi understands what this means, repaying a debt that continues to grow. Their lives as incidental collateral. Simply put, the Owner now owns them.

They have a job right away, he tells them. He rips a corner from the newspaper and scribbles something, then thrusts the scrap at Chandra.

"Appear here," he says, "at midnight." Chandra reaches for the paper and the Owner pulls it back. He offers it again and pulls it back once more like a child taunting a stray. On the third try he allows Chandra to take it.

"You should know, Chandra," the Owner says, "that I would have been the one to do it." He leans his head left and smiles. "Who knows?" he says. "Any mistakes and I still might."

When they are nearly to the door, the Owner calls to Tulsi. "Your girlfriend," he says. "She asks about you." His waxy lips contort into a smirk, cellophane skin stretched unnaturally. "You should come and visit her sometimes."

•

They drive out of the city like it's doomed. The Fort Pitt Tunnel swallows them whole, its track lighting and tubular construction something out of a science fiction novel. The city's western suburbs sail past: Dormont, Green Tree, Robinson, Moon. The parkway cuts through the low-lying valley between them. In the hills above, shopping centers and chain restaurants glow like outposts.

Neither of them speaks until they've been driving for nearly half an hour. The radio is off and the road empty. It's almost eleven.

"I'll pay you back," Chandra says, eyes straight ahead. "If it takes me the rest of my life."

Tulsi says nothing. Everything is silent except for Chandra's breaths, shallow and rapid. Tulsi rolls down his window to keep from hearing them.

They drive on, following Route 22 as it weaves its way through the darkened hills of western Pennsylvania. West Virginia announces itself with a pockmarked steel sign: MOUNTAINEERS ARE ALWAYS FREE, in fading white letters.

Twice they stop to check the directions Chandra brought up on his phone. The Turnpike would have saved them time but both thought it wise to avoid. Still, they have less than an hour to get where they need to be.

They merge onto Route 2 heading south, the Ohio River a wide expanse of darkness beside them. Chandra drives in the right lane at exactly ten miles over the speed limit while Tulsi scans the berm for cops. Across the river, the lights of Ohio's small towns burn above the black water. Rayland. Yorkville. Martins Ferry. Each a world unto itself. Tulsi tries to imagine what any person in any one of them might be doing at that very moment and finds he cannot.

By midnight they see the lights of the casino on Wheeling Island, a neon castle anchored right in the middle of the river. They head east past a suspension bridge, twisting along the narrow streets of Wheeling's downtown. Fifteen minutes later they arrive at the address, a two-story clapboard house adjacent a hillside on the town's outskirts.

The woman who answers the door looks as though she's been sleeping, scorched yellow hair matted on one side. She beckons them in wordlessly. They follow her through a darkened front hallway and into a living room, the whole house reeking of cat litter and weed.

"Wait there," she says, pointing at a couch, before disappearing up a set of stairs. The room is dingy and mostly bare, lit by a few randomly arranged floor lamps. A TV in the corner plays an infomercial, a studio audience watching mesmerized as the host saws through a hammer with a steak knife. Chandra seems as nervous as he was when they spoke with the Owner. He clamps his fingers over his knees to keep them from bouncing.

"What are we doing here?" Tulsi asks. The couch is deep and worn. Tulsi slides to the edge to keep from sinking in.

"I don't know," Chandra says. "I've only ever done pickups. I'm guessing that's what this is."

"You're *guessing*?" Tulsi fights an urge to sprint for the door. He closes his eyes and sees himself driving Chandra's Mustang back toward Pittsburgh, toward home. He tries to imagine the route, every turnoff and dark stretch of pavement that led them here. When he opens his eyes, a man is standing in the entryway watching him.

"What are you thinking on?" the man asks. He is thin in a T-shirt and canvas cargo pants. A buck knife is sheathed at his belt. He stares directly at Tulsi.

"I asked you something," he says. "You got your eyes shut like you're deep in thought. What are you thinking on?" The man holds his gaze, waits for an answer. His nose is hawkish, slightly crooked. He tilts his head to one side, his neck releasing a muffled pop.

"The Owner sent us," Chandra says. The man turns to him and Tulsi releases a breath he hadn't realized he was holding.

"Did I *ask*? I know who sent you." The man leans into the archway. "You think I'd let two strangers into *my home* without knowing why? You think I'm thick?" He straightens and adjusts the knife on his belt.

"No, sir," Chandra says.

The man smiles, spreading the edges of his patchy goatee. "*Sir*," he repeats, drawing out the syllable, "that's good." Tulsi thinks again of the Mustang parked outside. If there was a chance to leave, it is gone now. The man looks at him and Tulsi feels the appraisal of his stare, its deliberate registering of how he is different.

"One thing I hate," the man says, tapping his bare wrist, "lateness. A man can't be on time, what's that say about him? What's that say about how his people view obligations?" Upstairs, a dog barks, high-pitched and insistent. The man glances at the ceiling. "Where you all from anyway? Never had two looked like you down here."

Chandra is about to answer when Tulsi interrupts. "Pittsburgh," he says.

The man gives him a bemused look, a trace of pity. "Sure," he says. "Whatever you say." A ceiling fan stirs the warm air in the room, its blades throwing shadows over the man's gaunt face.

"I don't give a good goddamn who he has working for him so long as the money's right," the man says, stepping into the room. "Have her there by tomorrow morning and for Christ sakes don't let her out of your sight." He takes a seat in a folding chair opposite them and adjusts the knife so that the sheathed tip points outward. There is more barking from above, though this time the man ignores it.

"I don't give a shit if you take her for a test run, that's between you and your boss." He leans toward them, his spine curved like a cat's. "But you deliver her same as you found her or I'll tell him you fucked up." A grimace flashes across his face. "You don't want that." He takes a pack of cigarettes from his pocket and shakes one loose, then pulls a book of matches from the cellophane.

Tulsi feels himself sliding back and sidles forward. He smells the sulfur from the man's struck match. He is still unsure what they are there to do. He does not want to appear uncertain, but when he turns to Chandra he sees the confusion spread across his face.

"I'm sorry," Chandra says, "I'm not sure I'm following. What is it that you need us to do?"

The man smiles as though Chandra is joking. He takes a drag and points the cigarette forward to signal he gets it.

"We were given this address…" Chandra begins and trails off.

The man's smile disappears. "You're serious?"

"The Owner told us to be here."

"No shit," the man says. He stands as though ejected from his seat. "Can you believe this?" he asks, directing the question to no one in particular. He picks at his goatee, tugging the hair as though to pluck it loose.

"I'm sorry," Chandra says. "We were told to be here by midnight. Nothing else."

"Yeah, and you even fucked *that* up."

"We normally just do pickups," Tulsi says.

"Well, now we know who the brains of the operation is." A look of disgust appears on his face before he walks to the entryway. "*Linda*," he calls out, "*let's go*." He returns, shaking his head. "This is some bullshit."

There is the sound of footsteps on stairs, more barking, and then the woman who let them in reappears. Beside her is a young girl, a teenager. The woman leads her into the room by her elbow like a disobedient child. The girl stares at the ground and sways in front of them as though rocked by an invisible hand. Jet-black hair curtains her face. Tulsi looks to Chandra for some sort of reassurance, but Chandra is watching the man make his way to the girl. He wraps an arm around her waist and pulls her close, steadying her. With his opposite hand he swipes the hair from her face, tucks it behind a studded ear. Then, with his thumb and pointer finger, he lifts her head by the chin. Narrow dark-rimmed eyes, the irises small and cerulean. Flecks of sapphire in stone. Her nose, a sharp cut down the center of her moon-shaped face. Tulsi tries to meet her gaze but it is impossible. Her vague expression, the glassed stare, she is somewhere else.

"Gentlemen," the man says, "meet your pickup."

•

The girl sits motionless in the backseat, head resting against the window. Her book bag is in her lap where the man placed it. Chandra drives, his eyes fixed straight ahead. The man's directions were simple: have the girl and her belongings to the houseboat before sunrise. They drive back the way they came. Beside them are wide fields, some thick with corn, others striped by windrows of hay.

"What are we doing?" Tulsi asks quietly. The road is mostly vacant, only the occasional semi or car passing in either direction.

"What we were *told*." Chandra's hands are locked on the steering wheel. Concrete barriers dividing the highway disappear behind them into darkness.

"We can't," Tulsi says.

The outline of Chandra's jaw looks carved from granite, skin bulging from the clench. He reaches up and adjusts the rearview, glances at the girl. A semi rumbles past in the left lane, the Mustang trembling in its wake. Tulsi turns back.

"What's your name?" he asks. The girl's head lulls against the glass. She does not look up.

"Don't," Chandra says.

"Your name. What's your name?" Tulsi asks, reaching back and brushing the girl's arm. She does not react to his touch.

"Stop it," Chandra says.

"She has a name. Not hearing it won't change that."

"Just stop and be quiet."

"Why?"

"Because I said."

"Because *you know* what they do there. You know what they'll do with her." Tulsi thinks of grabbing the wheel, wresting it from Chandra's control. He imagines them skidding across the berm, the car spinning, finally coming to rest in the fields. There, hidden among the crop, he could talk reason, could return the night to something recognizable, something to be made sense of.

"I know what they'll do to *us*," Chandra says. He looks at Tulsi and holds his gaze, then turns his attention back to the highway. Before he does, Tulsi sees it as clear as day, is as sure of it as he is his own breath. Beside him is no one he knows.

•

They pull off at the exit for Burgettstown. A quarter mile on the left sits a giant travel center and truck wash, floodlights illuminating a line of semis idling in the lot. Chandra drives past it without slowing. A few miles down the road is a small dual pump station. A sign in the window advertises Marlboros in sputtering neon. It is darker here away from the highway. Tulsi cannot think clearly. The world outside seems to be closing in on them, compressing the car like the pressure of deep water.

Chandra slows, the turn signal clicking like a tongue against teeth. He pulls in and shuts off the engine. The car's reflection glows in the front window of the gas station. Behind the counter, a teenaged girl sits flipping the pages of a magazine. Chandra pulls a twenty from his billfold and thrusts it across the console.

"Here," Chandra says, "go in and pay." Tulsi does not respond and Chandra pushes the bill against his chest, his knuckles biting into Tulsi's breastbone.

"*Fuck you*," Tulsi says. "You go." He wonders if the girl is watching from the darkness of the backseat. He wonders if she even speaks English, if she understands why they are arguing.

Chandra lets his hand drop. "I should have known," he says. "The moment things get hard, the moment the money's not easy, you can count on Tulsi Gurung to bail."

"This is *your* mess. You're the one who stole."

"That's right," Chandra says, grinning, "and you never did a thing wrong. You just picked up your packages and dropped them off, took your money like a good little boy. Kept yourself safe by never thinking about what *you* might be doing."

A mass expands in Tulsi's stomach, a solid, heavy thing. He feels he might be sick.

"Needed the money to find your sister," Chandra says, "so that makes everything all right." Tulsi thinks again of the girl in the backseat, hopes she cannot understand what is being said.

He is not bad. He is not doing this to her. He wants her to know.

"I wasn't expecting…" he begins. There is an explanation somewhere but he cannot grasp it. Somehow he has ended up here, but he cannot remember how. A pounding in his head, a swarm of images forming a horrid collage: his grandfather's beaten face, purple and swollen like some strange fruit, the scratch Rebecca's ex carved into his door, cast fishing lines like silver filament over the rippling Allegheny, Grace's tiny shoes beside his own. He sees dark woods burning.

What are they trying to tell him? What does he need to know? He opens his eyes to Chandra, staring at him with disdain. He reaches out, takes the money.

Chandra unscrews the gas cap as Tulsi enters the store. Inside, the smell of ammonia and burnt coffee. Florescent lights reflect off the laminate flooring, drink coolers hum. The attendant talks on her phone.

"That's what I told him," she says, "but he wouldn't listen to me. He never listens to me."

Tulsi lays the twenty on the counter and the girl looks up. There is a piercing beneath her bottom lip, a small silver spike that looks as though it was pushed through from the inside.

"Hold on," she says into the phone. Then to Tulsi, "Whaddya need?"

"Pump three," he says, sliding the money forward. The girl considers him warily. It is a look he has grown accustomed to, this deliberation by others. As though trying to decipher his intentions. He registers it now, and a hatred for this girl momentarily overcomes his fear and confusion, the feeling of helplessness that has clung to him all night. The girl takes the money with her free hand and opens the cash drawer. A rash of acne stretches across her cheekbone like a streak of blush. There are more piercings in her left ear, a series of gold studs spiraling the cartilage. With practiced efficiency, she shuts the drawer and switches on the pump in a single motion.

"You want your receipt?" she asks, but Tulsi is already at the door.

•

Back in the passenger seat, he watches Chandra in the sideview. His back is to him, the pump's hose dangling near his feet. The girl's eyes are closed and Tulsi believes she has fallen asleep. He studies her in the yellowed dome light. Her complexion is pale, so much so that he can make out the threadlike blue and green veins running along her jaw and cheeks. Her narrow chest expands and contracts almost imperceptibly. Pinkish hands rest one atop the other. A silver Claddagh ring is on her right index finger, the heart facing out. She is maybe sixteen years old.

Tulsi leans against the console. The steady flow of gas reminds him of the pressurized cabin of an airplane ready to take flight. If he does nothing now they will be back in Pittsburgh within the hour. They will deliver the girl as told and that will be that. If he does nothing now.

A charm bracelet, partially hidden beneath her right hand, catches Tulsi's eye. He cranes his neck. Attached is a silver castle, a wand with a star at its tip, a tiny crown: a child's fairy tale kingdom looped at her wrist. Tulsi leans back, draws a slow breath. Before he fully realizes what he is doing, he drapes his body over the console, reaches under the driver's seat, and retrieves the pistol. The grip is cool to the touch. It is the first time he's ever held a gun. In the sideview Chandra is finishing, pulling the nozzle from the tank and setting it back in the pump. Tulsi opens the door and steps out. The gun feels weightless in his hand. He looks down to make sure he's still holding it.

"What are you doing?" Chandra asks.

"Stop," Tulsi says, though Chandra hasn't moved.

"Don't be stupid, Gurung. We're almost home. It's almost over." Fire pulses in Tulsi's cheeks. Something about Chandra calling him by his last name, the sound of it.

"No," he says. "You know it's not."

Chandra moves his hand off the pump and Tulsi raises the gun to chest level.

Chandra's eyes drop to the gun then back to Tulsi. He smiles, slightly amused like an adult humoring a child. "You don't even know what you're doing, do you? You don't even know how to do it."

Tulsi extends his arm, as though this somehow proves him knowledgeable. He tilts the gun slightly to the side as he's seen in movies. Chandra takes a step forward.

"Quit fucking around," he says, no longer amused. "The sooner we get back to Pittsburgh, the sooner…"

Tulsi points the gun skyward and fires. The bullet strikes the steel canopy above the pumps, the single crack of the shot echoing out across the road. Tulsi's arm vibrates. It takes all he has to keep from dropping the gun. Chandra covers his head with both hands. Tulsi is just as surprised, had no idea if it would actually fire. He lowers it and glances to his left. Inside the store, the girl rounds the counter, makes a beeline for the back.

Chandra's elbows are in front of his face.

"Turn around," Tulsi says, though they are someone else's words. He senses that and not much else.

"T," Chandra says, dropping his arms.

"*Turn around*," Tulsi repeats, thrusting the gun once more. This time Chandra listens. Tulsi instructs him to walk toward the edge of the asphalt lot and follows at a distance. They step into the overgrowth of the neighboring field, scrub grass and goldenrod rising above their knees.

"Lie down," Tulsi says, "facedown." They are ten or so yards deep in the brush, but still within sight of the access road.

"Do you know what you're doing?"

"*Now*," Tulsi says, speaking to Chandra's back. With his hands at his sides, Chandra kneels slowly.

"You might as well kill me," he says, his voice steady, deliberate. "That's what you're doing, you know? Killing me. It's you."

"Lie down," Tulsi says, "with your face on the ground."

Chandra leans forward, head on the matted grass like a penitent in prayer. "I'm as good as dead and you're the one who's doing it, Tulsi. *It's you*."

Tulsi turns and runs for the car, Chandra's words chasing him in the dark night.

•

Back in his room on the North Side, he scans the nightstand, the dresser, the table near the door: all of it unfamiliar as though the space belongs to someone else. He'd made it back to the city in just over twenty minutes. Near the highway, Tulsi spotted Chandra's cell on the dash. He waited till they were well clear of Burgettstown and pitched it from the open window. The girl slept through it all: the gunshot, the frantic drive. She was still asleep when Tulsi left her in the Mustang, hidden in a side alley two blocks away.

Now he feels hurried and disoriented like a child lost in a crowd. His canvas duffel bag lies open on his bed, but he cannot think of what to fill it with. Clothes, textbooks, his shaving kit. All of it seems necessary and completely extraneous at the same time.

Draped over a chair is the blanket Susmita knitted for him before he left Nepal. He grabs it and stuffs it into the bottom of the bag. There is a picture of him and his grandfather in front of the apartment on Eleventh Street. He takes it from its frame and slides it between the pages of a book. On top, he places as many clothes as he can fit, what little money he has left, rolled and banded in the back of a dresser drawer, and his passport and papers.

He is tugging the bags' sides together and trying to zip it shut when he hears the knock. He freezes, hoping that whoever it is has not heard him moving. A distant streetlight helps dilute the darkness in the room. He considers the window as a mode of escape but it's a three-story drop to the concrete sidewalk. He weighs the possibility that the fall may not be worse than what awaits him outside his door.

Another knock, and Tulsi lifts the gun from the dresser, hides it behind his thigh before twisting the knob. In the crack is his neighbor, the old man from across the hall.

"Hello," the man whispers.

Tulsi slides the gun into his pocket and opens the door wider. The man is dressed for the coming day: threadbare cotton slacks and a patched sweater. He smiles, exposing toothless gums, silvery slick as earthworms. Tulsi suspects that the man heard him moving about and has come for one of their talks or to offer him some tea.

"Hello," Tulsi says. He shakes his head apologetically and adds, "Not a good time." The man nods as though he knew this to be the case. He raises the bony crook of a finger and points it at Tulsi's chest.

"Leaving," he says, his smile replaced by concern. Before Tulsi can ask how he knew, the man lifts a bundle and extends it gently as though handling an infant. "*Take... care*," he says with great concentration, a pause between the two words so that they sound like a pair of instructions. Tulsi accepts the bundle and the man smiles again, this time laying a wilted hand on Tulsi's shoulder. He turns and disappears down the dark hallway.

Tulsi closes the door and lays the bundle on his desk, untying the twine that holds the brown wrapping paper in place. Atop a loaf of bread sits a small rectangular prayer card with the depiction of a saint, a young man with milky white skin. He wears a long red robe and matching cap. A rosary is twined through the fingers of his left hand. In his right he holds a lily, blooming white at its tip. A second right hand stems from the first, holding an identical flower. Tulsi brushes his fingers over the likeness, then sets it aside. Next to the bread are cheese and boiled ham wrapped in wax paper, two apples, each shrouded in its own damp paper towel, and a thermos.

Tulsi slides the prayer card into his book alongside the picture of him and his grandfather. He zips the duffel shut and then, taking great care not to tear the paper, rewraps the package his neighbor gave him, crying silently as he does.

•

The bus station is mostly empty. An elderly couple stands near the ticket counter; a homeless man on a bench rolls a cigarette. Tulsi wishes the station was packed, swarming with travelers headed in every direction. The anonymity of a crowd is what he desires now, and now that he needs it, it's nowhere to be found.

He'd parked the Mustang a few blocks away near the Convention Center and woken the girl. He helped her from the car, then grabbed her bag from the backseat. She was still dazed, her eyes glassed by whatever drug they'd sedated her with.

"We need to go," he told her. "It's not safe here." He was not sure if she understood, but she allowed herself to be led.

The Owner will be searching for the car, and when he finds it empty, he will not stop searching. Tulsi understands that by now Chandra has made a decision. Call the Owner and plead his case, explain how he was betrayed and beg forgiveness. Or run. Tulsi pictures the Owner's scarred neck, remembers the satisfied expression on his face when he held his cigarette to the girl's thigh.

He hopes Chandra has chosen to run.

Across from the bus terminal stands Union Station with its great arched entryways and stone rotunda. He wonders about the Amtrak trains, if they might be a safer bet, but he has no idea of their timetable or where they go. Instead, he scans that day's bus schedule, destinations scrolling across a ticker in neon green. New York, Detroit, Providence, Cincinnati; cities he has never been to and cannot imagine. What would he do in these places? Who would he know?

When he first arrived in Pittsburgh, Malcolm told him how much he loved it. How it would be the perfect place to put down roots. Tulsi remembers how it was a metaphor he couldn't help but imagine literally: thick green tendrils sprouting from arms and legs, diving into rich soil to divide and search and surface again, blooming and fruitful. The thought had left him happy, filled him with a reassuring hope. To belong to someplace. To have it belong to you.

He drops his duffel in a corner and sets the girl's bag beside it. Other destinations continue to roll along the screen: Cleveland, Buffalo, Erie. The last is a welcome sight but Tulsi isn't sure it would be safe. He wonders if they might look for them there, how far the

Owner's influence stretches. He wonders where Chandra is now.

Near the sliding-glass doors, a pigeon follows a woman into the station. It skitters along the linoleum floor pecking, head swiveling detachedly. It passes Tulsi and the girl, beats its wings once and disappears down a terminal hallway.

The doors open again, then close with no one passing through. A sourness rises in Tulsi's throat. The predictability of his choice to go to the bus station strikes him all at once. Someone will be coming to check. He is sure of it.

The girl is seated on his duffel, eyes closed and chin resting on her chest. Tulsi hurries to the ticket counter. The bus for Erie leaves in half an hour, the soonest departure of any. It sounds like an eternity but he is unsure what else to do. He considers again the dangers of returning, weighs them against the risk of waiting for a later bus. After a moment, he slides his money below the cage and takes the two tickets.

Every time the sliding doors open and someone enters, his stomach drops. He shuts his eyes and sees Chandra staring back: wide mouth and dark irises, bushy eyebrows nearly touching. He sees the gold crucifix swinging from Chandra's neck, hears the words he spoke as he knelt with his back to Tulsi in the dark field.

You're the one who's doing it. It's you.

Tulsi opens his eyes. There is danger everywhere. In the desolate station. In his abandoned apartment. Even in his own thoughts.

•

He holds the girl close by the waist as they board the bus. The driver eyes him suspiciously when he takes their tickets.

"Long night," Tulsi says.

"Looks like it." The driver tears their tickets and hands back the stubs. "Bathroom's busted, so if she's gonna be sick you better not make a mess."

"Got it," Tulsi says.

The air inside the bus is humid and oppressive. It smells vaguely of charred meat and coffee. When they're halfway down the aisle, the girl lifts her head and looks at him.

"Where are we going?" she manages. These are the first words he's heard her speak. Though they come out slurred, he knows immediately that she is not foreign. There is the slightest country lilt, but the accent is undoubtedly American. For some reason this makes him even more wary. "Where are we going?" she asks again, slow and easy, as though inquiring what he'd had for lunch. He leads her to the back row of seats.

"Home," he says.

The bus makes its way through the sprawl of downtown, the sheer spires of Pittsburgh Plate and Glass reflecting the early morning light. The city opens onto its northern suburbs, houses built into the sides of hills like steps on a staircase. The interstate is under construction, milled asphalt rumbling underneath, concrete barriers dividing the northbound lanes. Tulsi has not traveled I-79 since moving to Pittsburgh nearly seven months before. They pass McCandless and Cranberry and soon the strip malls and office parks give way to cornfields, tree lines making dark green smudges in the distance. Farmhouses and weather-beaten barns in the rolling pasture on either side. The thought occurs that not only is he running away, but also backwards, regressing into a life he thought he'd escaped. Pittsburgh had been a goal he set for himself: a bigger city, better schools, new people.

A fresh start, Malcolm had said. May we make the most of them. And what had he made of his? What does he have to show for it? Fear. A friend in peril. Memories that will haunt him like ghosts.

He concentrates on the hum of the bus's wheels. Beside him the girl is once again asleep. Several rows up, an elderly man dozes, his head bobbing and jolting upright with each bump and bend. For the most part the bus is empty, a few scattered passengers nodding in rhythm to the surface of the road.

In a couple of hours he will be back where he started, back where he first arrived nearly seven years before, alone and afraid and entirely unsure of the new life awaiting him. He pictures himself exiting the plane, emerging from the gangway into the tiny airport. Sees himself waiting uncertainly near the baggage claim, avoiding the glances of his fellow travelers. Would they have known he was a refugee, a boy without a home? He recalls walking out into the damp afternoon, the asphalt glittering in the rain like crushed diamonds. His first fresh start. How many did you get in a lifetime? He was going to a new world. That's what they told him before he left the camp. A different world, they said, and though he was frightened, he believed them.

Now he rests his chin on his chest and waits for sleep that will not come. How young he'd been then. How foolish.

Dear Brother,

I take a moment to write you. It is many months since we have left Qatar, and though we are once again in exile, our hearts are lighter. Half a dozen others joined us. They too had fallen victim, and like thieves, we stole out in the night.

It has not been easy, brother. We have little, though such has long been the case. Some days we move without ceasing. Others we hide away, unable to emerge for fear of arrest. Many have helped us. For everything I have seen I still possess a belief I've always held: a wicked world can be filled with good people. Do you believe it, brother? I hope that you do. I hope your own path has proven as much.

We near Jordan and from there will consider options. But I do not write to trouble you with half-formed plans. This is not what weighs on my mind. I write for another reason. It is too much for me to hope that this will find you. I may not even have opportunity to send it. Still, as I've written, so would I speak.

Brother, know that wherever you are, you will soon be an uncle. I carry a child born of love and hardship, a blessing in the midst of tribulation. Purna is overjoyed but fearful. He worries our baby will arrive while in transit, a refugee like us. Cast out by a world it has yet to know. I fear the same but try to keep it hidden.

A thought has occurred to me over and over again on our journey. There are days the horizon seems endless, the earth an infinite place. What I ponder is this: in a world so vast and unknowable, how is it that so many are prevented from finding a place of their own?

I hope you have found yours, Tulsi.

Susmita

TULSI IS LOST AMONG UNEASY dreams. He is in a casino, row upon row of slot machines echoing their unbearable symphony of bells and clanking coins. He walks past, scanning the rows, but each is empty, the casino abandoned. There is no one but him. He tries to find an exit but cannot. Every turn and corner, every archway, leads to a new room of empty tables and slots, deserted bars, ceaseless noise. Domed cameras monitor him from the ceiling, twisting to mirror his movements. He stops, yells upward at them, at whoever is controlling them, but when he stands still, they pause.

In the distance, beyond the flashing lights and felted tables, he spots a man seated with his back to the wall. The man's head rests between his knees, his face hidden. Tulsi calls out to him and when he does the man looks up and Tulsi sees that it is himself. They differ in appearance, the seated man older and bearded, but Tulsi knows without question that he is looking at himself, feels it in the marrow of his bones. He runs forward, the cameras reeling to follow. His legs churn beneath him, his feet touch only air, but when he is almost there, less than an arm's length away, something grabs him, tearing him up and out of his dream.

He jolts awake, the bus slowing. Ahead of him, down the long center aisle, he sees the exit ramp they've taken. They're stopping, though he isn't sure why. The sign reads Meadville, still more than half an hour from Erie. A shock wave of fear moves through him. Are they being pulled over? He turns to his left to scan the shoulder for police, or worse, an unmarked vehicle, and finds the girl awake, watching him.

Something is different. The glassiness of her eyes has faded, the pupils no longer inky blotches. Her black hair is tucked back, revealing her round face.

"Bathroom break," she says quietly, the country lilt clearer now. She points toward the front of the bus, where a couple of elderly riders lean into the aisle.

"I see," Tulsi says. The bus pulls into a truck stop and the driver tells them to be back on in fifteen minutes. The older passengers maneuver for the door. "Looks like we're in Meadville," Tulsi says.

"Which is in?"

"Sorry. In Pennsylvania. We're headed to Erie, about a half hour from here."

The girl absorbs this, running the pads of her fingers across her forehead. "Pennsylvania," she says. She works a circle into her temple, her charm bracelet jingling. She shakes her head and smiles, laughs dryly. Tulsi is uncertain how he expected the girl to react after emerging from her haze. Screaming perhaps, accusations of kidnapping, maybe tears. He did not anticipate laughing. The sound unnerves him.

"Pennsylvania," she repeats. "Looks like my mom was right. I didn't make it too far after all."

•

Tulsi buys two bottles of water and some chips and waits for the girl to use the bathroom. He wonders how much she remembers, if she even recognizes him from the house in Wheeling, the drive to Pittsburgh, the bus station. All of it seems distant, like something that happened a long time ago, not just a few hours earlier. A mother walks by with two children. The older, a boy, chews on a stick of beef jerky and stares at Tulsi. Across the parking lot, the last of the passengers board the bus.

The girl has been in the bathroom since they arrived. A few minutes more and they will be left. It occurs to Tulsi that he could tell the driver the girl is staying behind, that a friend is picking her up. He could leave her and cut his losses. The possibility is still unfolding itself when the girl emerges. She spots him and walks over. He can tell she's been crying.

"Where are we going again?"

"Erie, Pennsylvania," Tulsi says, "about forty miles from here. But you don't have to go. I'm not making you. You don't have to do anything you don't want to."

"I don't even know where I am," she says. She glances at him, then looks away. "Or who *you* are."

Tulsi stares out at the parking lot. He knows he is implicit in whatever this girl was mixed up in, that not delivering her is insufficient penance for the things he has done. He feels the heft of his guilt, something solid strung round his neck. Worse, he knows the girl senses it too.

He remembers the chips and hands them to her, along with one of the waters. "I just don't know how safe it would be for you to stay here. I think we're both in some trouble."

The girl opens the water and takes a long drink. "Erie," she says. "Isn't there one in Indiana?"

"I don't know," Tulsi says. "This one's on a lake."

The girl considers this, caps her water and rolls the cool bottle across her brow. "Do you have a cigarette?"

Tulsi shakes his head.

"Can you buy me some? Anything but menthols." She wrinkles her nose. "They give me some kind of headache."

"All right," Tulsi says, barely registering the request, and then, "Are you coming or staying here?"

The girl looks out at the idling bus. "Erie bigger than wherever this is?"

"Than Meadville?" Tulsi says. "Yeah, it's a lot bigger."

"All right then."

●

Tulsi rents a room at the Knights Inn at Tenth and Sassafras. Rust-colored stains bloom upon the lobby walls and the floor is missing tiles, but for thirty dollars a night it's the best he can do. Through the front window he watches the girl smoke. She lit up the moment they got off the bus and has been at it ever since.

"Here you go." The young woman working the front desk slides Tulsi a key beneath the Plexiglas partition separating them. She smiles apologetically as though embarrassed they've both found themselves in such a place, an accident of fate. She returns to her textbook, highlighter at the ready. Tulsi tries to catch a glimpse of the subject: biology or chemistry, some type of science. He thinks of his own textbooks, abandoned in his room in Pittsburgh. The spring semester feels so long past he cannot even remember the classes he'd been enrolled in.

●

He and the girl take the exposed concrete stairwell to the second level. A fenced-in pool sits at the center of the motel's courtyard, its white lining torn, a skim of oily filth on its surface.

Their room is at the end of the walkway. Tulsi unlocks the door and flicks on the light. Inside are gray carpet and two narrow beds. Faded wallpaper displays an ear of corn alternating with a tuft of wheat, repeated in diagonal lines over and over. A beige acrylic bathtub sits in the corner atop a section of tile, a shower wand mounted to the wall.

Tulsi tosses their bags on the floor and finds the toilet in a closet-sized room in the corner. A used condom, translucent and shapeless as a jellyfish, floats on the surface. Tulsi flushes it quickly, his cheeks burning with shame.

When he emerges, the girl is sitting on one of the beds, flipping through the channels on the old box television set.

"This place is a shithole," she says without looking up.

"I'm sorry."

"Don't be. Makes me feel right at home."

Tulsi pulls a towel from the wall rack and dries his hands.

"All it needs is some loud music and people arguing. A couple cousins flinging their shit at each other, and I'd swear I was back in Pikeville."

Tulsi hangs the towel and sits on the bed opposite hers. "Is that where you're from?"

The girl eyes him suspiciously. "Sure," she says, "why not."

"What were you doing in Wheeling?"

"I don't know. Vacationing. What's it matter?"

"Those people you were with," he says, "they're not good people."

The girl tosses the remote on the bedspread, scoots up until she's leaning against the headboard. "So how do *you* know them?"

Thin curtains billow above the air conditioning unit near the door. Light filters through the gap, illuminating the girl's face and a patch of wallpaper above her head.

"I used to work for the same man they do. At least I think that's who they work for. But not anymore."

"And your friend?"

Tulsi feels the blood rush from his face. "You remember him?"

"I remember there were two of you. Not much else." The girl pulls her knees to her chest. "I'm not supposed to be here, am I?" She shakes a cigarette loose from the pack and lights it.

Tulsi watches the smoke trail to the ceiling. He considers telling her about the houseboat, what would have happened to her there. Instead he says, "Neither of us is supposed to be here."

"I kind of figured," she says. "You looked scared as shit when the bus was pulling over. I knew something was wrong." She takes a drag, then rests her cigarette on the edge of the nightstand, extends her hand across the space between the beds. "Bronagh," she says.

Tulsi shakes her hand. "I've never heard that name before."

"No one has. We've got Mick ancestors, which is how I got saddled with it." The girl's gaze grows distant. "I was gonna change it, if I ever made it somewhere worth changing it for."

"I'm Tulsi."

The girl laughs and shakes her head. "Like in Oklahoma?"

"No," he says, smiling, "but I've heard *that* before."

•

They both fall asleep in the late afternoon, the air conditioner humming noisily. Around five Tulsi startles awake, a parting gift from a nightmare he has already forgotten. After having barely slept in a day and a half, the few hours' rest leaves him feeling underwater. He props himself on his elbows and takes in the still, unfamiliar surroundings. The TV is on mute, some talk show with a panel of hosts. A thin band of sunlight divides the curtains and cuts the room in half. All around him is silence, the air dank with sleep. He turns to his left and finds the other bed bare, sheets tucked neatly beneath the pillow. The corners of the room are empty. Behind him the bathroom door is open, the light off. Bronagh is gone.

For a moment there is relief, a loosening in his limbs. She is the one they wanted. She is the one they are after. He shakes his head at the guilt that follows. It has been with him all his life, familiar as a scar.

He had fallen asleep in his clothes, but the girl must have removed his shoes. They sit at his bedside, upright and untied. He puts them on and steps out onto the walkway where a warm mist falls from a cloudless sky. A bread truck sits unoccupied across the street, a ramp protruding like a long steel tongue from its back. Tulsi's phone chimes from inside. He goes to retrieve it and notices that the girl has left her cigarettes. Her bag sits beside the bed where he'd left it.

The text is from a number he does not recognize but for the area code. 412. Pittsburgh. He reads the number to himself silently, some secret code he cannot decipher. It strikes him that were he blameless he could open the text without worry, a man unburdened by the world. But he is not blameless and his fingers tremble as he taps the okay button.

The screen fills with a picture, an empty room bathed in light. At first it is hard to comprehend the scene. A yellowed rectangle on a sheet of gray is a bare mattress in the center of a cement floor. A felled tree with outstretched branches is a body, arms splayed and wrists bound. At the top of the body is some burst fruit, overripe and split by the ground, purple and red spilling from its insides in a sick dark stream. It is a face beyond recognition as a face, a piece of a puzzle that only makes sense when complete. Looped around the neck is a thin chain, a fraction of the width of the chains that bind the body's wrists. At the end of the chain is a crucifix, its shape unmistakable against the battered mattress.

Tulsi's stomach heaves. He drops the cell and makes it to the bathroom just in time to empty yellow bile into the bowl. He grips its sides, his throat constricted.

He returns to his phone and exits the picture without looking again, the disgrace of cowardice burning through him. No text accompanies the picture and none is needed. It is Chandra. Tulsi left him behind and now this thing has happened to him. Tulsi is responsible and soon, it will happen to him.

•

Tulsi sits on the edge of the bed staring at the painting hanging opposite him. He does not know how long the girl has been gone. He does not know what time it is. The painting is a faded print the size of a shoebox. It depicts an empty skiff at the bottom of a dry lakebed. White paint peels near the boat's rails and the oars are missing. The red lettering along its side is illegible. From the front of the room comes the sound of a key finding its lock, a door swinging open, footsteps. Tulsi cannot bring himself to look away from the painting. The door clicks shut, muffling the noise of traffic.

"Are you all right?" a voice asks, but he cannot answer. He is too intent on the painting, on the mystery implicit within it. There is a story behind the skiff that he is desperate to know. Over and over again he works it in his mind. He cannot decide if the boat sunk or if the lake drained beneath it. A less likely scenario occurs to him as well. Someone has dragged the boat there to rot.

Bronagh steps between Tulsi and the painting, breaking the spell. "Tulsi," she says. A fine slick of rain coats her face. She tilts her head and offers a nervous smile. "How long have you been awake?"

"Where were you?" Tulsi asks. She has brushed her hair back, pulled it into a neat ponytail. Again, he sees the broken face, the bound wrists. This time it is not his friend lying there, but this girl. He stands and in one quick step is inches from her. He grabs her forearms, squeezes tightly. "Where'd you *go*?" She tries to twist away. "Do you know how much trouble we're in?"

"I'm sorry," she says. "I was hungry. I brought us food."

"Do you know what they'll do to us?" He squeezes harder, feels her bones viced in his grip. "*Stupid*," he says, saliva sparking from his mouth. "*Stupid*, Chandra. Never enough."

Something drops from the girl's hand and lands at his foot. He looks down to see a crumpled McDonald's bag, fries spilling out. When he looks back the girl flinches. It's only then he realizes he's been screaming. He is shaking when he lets her go. She stumbles back against the far wall, bumping the picture of the boat, unsettling it. He opens his mouth to apologize but says nothing.

"I'm sorry," she says again, rubbing her arms where he gripped them, the finger marks paper white. "I wanted to surprise you. As a thank you. But there was a line and..."

"*No*..." Tulsi says, shaking his head. "No, it's not your fault." He lifts the bag of food from the floor. "Here," he says extending it toward her, but she does not move. She is still rubbing her arms, her charm bracelet clinking like a wind chime. "Here," he repeats. "I'm sorry."

When she finally straightens and separates from the wall she approaches him hesitantly, the way one might approach a stray dog at the edge of a wood. While handing her the bag he sees something new in her eyes: the shading of fear, a flickering of uncertainty, the proper pause for a man not worthy of trust.

•

In the bathroom he rinses his face and looks at himself in the mirror. His cheeks are sunken. Sallow crescents rim his red eyes. He looks older than he is. Feels it. His cell phone rests on the glass shelf above the basin. He holds the power button until it shuts off then wraps it in a hand towel and lowers it to the floor. Balancing himself on the sink, Tulsi stomps on the phone repeatedly, feels it come apart beneath his heel. If there's any way they can use it to find him, it's not worth the risk, and if his past has taught him anything, it is this: they will always find a way.

Bronagh sits on the edge of the bed, finishing a burger. She has mostly recovered from his fury, but a loose strand of hair from her ponytail brings a flush to his cheeks. She offers him the bag of food and he shakes his head no.

"We can't stay here," he says. "It's not safe anymore."

"What happened?" she asks. "When I was gone." He can't bring himself to look directly at her and begins to pack the few things he took from his bag. She seems to understand and bends down to slide on her sandals.

"Don't forget your things," Tulsi says.

"What things?"

"Your bag," he says, straightening. "I carried it for you from the bus." He points at the red book bag in the corner. She has left it untouched since they arrived.

Bronagh shakes her head. "Not mine," she says, and bends to finish securing a strap. Panic gathers in Tulsi's gut, threads itself upward through his chest.

"It is," he says. "The man you were with gave it to me when we picked you up." He flinches at the word *we*, tries to focus on anything but the picture that fills his mind. "He said to make sure it stayed with you." Tulsi already knows what is happening but is hoping somehow he is wrong.

"All I took when I left was my ID and a few twenties from my mom's purse. It was kind of a quick exit."

Tulsi lifts the bag and lays it on the bed, feels the heft he'd taken for granted earlier. Bronagh watches as he unzips it. Inside are four rectangular bundles wrapped in aluminum foil. He takes one and peels it. Beneath is clear plastic covering a solid white brick of cocaine.

In all the field trips he made for the Owner, he never once looked inside a package. He remembers Chandra instructing him not to. *What you don't know can't hurt you*, he'd said. Of all the lies he chose to believe, this one stings the worst.

Tulsi slips the bundle back inside the bag and zips it. He presses his hands flat against the bedspread to stop them from shaking.

Bronagh's eyes are wide, the corners of her lips curl slightly upward. "You think they're gonna want that back?" she asks.

"Yes," Tulsi says and nods. "I'm thinking yes."

•

The rain has stopped, the sky even clearer than before. The city's streets steam. Tulsi holds Bronagh's hand, tries to quicken her pace as they round the corner onto Sassafras. The red book bag bangs against his back with every step. He'd considered leaving it in the room, sliding it beneath the bed where it would eventually be found by housekeeping or another guest. Then he'd recalled the video camera mounted in a corner as he checked in, the red light flashing as he paid. It was bad enough having the Owner searching for him without the cops wanting him too. There is something oddly funny about it, opposite sides of the law with him as shared enemy. Gallows humor, he knows, but still, he has to shake away the smirk.

"Where are we going now?" Bronagh asks. A woman in a motorized wheelchair passes in the opposite direction. Since leaving the motel Tulsi has been on high alert. Every car is one of the Owner's enforcers eager to cut him down, every pedestrian an undercover cop ready to stop and frisk.

"We've got to get rid of this," Tulsi says. He takes another step but feels the sluggish weight of the girl holding him back. She's barely moving.

"Are you sure that's a good idea?"

The woman in the wheelchair looks over her shoulder. Tulsi imagines what they must look like standing there in the middle of the sidewalk, the odd couple they must make.

"What do you suggest I do? Sell it? I'm not a drug dealer."

Bronagh tilts her head, and again Tulsi feels shame burn through him. He remembers his grandfather, his hajurba. A hardworking man of simple pleasures. A man who at the end of his life longed only for the mountains of his youth. What would he think of his beloved grandson now?

Bronagh frees her hand and reaches for her cigarettes. "That's not what I'm saying, but what if they find us and we've tossed it. Imagine the trouble we'd be in then."

Tulsi does not want to consider the ramifications of being caught, does not want to revisit what the Owner and his men are capable of. Still, he knows that the girl has a point. If the Owner's men were to catch up to them and the drugs were gone, there'd be no reason to let them live. Stashing them might provide time, a means to escape if it came to that.

"I don't know," he says. He thinks again of the list of options he has left and finds it lacking. The Owner probably hadn't thought him stupid enough to return to Erie, but between the drugs and the girl it would be worth checking. No stone left unturned.

"We need a plan. We can't just run around with *that* hanging off your back."

A line of cars rides past, a dark blue police cruiser among them. Tulsi watches it from the corner of his eye. "We've got to keep moving," he says.

"Fine, but are you gonna tell me what we're doing?"

The cruiser pulls into a McDonald's on the corner and joins the line of vehicles at the drive-thru. "All right," Tulsi says, "but please, let's just keep moving."

•

They head farther downtown, past the banks and barbershops and boarded-up storefronts. A group of teenagers loiters near the Dollar Store, their collective mass expanding and contracting rhythmically. Tulsi and Bronagh pass the old Warner Theater, its Art Deco marquee providing shade to a pair of men smoking thin cigars. When they reach Third Street, Presque Isle Bay opens beneath them, a wide blue tarp upon which the whole city seems to rest. Tulsi feels the girl's hand go slack, looks back and sees her staring. For a moment they stand there looking out over the water, its rippling surface reflected in the windows of office buildings. Boats glide past, the white triangles of their sails brilliant. He knows what the girl is thinking, the sudden shock of beauty. He is about to say something when a truck towing a trailer full of landscape equipment rattles past. He looks up and sees the wonder gone from Bronagh's eyes and so they keep moving.

At the bottom of State Street, they duck into a coffee shop. A few patrons sit leafing through magazines or staring at their phones. They find an open table near the window and Tulsi takes a twenty from his wallet.

"Here," he says, "get whatever you want and wait for me."

"You're gonna leave me here?" Bronagh's voice goes high, desperate, and for the first time Tulsi understands just how young she must be.

"Look," he says, "I'm only going across the street. You can watch me the whole time. I'll be right back."

"What's across the street?"

Tulsi stands and lifts the book bag. "The library. They have lockers there. I'm going to get rid of this and then we can go."

Bronagh looks uncertain, but Tulsi presses the creased twenty into her hands and leaves.

•

He passes through the stacks, the musty smell of old books somehow calming. The library is just as he remembers it from when he used to come and research schools: algae-colored carpet, squares of fluorescent light, and then, through the towering corridors of books, a wall of floor-to-ceiling windows facing the bay. He remembers afternoons spent casting a line over that water, the sun warming his face as he waited for a bite with a relaxed anticipation he has not known since. He brushes away the thought and continues to the rear of the library, where a bank of aluminum lockers rests against a wall. The room is nearly empty. A teenager in oversized headphones sits transfixed by a laptop. A young woman turns the pages of a novel.

Tulsi fishes coins from his pocket and deposits the bag in a small locker along the bottom row. The locker's key is attached to a black rubber coil. He loops it over his wrist.

Walking back through the stacks he feels a slight unburdening, the temporary absolution of separating himself from his sins. He emerges into the library's high-ceilinged lobby. Passing the glass-walled periodical room he feels eyes on him. He quickens his pace toward the circulation desk in front of the exit. He is nearly there when he hears his name from behind.

It is the voice that makes him stop, the way his name is pronounced perfectly but spoken as a question, the accent unmistakably Nepalese. He turns to find an elderly man peering at him. A newspaper attached to a wooden rod dangles from his hand. It is Mr. Bhandari, his old neighbor, his grandfather's stubborn friend.

"Tulsi," he says. "I wasn't sure it was you."

Tulsi sees how the years have aged him: bent spine hunching him into a partial bow, eyes clouded by cataracts. He cannot help but think of his own hajurba, how he might have looked were he still alive. Sadness pools within him, and he has to concentrate on the carpet as he approaches.

"Mr. Bhandari," Tulsi says, "it's good to see you." He means it. Even this man, who had scolded him with every glance, admonished his fascination for all things American. He is a part of Tulsi's past, a tangible reminder that he does exist.

"And you." Mr. Bhandari smiles, revealing several missing teeth below darkened gums. There is a tenderness about him that Tulsi does not recall, time softening even the hardest of men.

"And Mrs. Bhandari?" The smile fades, and Tulsi sees that he's made a mistake, touched upon a sorrow never far from the surface.

"A year after your grandfather," he says, his voice tremulous. He clears his throat with a cough. "Also from cancer."

"I'm sorry," Tulsi says. The old man nods, looks left where a semicircle of glass above the fire exit lets in the afternoon sun.

"I always blamed this place. Said it corrupted our people, made us sick. My wife did not agree. I don't know that I do anymore either."

Near the media section, a young couple debate which DVD to rent. Mr. Bhandari lifts the wooden rod at his side. "I come here to read the newspaper from Bhutan. *Kuensel.* It reminds me of home." The old man's smile returns. "Even the advertisements I like."

"I remember it from Goldhap," Tulsi says, and just speaking the place awakens it for him. He remembers the way the camp's elders would swarm newcomers from Bhutan asking for news of their country. The way letters and newspapers were treated almost as contraband, read communally in the close heat of crowded huts. There had been such desperation to find out what happened to those left behind. Like the camp's other children, Tulsi could not comprehend the urgency. They had been born in Goldhap; their histories began and ended there. How thoughtless he had been, he realizes now, not to understand the suffering of separation from what one knows and loves.

Mr. Bhandari folds the newspaper shut and rests the rod across his forearms reverentially. "Tulsi, you must come for dinner. I am not the cook my wife was, but every week I make her dal. I am getting quite good." The old man's clouded eyes are steady, his face hopeful.

"It's a very kind offer, but…"

"You would honor me," Mr. Bhandari says. "Your grandfather was my closest friend, though I know I burdened him with my worrying. You bring his memory close."

Tulsi thinks of the girl waiting for him in the coffee shop, the trouble they're in. He does not want to involve his grandfather's friend, but he has also not planned beyond what he's just done. He understands they have nowhere to go. He imagines Mr. Bhandari going home, eating his soup silently in his darkened kitchen. He reaches out and holds the newspaper for him.

"All right," he says, "but may I bring a friend?"

•

The old neighborhood is much as he remembers it. The close-set houses and apartment buildings, clothing lines sagging between them. The small rectangles of grass along fractured sidewalks, families gathered on porches. They pass his old building and a knot forms in his stomach. He thinks of summer evenings spent sitting on the concrete stoop with his grandfather, eating pizza after soccer practice, or simply talking. It seems so long ago that it's hard to accept the place still exists. When a small girl emerges from the front door and rushes to join her friends, a pang of ownership fills Tulsi with unreasonable envy.

Mr. Bhandari still lives in the same apartment, two buildings down. Together they climb the stairs to the second-floor landing. He unlocks the door and they follow him into the small living room. The smell is instantly familiar: the tang of curry mixed with the sweet, earthy scent of tobacco. A pang of guilt strikes Tulsi for the recklessness of having come here. He does not want to endanger anyone else, but his lack of options has left him weary. Mr. Bhandari instructs them to sit and turns on the television before shuffling off to the kitchen to prepare their meal.

Bronagh seemed hesitant when Tulsi showed up to the coffee shop with Mr. Bhandari in tow, but now she lifts the remote and clicks through the channels. She settles on a cooking show, where a man with an enormous beard gushes over a vat of chili.

"I'm starving," she says. "I could eat a horse."

"That's probably what we're having," Tulsi says. The girl gives him a confused look. "Bhutanese delicacy," he says, then smiles, forgetting for a moment the trauma of the last two days.

"You're funny," Bronagh says. "A real ham." She turns her attention back to the show, a sly smile settling briefly on her lips.

They eat gathered around a small circular table, Mr. Bhandari regaling them with stories of Bhutan: his youth spent cultivating cardamom in the southern foothills, surreal encounters with European backpackers searching for Shangri-La, and then the dark times, the census and the struggles that followed. Men coming to his home and expelling him as an illegal immigrant.

"Three generations my family had lived there, but I had a Nepalese name," Mr. Bhandari says. He lifts his hand to his brow. "A Nepalese face. This was enough."

Bronagh lowers her soupspoon. "Why did they want the Nepalese to leave?"

"In the south, there were many of us. We spoke our own language, followed our own customs. These differences were seen as a threat."

Mr. Bhandari reaches across the table and lays a hand on Tulsi's, his skin thin and brittle. "This was long before you were born," he says, "but the king began a policy: one nation, one people. Unfortunately for the southerners, that 'people' was not us." Mr. Bhandari pauses, looks down at his dal as though trying to conjure some meaning from the steaming soup. "None of this matters anymore," he says, steam condensing on his aged skin, causing it to glisten. "I waste your time recounting ancient history."

"It's not a waste of time," Tulsi says. "It's important."

Mr. Bhandari smiles and pats his hand again. "Your hajurba was very brave," he says. "The soldiers came and told us not to speak our language, tried to force us to dress as the northerners did. Your grandfather refused. He wanted to stay and fight." Mr. Bhandari's gaze wanders off, his clouded eyes recalling some episode a lifetime past. "In the end we could not. We were forced to leave."

"How could they do that?" Bronagh asks, her tone incensed as though the outrage has just occurred. "If you lived and worked there and it was your home? It's not right."

Mr. Bhandari smiles faintly at the stranger sitting across from him, this young girl he's just recently met. "Men do many things that are not right."

•

Once dinner is finished, Mr. Bhandari disappears into the kitchen. He returns with a tray upon which sit a kettle of butter tea and an unopened package of almond cookies from Nepal. When he goes to open the package, Tulsi tells him to save them.

"Nonsense," Mr. Bhandari says, "this is the manner of occasion I've been saving them for."

The three of them sit there a while, softening their cookies in the hot tea, refilling their cups from the porcelain kettle, a motley trio savoring the final moments of their meal.

Once the table has been cleared and the dishes washed and put away, they descend the stairs and stand on the concrete landing in front of the apartment. Tulsi leans against the railing while Bronagh slips a cigarette from her pack. Mr. Bhandari rolls his own as Tulsi's grandfather had, his hands holding the paper delicately, smoothing the tobacco evenly from one end to the other. Once he's sealed it, he hands it to Bronagh.

"Nepalese tobacco," he says, striking a match and lighting it for her. "Much better for you." He begins to roll another for himself.

Tulsi watches them smoke, these two contrasting figures. A runaway encountered through his own sins and an old man expelled from his rightful home. What suffering one has already seen, he thinks. How much yet for the other?

The cool night air feels good against Tulsi's skin after the spicy dal. The familiarity of his old street, of being with someone from his past, fills him with a sense of tranquility he knows is dangerous. He's let his guard down and more than anything he wants to leave it that way, to rest if only for the night. Still, he understands the peace he feels is false, a delusion he's too eager to embrace.

"We should be going," he tells Mr. Bhandari.

"Where?" the old man asks. Tulsi was not ready for the question. He and Bronagh exchange a look.

"Exactly," Mr. Bhandari says. Tulsi understands at once that he's not hidden his uncertainty or fear nearly as well as he thought. The old man knows they need help and he's offering it. "You should spend the night here," he says. "In the morning, once you're rested, then you can go."

"It's very kind of you to offer, but…"

"Nonsense," Mr. Bhandari says. "This is the best night I've had in ages. You grant a lonely man a true kindness." Across the patio, Bronagh hunches her shoulders, leaving it up to Tulsi.

"All right," he says, too tired to argue, "but only for the night." Mr. Bhandari reaches out and pats his shoulder.

"Excellent," he says, and takes the tobacco pouch from his pocket. "In that case, I'll indulge." He rolls another cigarette for himself, and one for Bronagh.

The neighborhood is quiet, with only the occasional car rolling by. In the graying sky, the signal lights of an airplane blink steadily, a trio of red dots against the growing darkness. Two buildings down, a door opens and Tulsi watches an elderly Black woman emerge from his old apartment. The girl he'd seen earlier follows her out, dressed in a cartooned nightgown. They sit on a gliding aluminum bench. A vision strikes him: his grandfather trudging home through the snow, sandaled feet covered in plastic bags cuffed with tape. Tulsi shakes it away and concentrates on the rhythmic squeaking of the bench. The girl holds a doll, combing its hair in long careful strokes. Mr. Bhandari has noticed Tulsi watching.

"How long have they lived there?" Tulsi asks.

"Since shortly after you left."

"Do you know them?"

"Only to wave and say hello. Not by name." Mr. Bhandari surveys the street. "They are good neighbors. Neat. Considerate. This is not always the case."

Tulsi recalls the many nights he fell asleep with police lights strobing the cracked ceiling, a fight spilling out from one of the seedy bars along Parade. He remembers waking in the night to the shattering of bottles.

Across from him, Bronagh stubs out her cigarette. "I think I'm going to turn in, if that's all right."

"Of course," Mr. Bhandari says. "I'll fix the spare room." He follows, then turns to see if Tulsi is coming.

In the street a man on a bicycle rides past, a chain lock wrapped around his waist like a belt. Tulsi watches him pedal away. "I'll be right up," he says.

•

The woman hums softly to the girl as Tulsi approaches. He senses he is intruding upon a nightly ritual, something private and safe. Still, he is compelled to speak, to inform them of their connection.

He greets them from the other side of the railing. The girl looks up, eyes heavy in the dim light. She does not seem startled to find this man, a stranger, standing in their yard speaking to them. The woman stops her humming and offers Tulsi a half smile. Her gray hair is cut close to the scalp. She has on a blue cotton nightgown with a scalloped neck. Behind them, the darkened living room window flickers with the light of a television.

"Is there something I can help you with?" the woman asks. Her voice is friendly enough, but Tulsi understands the impropriety of the moment. His eyes settle on the wrought-iron railing.

"I'm sorry to bother you. It's just…I used to live here. I haven't been back in a long time."

At this the woman's face opens as though she's just recognized an old friend. "You don't say." She shakes her head once and laughs. "I was worried you might be selling something. Religion or steak knives. You never know." She strokes the girl's hair and smiles. "We've been here a year now. Just signed the lease for another. Landlord tried to bump the rent, but we threatened to leave and he backed off."

"He pulled the same thing on me," Tulsi says, leaning against the railing. "I should have done what you did."

"Tricks of the tenant," she says. "Where do you live now?"

"Pittsburgh," Tulsi answers reflexively. He realizes once he's said it that this will never again be true.

"I have some family down that way. Always loved how the rivers cut that city up. Must be hell for getting around, though."

"You get used to it," Tulsi says. He remembers the awe he felt watching a coal barge power its way up the Allegheny, the pleasure he took following the bending riverwalk to work.

"I imagine you do," the woman says and peers down at the girl, whose eyes have closed. "I'd invite you in for some tea, but I need to get her to bed." When she looks up again, her face is bright with pride. "My granddaughter," she says. She nods at the door. "Feel free if you want to take a quick look around, for old time's sake."

"That's all right," Tulsi says. "I just thought I'd say hello." The girl nestles her head in the woman's lap, and Tulsi thanks her and turns to go.

He is nearly to the sidewalk when he hears the woman's voice, a raised whisper reaching out to him from across the lawn.

"Hold on, what's your last name?"

•

Tulsi sits in the living room of Mr. Bhandari's apartment staring at the letter in his lap. Mr. Bhandari had fixed the couch for him to sleep: white sheet tucked firmly in the gap behind the cushions, crocheted blanket folded neatly overtop. A set of towels and a pillow rest on the coffee table. Both Bronagh's and Mr. Bhandari's doors were shut when Tulsi returned. The only light comes from the dim lamp on the end table.

The letter arrived a few months back, the woman told him. There'd been some other mail addressed to a Mr. Gurung: circulars and credit card offers, stuff she felt comfortable throwing away. But this looked official, figured she better hold onto it in case anyone ever came by. She smiled when she handed it to him.

"Probably nothing," she said, "but I'm glad I kept it."

•

The letter is from the Office of the UN High Commissioner for Refugees. It is postmarked Geneva. Its manila envelope is ink-smudged and wrinkled at the corners. Tulsi's name and address are typed on a white label at the envelope's center. He knows it could be nothing. A questionnaire or survey, a fundraising campaign beseeching him to send money. Still, he's been staring at the envelope for half an hour, unable to open it. He turns it over again in his hands, studies the sealed flap, and then, before he can stop himself, slides his index finger into the gap and tears. Inside is a single sheet of paper, a lone paragraph a third of the way down. At first it will not come into focus, the words bleeding together to form a jumbled blur. When he can concentrate, he reads slowly.

Dear Mr. Gurung,

We are writing with regard to your numerous correspondences dated between September 2008 and October 2012 concerning your inquiry into the whereabouts of your sister [previously Susmita Gurung, married name Susmita Khalishar]. It has come to our attention through the Central Tracing Agency of the International Committee of the Red Cross that the individual and/or extended members of her husband's family may be living in Canada, specifically the Greater Toronto Area. We are unable to provide an exact address nor confirm the certainty of Mrs. Khalishar's presence in Toronto, as it was not the assigned relocation site. We hope you will accept our deepest sympathies for your ongoing separation and our sincerest wishes that your family be reunited.

Sincerely,

Mr. John T. Isserman, Secretary to Regional Director Sandra Belle
UNHCR Bureau for Asia and the Pacific

Tulsi rereads the letter once, then again. What strikes him first is simply seeing his sister's name in print, as though this itself somehow ensures her existence. The rest of the letter comes next. Susmita's husband: soft-spoken Purna, scholarly and meek. Tulsi's endless correspondence with the UN, the simple relief of knowing it was received, read, considered. The city of Toronto, a frosted metropolis in Tulsi's mind, its residents bundled and jostling beneath a glittering skyline. Though he has never been there, he knows it is not far, lying just beyond Lake Erie. Hopefulness ascends from some deep abyss. He has the sudden urge to awake Mr. Bhandari and show him the letter. But before he can even lift himself from the couch, his optimism is quelled by the heavy weight of the words before him.

unable to provide

not the assigned relocation site

deepest sympathies

He sits and reads the letter again and again, the text growing hazy. He reads until the words cease to make sense, until they exist only as a series of scratches and grotesque forms, shapes mutated into ancient hieroglyphs. The prophesy of a fool.

•

Tulsi awakes to a truck rumbling over the ruined street below. He fell asleep sitting up and his neck is cemented in place. Stretching it slowly, he searches for the letter, finds it beside his feet where it must have slipped from his hand in the night. The apartment's bedroom doors are still closed, and Tulsi cannot tell whether it is predawn or whether the darkness beyond the curtains is an overcast sky. He stands, his legs needling as the blood rushes through.

He washes his face and relieves himself, then steps from the bathroom to find Mr. Bhandari adjusting the burner beneath a kettle of tea. He is already dressed in slacks and a tan shirt.

"I thought you might like some breakfast," he says. "I didn't want to wake you earlier, but I heard you moving about."

Tulsi takes a seat at the kitchen table. "How long have you been up?"

"Only an hour or so," Mr. Bhandari says. "I try to sleep more but it's no use. As a young man there was never enough time in the day. Now," he says and raises his palms skyward, "I have more than I need."

Tulsi thanks him again for letting them stay.

"It is nothing," Mr. Bhandari says. "I only wish you could stay longer." He moves along the counter and opens the refrigerator. "I'm embarrassed to say I've run out of eggs. I could make some hot cereal."

"That's very kind, but we really should be going."

The kettle releases its slow whistle and Mr. Bhandari lifts it from the stove. "Your friend already stepped out," he says. "You could have something while you wait for her return."

It takes a moment for the words to register, and even then Tulsi is confused. "Stepped out?"

"I heard her leave a little while ago," Mr. Bhandari says, "before you were up." He pours steaming green tea into a white mug and slides it toward Tulsi. "I thought maybe she was going for coffee or for more of those awful American cigarettes."

Tulsi rushes to the spare room and throws open the door. The bed is perfectly made as though unslept in. There is no sign of Bronagh. He returns to the living room and begins to pack the few things he'd taken from his bag, slipping the folded letter into his front pocket.

"I'm sorry, but I have to go."

Mr. Bhandari looks confused, but nods in understanding. "I would have woken you had I known this was bad," he says. "I apologize."

Tulsi stops what he is doing and looks up. "No," he says, "you have nothing to apologize for." He is about to say something else, to explain to this man what his help has meant, but he cannot. A torrent of gratitude and sadness fills him so abruptly he is certain one more word will leave him in tears. He breathes in, concentrates on the deep creases running from the corners of Mr. Bhandari's eyes, the fine white hairs like strands of silk on his head.

Tulsi returns to his packing, leaning into the bag's side to shut it. He is buckling the duffel when he notices his bare wrist, the rubber loop that held the locker key, gone.

•

The library is nearly unoccupied at this early hour. A pair of old women use the computers near the front. A young man in thick black glasses sits at the circulation desk, head resting on propped elbow. Tulsi tries not to draw attention as he rushes toward the stacks. The aisles are narrow and his elbows catch jutting books, causing a few to spill out behind him. He emerges into the back room and finds it empty. Turning to face the bank of identical, lockers he cannot remember which is his, only that it was along the bottom row. He begins at the left, scanning to see which are in use and which still have a key attached. Only one has its key missing, but he cannot be sure it was where he left the bag.

Beside him a line of windows faces the bay. A lone seagull glides on a current of air. The city's Bicentennial Tower looms above the water like a giant unlit candle. Tulsi stares out at the white-capped waves, at the brilliant green of the park beyond. For the past two days he has existed in a near-constant state of uncertainty. The blinding bouts of panic have left him numb. He watches a fishing charter idle toward the channel. Across the water, the sun sets fire to the tops of the trees. Tulsi looks around, hands trembling. All he wants in this moment is for someone to tell him what to do.

He sits on a bench in the lobby, his duffel perched beside him. There is still a chance he has beat Bronagh here. She might have gotten confused retracing their steps from Mr. Bhandari's to the library, or had a pang of conscience and returned. Either way he must wait. What choice does he have? He rubs his sleep-crusted eyes, sickened by his own stupidity. He should have known. Tulsi recalls the girl's insistence he not discard the bag. What must those aluminum-wrapped bundles have looked like to her? A once-in-a-lifetime windfall? A first-class ticket anywhere? She'd never met the Owner, had no idea what he was capable of. Tulsi should have explained things to her, warned her. He shakes his head, his stomach riled with regret.

Tulsi studies the clock on the wall, the seconds ticking away. The young man working the circulation desk has given up all pretense, his head resting cheek down. Tulsi's knee bounces a staccato rhythm. He cannot stay seated, feels the urge to pace if only to keep from going mad. He stands and walks to the entrance, stares out across the mostly empty parking lot. Beyond it, a few early commuters drive along the Bayfront Highway. A gleaming fire engine catches the rising sun and casts its glare. When it passes, Tulsi notices something he had missed. Near the parking lot's exit, partially hidden by a trio of saplings, stands a glass-walled bus stop, its metal roof glinting. Tulsi squints and steps forward. Inside, wedged so tightly into one corner that she seems a part of the structure itself, sits a girl. Clutched to her chest is a red book bag.

Even before he's outside, relief brims, fills him like a vessel. He is not too late. As he pushes open the library door, he imagines what he will tell her: that he understands. That he'd have done the same. That in some ways, he has.

A few steps and he is certain that it's Bronagh, black hair swept over one shoulder. He walks carefully across the wide parking lot. He's still a good fifty yards away and she has not spotted him yet. He wants to keep it that way. If he spooks her she might run. That is not what he wants. He recalls his reaction at the motel, how he gripped her forearms, demanded to know where she'd gone. That is not who he is.

"It's okay," he says unconsciously, as though already reassuring her. Such a small thing to offer. Maybe it will be enough.

Suddenly the air around him fills with a howl, the unmistakable sound of rubber flayed by road. In front of the bus stop, a dark truck skids to a halt, two of its wheels resting on the sidewalk. In the second it takes Tulsi to realize what is happening, a man leaps from the passenger side. In his hands is a canvas bag. Before Bronagh can react, he is upon her.

Tulsi begins to run, the distance between himself and what is happening all of a sudden impossible. The man, intent on his awful errand, does not spot Tulsi. Instead, he lifts the bag and rips it down over Bronagh's head. With one hand, he secures the red book bag to Bronagh's chest, and with the other, hauls her backward toward the cab, her legs churning wildly like a swimmer kicking to the surface for air.

Tulsi runs toward the truck, is at a full sprint when the door shuts. His footfalls send shockwaves through his body, reverberate through his skull like the crack of a rifle. The air feels thick and stifling, an obstacle to overcome. The truck's tires release their hideous whine and spin in place over concrete sidewalk and shoulder. Dark smoke billows. The infinitesimal pause before the treads catch is the worst kind of hope.

There is time, Tulsi thinks. There is time.

The truck tears onto the highway, rocking violently when it jumps the curb. Tulsi watches it right itself, watches it fishtail across the center lane and back. When the truck disappears around a bend, he is still running.

PART FOUR

IN HIS DREAMS CANADA HAD been a barren tundra, flat and white as paper. On the bus traveling north it was all he could imagine, how as soon as they reached the border the green fields and burgundy leaves would give way to a pallid horizon, the world drained of its color. Crossing over from New York he saw the same burnished golds and crimsons in the trees and felt not relief but foolishness. He remembered the fears he'd had arriving from Nepal some seven years past, the bigness and strangeness of the world waiting for him in Pennsylvania. He remembered the boys in the camp warning him of the vampires he'd find there.

The border agent who'd boarded the bus to check passports asked him to disembark. He waited in a bare room for two hours, after which another agent asked him the same series of questions the first had put forth. Once he was cleared, he emerged from the station to find that his bus had left without him.

•

Before Canada he'd spent two weeks in Buffalo, staying in a motel off Genesee. Each day he visited a different payphone and placed an anonymous call to the Pittsburgh police. Every time he rattled off the exact same list of locations and crimes as though reciting scripture. The upper room at Jack's, the houseboat off the Strip: drugs, prostitution, kidnapping. Did he have names, one officer had asked him. Another demanded to know his country of origin, whether or not he was an illegal. Each time he was dismissed until finally the dispatcher knew his voice and simply hung up.

Nights he lay in bed unable to sleep, eyes fixed on the dark curtains until they paled with dawn. He ate intermittently, venturing out for little more than his phone calls. In his exhaustion, the ghosts of his past visited him, filling the cramped room like spectators to his demise. He saw Abigail, his first American friend, her copper eyes filled with sadness. She was the wife of a preacher and yet he knew she'd cursed God. He wondered if she ever became a mother. There was Malcolm, whose family and friendship had provided him a temporary solace, something he feared was gone forever until Rebecca and Grace filled his days with a lightness he'd never known. All of it vanished now. He saw Chandra, beaten, and Bronagh, taken. Both of them dead or worse. He could feel the presence of his grandfather by his bedside: gentle, kind. How the world treated a man like that.

Each of them had come into his life and left it. Watching the shapes of the room sharpen in daylight, he had never felt so alone. He shut his eyes against the coming hours and imagined a vast field burning, windswept flames spreading in every direction as though spilt from the sky. And somewhere, behind it all, a single house ready to be swallowed by the conflagration, once lived in, now unreachable.

•

Tulsi arrives in Niagara Falls at night, the small downtown choked with tourists. He walks down Queen Street, invisible among the weekend revelers. There is something grotesque about them he cannot quite put his finger on. He fixes his gaze and moves past the restaurants and arcades, a Ripley's Odditorium promising shrunken heads and deformed animals. He passes a haunted house adorned with gargoyles and a crumbling green façade. There is even a Ferris wheel, its left half protruding from behind a high-rise like a waning moon. Beneath it all, the chatter of the passing crowds, the music leaking from the clubs and bars, there is something else, a low hum that begins beneath his feet and travels upward through him. It fills the crevices of silence, saturating the air, constant and embodying a powerful restraint, like the vibrations of the Earth itself.

Several blocks from the strip he finds a motel, an arc of red doors surrounding a crowded parking lot. At the front desk a matronly woman in an orange sweater informs him there are no rooms.

"Busy weekend," she adds, "with the holiday and all."

"Holiday?"

The woman regards him askance, as though he might be trying a joke at her expense. "Halloween," she says after a moment, her face softening. "Didn't you see all the people dressed up? It's always a big weekend for us."

Tulsi thinks of the tourists clogging the sidewalks, recognizing only now the grim robes and gruesome masks, those wielding plastic scythes and swords. Others dressed scantily as nurses or devils. How had he not made the connection?

"Of course," he tells the woman. "I should have planned ahead."

She offers him candy from a plastic jack-o-lantern and he raises his hand no.

"You might have better luck at the casino," she says. "They've got plenty of rooms."

Seventy dollars is more than he intended to spend but the bus stop is closed for the night and so the alternative is sleeping outside. His room is on the ninth floor. A plush king bed stands centered against one wall and adjacent to it, set on a raised platform, is a large mint-green hot tub. There is something ludicrous about its presence in the bedroom, but Tulsi is too exhausted to care. He removes his shoes and collapses in bed, not even bothering to get beneath the covers.

●

He is awoken by the same vibrations he felt the night before, a powerful white noise that coils into his dreams like a snake, its sudden presence shocking him from sleep. He finds himself fully clothed and stands to stretch. Coppery light paints the corners of the room, filtered through a set of taupe drapes that span the length of one wall. The noise that woke him is more powerful now, separate and above his own shallow breaths. He walks to the drapes, pulls them apart, and is barely conscious of the gasp he releases. Nine floors below he sees what he's been hearing all along, the thundering semicircle of Horseshoe Falls, its cascading water pouring endlessly over the edge. Tulsi can hardly believe the sight of it, white mist ascending from below as though in rebellion, climbing eye-level with where he stands and then higher, communing with the heavens. He gazes at the great absence that creates the Falls, the namesake curve stretching from one border to the other as though some unfathomable giant had reached down and scooped the earth out. Tulsi leans forward, bumps his nose against the cool glass and pulls back, surprised. He cannot help but laugh, the sight of it all so magnificent past the smudge of his mistake. He laughs until his sides hurt, until he is crying, then weeping, alone in a room he can barely afford, staring out over a sight he might never have seen. He continues to watch, sleeving the tears away quickly when his vision blurs, for fear of missing a thing.

•

Walking through the streets of downtown Toronto, Tulsi can scarcely believe how clean everything is. Sidewalks and roads are clear of trash, buildings free from graffiti. Even the storm drains and gutters seem as though someone has polished them. The pristine appearance was the first thing he noticed after disembarking at Union Station. He'd taken a train named the Maple Leaf and spent the entire ride staring out the window, Lake Ontario stretching before him like a still ocean.

Before leaving Niagara Falls, he contacted the Nepalese Canadian Community Center. They did not keep records of all Toronto-area refugees, they told him, only those who used their services. Still, he cannot think of where else to go.

The early evening air is crisp and it's already grown dark, but Tulsi is glad to be outside. An old man stands smoking near a bar and nods as Tulsi passes. Couples walk by hand in hand. Rounding a corner near Front Street, Tulsi catches a glimpse of a towering structure dominating the horizon, splitting the sky in half. Lit in red and white, it looks as though a giant syringe has been erected, pointing toward the heavens. An older woman laden with shopping bags nearly runs into him as he stands there gawking.

"I'm sorry," he says, stepping from the center of the sidewalk, and then, "what is that?"

The woman slows and turns. "CN Tower," she says. "Go up if you have the chance. View's incredible."

Tulsi continues to stare, amazed by the sheer audacity of the structure, its slender frame strangely elegant. "People can go up there?" he asks, but the woman has already moved on. Tulsi looks back up at the tower, the white circle of light surrounding what must be its observation deck. He remembers vaguely the dreams he harbored of one day becoming an engineer, of having some part, small as it may be, in creating structures that could serve to connect. That is what this is. Not a bridge or a highway or a trestle, but a tower. Man's humble attempt to gain the attention of God.

●

By the time he reaches the Nepalese Community Center, it has long since closed. Through the glass double doors he sees an empty receptionist's desk, a small waiting area with chairs and tables stacked with magazines. Arriving and finding the office empty strikes him as a bad sign. He rests his palm against the cool steel frame before turning to go.

Rummaging through his pack in the dark, he pulls out a square of cardboard stock. It is the likeness of the saint his neighbor in Pittsburgh gave him. Tulsi runs his fingertips over its glossy surface, the saint's two right hands holding their lilies, his left wrapped in a rosary. He studies the saint's face but it betrays nothing. Neither compassion nor contempt. It is bare, expressionless. He puts back the card and finds the envelope with the last of his money. Two hundred dollars in crumpled twenties and tens, all he has left.

•

Tulsi sits in the fluorescent light of the all-night diner. A cup of coffee cools before him, his third since arriving. For the past few hours he's watched the other patrons come and go. An old man who sips his soup delicately and makes small talk with the waitress. A young couple who cling to each other as they share the same side of a booth. A group of drunken college-aged men whose loud voices shatter the stillness of the place. All of them eventually pay their bills and leave, while Tulsi remains.

Around one in the morning, the waitress stops by to refill his coffee.

"Look," she says, setting the pot on the table, "I don't mind if you sit here all night. We're open anyway and you wouldn't be the first. But you're gonna have to order something other than coffee."

She is tall with a slender neck and big dark eyes. She removes a pen and tablet from her apron. Tulsi runs his hand over the pocket that contains what's left of his money.

"Would a side of fries be okay?" he asks. The woman puts the pen away without writing anything. She glances at the duffel that sits across from him in the booth.

"I'll do you one better," she says, and walks away. A little while later she returns. "Plate's hot," she says, setting it in front of him. "Don't burn yourself," and then, "welcome to Canada."

A heaping mound of fries sits on the plate, covered in brown gravy and sprinkled with hunks of cheese and bacon. Tulsi takes a bite and then another. The food is delicious and warm and filling. He eats it slowly, covering each fry with a perfect combination of gravy, cheese, and meat. When he looks up, the waitress smiles at him from behind the counter. Tulsi nods in thanks. Past the diner's blackened windows, a row of streetlights shine against the night sky like a string of pearls.

•

Tulsi gets to the Nepalese Center half an hour early and finds it still closed. He waits in the chill morning, clutching the straps of his bag. At exactly nine o'clock an elderly man arrives and walks past him without a word. The man unlocks the glass door and enters. Tulsi waits, then follows him in. The man disappears down a hallway and Tulsi, unsure what to do, takes a seat in the waiting area. The walls are covered with framed posters of the towering Himalayas shrouded in snow. Even in miniature they are something to behold, rising majestically above the clouds. He remembers the way his grandfather longed for mountains at the end of his life, spoke of them the way one might recount a first love.

For a while he sits waiting. He leafs through a pamphlet on proper etiquette for job interviews, then an old copy of Reader's Digest. Finally, the man emerges from the hallway.

"Okay," he says, "ready," and then disappears back down the hallway, leaving Tulsi to hustle after him. Tulsi follows him to a small, windowless room near the rear of the building. The space is cramped with filing cabinets and stacks of books. A potted plant sits wilting in the corner.

"Well?" the man says. He is bald and unmistakably Nepali, his skin the color of sandalwood. His black-rimmed glasses have thick lenses that magnify his eyes; a bushy white mustache hides his top lip.

"I," Tulsi begins, but stumbles. Everything about the man is urgent. He glances from Tulsi to the open ledger before him, back and forth as though comparing the two intently.

"Out with it," he says. Tulsi reaches for his bag and begins to search for the letter from the UN. The letter that has led him here. The man sighs and Tulsi, unsure what to do, empties the contents of his bag onto the office floor.

"What are you *doing*? You're making a mess."

Tulsi finds the letter and hands it across the desk. "Here," he says, "I called about finding my sister."

"Who did you speak to?" the man asks. "You didn't speak to me." He snatches the letter and unfolds it, scanning it hurriedly. "This is vague at best, and we would only have a record of your sister if she's come to us for assistance. I wouldn't expect much. It will take me some time to check the records and…"

"I can wait," Tulsi interrupts.

"I might not get to it today."

"I'll wait anyway. As long as it takes."

The man removes his glasses and wipes his brow with a handkerchief. His face takes on a look of resignation. "Well, you can't wait in here," he says, "so…" He raises one hand, the fingers gnarled and thin, and motions toward the door, casting Tulsi away.

•

Tulsi awakens in the waiting area hunched over the duffel bag in his lap, his neck cramped. Sleep has gathered in the corners of his eyes and he rubs it away. The clock on the wall reads quarter past three and still the man has not emerged. At the receptionist's desk, an elderly woman sits watching him.

"Feeling rested?" she asks. Tulsi straightens himself.

"Yes," he says. "I'm sorry, it's been a long couple of days."

"Sleep is not a thing to be sorry for," she says, and then conspiratorially, "I sneak into the back sometimes. There's an empty office with a couch." She smiles, her dark skin rippling into a series of wrinkles. "It can be very boring here."

She too is Nepali, with expressive brown eyes, her head covered in a brilliant yellow wrap. Hooped earrings hang from stretched lobes; in her nose, a gold stud. "Is there something I can help you with, or are you waiting on my brother?"

"Is he the one who opened this morning?"

"Yes," she says, "he's very thorough. What they call 'by the book.'" Her expression turns serious. "Was he polite to you? I am always reminding him. 'Here, Prajun, we are polite. Here, we work only to help others.'"

Tulsi hears the reprimand in the woman's voice and cannot suppress a smile. "He was very helpful," he says.

The woman throws her hands in the air and sighs. "You are covering up for his rudeness. I *know* my brother." She nods at Tulsi and winks. "Now," she says, shaking a finger at him, "you are his accomplice."

●

It is past five when the man walks into the waiting room. He is wearing his coat and carrying a briefcase. When he sees Tulsi, he appears surprised.

"Are you crazy? I did not even begin to look into this matter. There are more pressing issues at hand. Tihar is less than a week away. I'm organizing performances, procuring permits from the city. I told you I might not get to this today. I am very busy."

Tulsi waits till the man is done speaking. "I understand," he says. "I'll come back tomorrow, and if you are busy then, I'll come back the next day." The woman at the desk laughs.

"Hard-headed," she says, "like you, brother. And stop with this nonsense of being busy. I find you dozing as often as I find you awake."

"*Ahhh*," the man says, and waves away his sister.

"And *you*," the woman says, turning to Tulsi, "where will *you* go now?"

Tulsi hesitates, a vision of the deserted diner flashing through his mind.

"Exactly," the woman says. "Exactly."

•

The woman, whose name is Devi, sets the table as Tulsi and Prajun look on. Tulsi had asked if he could help and she had lowered him into a seat with one surprisingly strong hand. On the way home from the Nepalese Center, they stopped for a bucket of fried chicken, and now she arranges the sides into individual bowls.

"This is my favorite meal in Toronto," she says, emptying a container of potato wedges. "Delicious."

"This man could be a murderer," Prajun says, shifting in his chair. "Have you considered that? To think, murdered in my own home after traveling all the way from Nepal."

"Shhhh!" Devi wags a finger at him. "You embarrass yourself, and worse, me." She disappears into the kitchen and returns holding a jar of chutney. "To add heat," she tells Tulsi. "For such a cold country, its cooks certainly fear heat." Seated across the table from her, Tulsi notices the darkened Bindi drawn between Devi's eyes, worn to mark widowhood.

"You are naïve, sister," Prajun says.

"Better naïve than a grouchy old man. A *rude* old man." She fixes her gaze on her brother, and Tulsi sees surrender the moment she does, Prajun's shoulders slumping in defeat. "Now," she continues, "we have a guest, a blessing in life, and what I would like very much, what would fill me with delight, is for him to enjoy his meal."

•

After dinner Tulsi helps Devi clear the table, placing leftovers in containers and stacking the plates by the sink. Prajun retires to the living room to read the newspaper and Tulsi watches him go.

"Pay no attention to him," Devi says. "Unpleasantness is his overcoat; he'll take it off once he warms." Tulsi hands her a plate, and she holds it beneath the hot faucet. "He did not always envision a life such as this."

"How long have you been in Canada?"

"Only two years," she says. "Before that, Camp Sanischare. Not so far from Goldhap. When my husband died, I asked to be relocated. He did not want to leave the camps. He believed we'd be repatriated to Bhutan." Tulsi watches Devi's frail hands as they turn the plate over and over beneath the water.

"And your brother?" he asks.

"The same. I forced him to leave when I did. He believed like my husband that one day we'd all be allowed to return home." She laughs and hands the plate to Tulsi. "Can you *imagine*? The king awakening one day and saying, 'We've made a grave mistake. Come home.'" Tulsi lets his eyes fall to the dish in his hands, dries it slowly.

"And if we did return, what would we have found? A place unchanged? Our world as we left it?" She shakes her head and shuts off the water. "Some *still* wait, refuse to go. I did not want my brother to die waiting."

A small window above the sink lets in the last of the twilight. A vase of dried goldenrod sits on the sill.

"My grandfather told me about Bhutan," Tulsi says. "Before he died, he talked about it all the time. I never saw it." Tulsi sets the plate in the rack to finish drying. Talking about his grandfather, about Bhutan, drains him, leaves him feeling hollow.

"It must be difficult," Devi says, "to be a refugee from a place you've never seen." She unties the apron at her waist. "It *was* beautiful," she adds, and then, "it must still be."

Tulsi stares out the window. Waits for the empty feeling to pass. Devi pats his cheek, her touch as soft and light as the wing of a bird.

"You are still young," she says, "and the world is full of beautiful places."

●

Tulsi awakes on the couch to find the house empty. A note on the coffee table informs him that Devi and Prajun have gone to the

Community Center, that he should make himself at home. Holding the bit of paper, a familiar sadness fills him, a kind of resigned embarrassment at having to rely on the generosity of strangers. He had not wanted to stay but Devi insisted, and of course he'd nowhere to go, no one in Toronto he knew. Only the faintest hope that Susmita is here, that somewhere in a city of two and a half million, his sister sleeps and eats and lives, or at least once did. That someone here knows her or what has happened to her. Foolish, he thinks. Though no more foolish than all the other things that led him here.

He rises and folds the blankets and sheets Devi arranged on the couch. The night before, he wished Prajun a restful sleep, thanked him for his kindness. The old man huffed and walked off to his bedroom down the hall. Devi reminded him to ignore her brother and then retired to her bedroom upstairs. For a long time he lay awake, the darkness of the living room softening, the sound of the wind and an occasional train whistle taking him back, lulling him.

He finds the washing machine in a damp corner of the basement, loads his clothes, then walks upstairs to shower. Afterward he dresses in the jeans and sweatshirt he set aside and switches the laundry to the dryer. When it is finished, he will pack his things and go. He will call the Community Center to thank Devi for her kindness and to ask Prajun what he has found and then he will make himself disappear. A ghost traveler come and gone in the night. He checks the timer on the dryer, forty-five minutes. He decides to take a walk.

A soft wind blows in from the water, drawing Tulsi toward the lake. He follows winding sidewalks past two-story homes set squarely on their lots, cars lining the curbs. There is an order here he appreciates, a consistency that does not go unnoticed. In the distance the downtown skyscrapers stand shimmering in the crisp fall dawn.

At the southern edge of the neighborhood, the residential lots and rows of uniform houses give way to a wooded park. Its entrance is bordered on either side by fenced-in tennis courts. They are empty save for a pair of teenage girls in leggings and sweatshirts striking the ball expertly. Tulsi walks past them down the park's drive. A little farther on, the drive ends in a small cul-de-sac at the center of a field. He follows a worn path past saplings, thin and tethered to the ground.

Through a stand of trees he finds what he'd been hoping for. Far below him, maybe some two hundred feet, is Lake Ontario. Its waters, a soft blue near the shore, deepen in color at the horizon. He stands looking over it, letting his eyes adjust to the unobstructed view. Below him, another park juts out into the water, a circular plot of land dividing the shoreline into two beaches. The cliff on which he stands is sheer and white like a sandcastle half collapsed. Tulsi recalls himself at the marina in Erie, staring out over the water in wonder at what might exist on the other side. Now that he is here, he is unsure how he feels.

Whitecaps roll in slowly and wash against the gravelly shore. Though he has crossed one, he's still never been to the ocean. Standing above the muted foam, it is hard to imagine the monstrous waves shown on television, the way they crash down onto themselves like buildings imploding. When he was still with Rebecca, they'd spoken about taking Grace to one of the boardwalk towns that pepper the coasts of Maryland and New Jersey. He wonders, had things been different, if they'd ever actually have gone. He tries to imagine them moving past burger stands and arcades, the sun warming their bare feet. How old Grace must look now, a different child than the one he walked to school. Would she even recognize him if he were to pass by? Would she turn and look back, the faintest flicker of remembrance?

Over the lake, a single gull soars level with the bluffs, coasting on a current of air. Tulsi watches it dip toward the water then disappear, indistinguishable against the chalk-white walls.

•

Back at the house he folds and packs his clothes. He was gone longer than he planned. While writing a note in the living room, he hears the mechanized grind of the single garage. He expects Devi, home early to check on him, but finds Prajun entering the kitchen through the side door.

"*You*," he says, "you're still here?" The old man lowers himself onto one of the stools that line the counter. He looks weary, his head angled downward as though suffering from a stiff neck.

"I was just leaving," Tulsi says. "Thank you again for letting me stay."

Prajun nods, his hands folded before him. "And where are you off to?"

This time Tulsi is prepared. "Downtown," he says. "The International Hostel." He'd called earlier and spoken to an employee. Rooms were cheap and he could arrive anytime.

"I see," Prajun says. His face is creased, dark folds of skin segmented by deep wrinkles like patches on a quilt. From his coat pocket he produces a bottle of pills. He loosens the cap and takes one, swallowing it without water. "And in this hostel, you will share a room? With strangers?"

"Yes."

Prajun replaces the cap and sets the bottle on the counter, his hand trembling slightly. "You are too young to remember, but when we first arrived in the camps there were not enough huts. People were coming so quickly. Families, two, three, sometimes more, would have to share." Prajun shakes his head and smiles, the first time Tulsi has seen him do so. "At the time, I thought, 'Look how little they think of us, to herd us together like cattle.' Now, when I remember it, I think of how in many ways it helped. How we shared our grief, each taking a little bit of the whole." The whites of his eyes are slightly yellowed, newsprint left in the sun.

"Are you sick?" Tulsi says, motioning toward the pills.

Prajun shrugs dismissively. "We are all sick," he says. "Some of us are just better at it."

Tulsi takes a half step forward onto the linoleum. Sunlight pours through the window above the sink. "In Nepal," he says, "I lived with my sister and her husband before moving to the States with my hajurba."

Prajun stares into his open hand as though reading his own palm. "And now," he says without looking up, "your hajurba has died and you do not know where your sister and her husband are."

Yes, Tulsi wants to say, that is my life put plainly. He watches the windowsill, studies the brittle bloom of goldenrod.

"It is a common story for our people. For many people. Families separated, strewn about." The light in the room dims almost imperceptibly.

"Have you had the chance to look at your files?" Tulsi asks. The shadow of the flowers lengthens on the wall opposite the window. Tulsi traces the silhouette with his eyes. "I was told she might be here."

"I have looked," Prajun says. "And if she is here, we have no record." Tulsi senses the man watching him, assessing his reaction. "I'm sorry," Prajun says. "I know this is not the answer you were hoping for. I will continue to look. I have friends who know many people."

Tulsi's arms hang at his sides, heavy, burdened by invisible weights. "Thank you," he says, "for looking."

Prajun lowers himself from the stool. "Have you told Devi you are leaving? She'll be sad to see you go. It is not easy for her with only myself as company."

"I was writing her a note, to thank her."

The old man walks to the refrigerator and takes out a container of orange juice. "She will be home soon," he says. "She dropped me here and went on to the grocery. Wait until she arrives. To say goodbye." He pours two glasses and replaces the pitcher.

"I should go," Tulsi says. "The hostel is expecting me."

Prajun hands him a glass. "Let them expect you a little longer."

●

Devi arrives in a huff, plastic grocery bags dangling from the crooks of her elbows. Tulsi helps her unload the car. When they are done, she takes a seat at the kitchen table, short of breath and smiling.

"I left you alone with the wolf," she says and winks. Prajun lifts his hands in annoyance, but there is the trace of a smile. It is an old act, this bickering between siblings. Tulsi has a front-row seat.

"He was preparing to go," Prajun says.

Devi looks alarmed. "Tonight?"

"Yes. I wanted to thank you…"

"Why so soon? You just arrived in Toronto."

"I'm staying in Toronto. I booked a room at the International Hostel."

"Why?" Devi shifts in her seat, an injured look on her face. "Are we so bad?" She has on an ivory sweater with lavender trim. Raising her arm, she lowers her nose to the cotton theatrically. "Are we so old we smell of death?"

"No," Tulsi says. "You've been wonderful. But I can't impose on you anymore. It's not right."

"Ha!" Devi removes some peppers from a bag and walks to the sink. "I am cooking tonight. Red rice, vegetable curry, momo dumplings." She opens the faucet and holds the peppers beneath it. "You *must* stay and eat," she says. "The rumblings of your stomach have scrambled your mind."

•

It is late and again the couch has been dressed, pillows and blankets stacked neatly at one end. Prajun excused himself after dinner and retired to his room. Devi sits in an armchair, finishing her chai. They are watching the end of a reality show, contestants left to fend for themselves in a desolate wilderness, scheming to eliminate one another. When the show ends, Devi shuts off the TV and lays the remote on the coffee table.

"Silliness, I know, but I love it. That anyone would choose to endure such things." She shakes her head, then takes a sip of tea. "There are crazy people in every corner of this world."

Tulsi laughs and settles into the couch. The food was delicious, spicy and warm, the familiar flavors revealing themselves like obscured memories. Once more, Devi has made him promise to stay. He knows he must leave tomorrow when the two are at work. His things are packed, and he will finish the note before he goes.

Devi looks down the darkened hallway toward Prajun's bedroom. A framed photograph of a small village hangs on one side of the hallway's entrance. On the wall opposite is a painting of a young woman wrapped in a sari. Her body is turned as she glances back over her shoulder.

"My husband painted that," Devi says. "In Bhutan, he was an artist. People traveled from far away to buy his work."

"It's beautiful."

"It's me," Devi says. She smiles mischievously, her cheeks rounding like plums. Her gaze grows distant. When it returns she looks at Tulsi. "I know you are going to leave," she says, setting her mug on the end table. "And I cannot convince you to stay."

Tulsi stares at the painting. He feels the old woman's disappointment and cannot stand to see it as well. He is sorry to be letting her down, but he cannot stay. He remembers Mr. Bhandari's kindness, the meal he prepared for him and Bronagh. He thinks of Malcolm and his mother, Rachel, feeding him after soccer practice, taking him in like another son. In his bag is the picture of the saint his neighbor in Pittsburgh gave him. He has already taken too much in this life. And because of it, things have been taken from him. He cannot stay. Devi speaks his name and it comes to him from a great distance.

"My brother is very sick," she says, "and very stubborn." She points at the painting. "I am not as young as I was then. I no longer have the patience for stubborn men."

"You have been very kind," Tulsi says, "but this is something I have to do."

She must see something in his eyes, the resignation he feels. "And what will you do for Tihar?" she asks. "Celebrate it alone in your hostel?"

Tulsi remembers the festival, now only a fractured relic of his childhood. He thinks of candles flickering from every surface, the colorful rangoli canvassing the packed-dirt floors, elaborate patterns of dyed rice and sand. He's forgotten the prayers, the order of the days. All that remains are scattered images.

"You must promise to come celebrate with us," Devi says. "It is a part of who you are."

"It's been a long time."

"You will find it similar," she says, and smiles, "though here we have fireworks." A single wisp of white hair falls across her forehead. She brushes it away. "I trust that you will come, but just in case." She stands and disappears into the kitchen, returns with a small jar containing a clay-colored substance. "Turmeric," she says, tapping the glass. "Not perfect, but the Gods will understand."

She unscrews the lid and dips her thumb. Leaning over him, she makes a single upward stroke on his forehead while speaking softly in Nepalese. She smells of vegetable oil and sweet floral perfume. Her shadow covers him, her words lull. She finishes and takes a step back, observes her work and smiles.

"There," she says. "Now you are blessed."

•

It is April and the city thaws. Water drips from the corners of roofs and gathers in clear puddles on the sidewalks. Most days, clouds still cover the sky, though occasionally a sunset will burn through, singeing their underbellies brilliant shades of tangerine and amber. The air blows in cool off the lake, no longer so frigid it burns the lungs. Inhaling it somehow refreshes. Quite simply, it is the purest thing Tulsi can imagine.

The winter itself was long and relentless. Still, Tulsi found beauty in it: cars buried beneath shells of snow, branches coated like delicate candies. Even the permanent overcast sky had come to feel familiar, a fat down comforter thrown over the entire city.

It was hard at first, staying at the hostel for two months before finding a place of his own. There were new roommates nearly every night, faces unrecognizable in the dark. Most of the travelers were from abroad: Europeans and Australians exploring the continent. Some had even been to Nepal and were excited to learn Tulsi had lived there. When they asked him questions, he no longer spoke sadly of Camp Goldhap, focusing instead on his trip through Kathmandu, the cleansing rains of monsoon season, summer days spent chasing friends through lush forests.

Tulsi's days have taken on a rhythm. Six times a week he travels to a bookstore downtown to work an eight-hour shift: stocking shelves, guiding customers, pouring coffee in the attached café. There are long spells of solitude where he does nothing but read. It is the antithesis of the casinos he worked in for so long, the carnival atmosphere and desperation replaced with solace. Sometimes, if it is late and he is there alone, his thoughts turn on him, worry and regret as sudden and suffocating as a cave-in. Over time, and with help, he has learned how to calm these attacks, how to step outside himself and begin to make sense.

Through their connections at the Community Center, Devi and Prajun helped him find a support group specifically for refugees. Tulsi had been skeptical of it all: the church basement where the meetings were held, the circled folding chairs and stale coffee, the soft-spoken counselor who greeted them by name each week. Early on, almost in passing, she referred to them as survivors. Tulsi was unsure if he liked the term. He sensed the weight of what it implied: difficulty, suffering, trauma. At first it made him feel guilty, undeserving. Now he is willing to accept it. He has come to look forward to the meetings, to the others who attend faithfully and share their stories. He carries those stories with him throughout the week, replaying them in his head. It is what quiets his mind when his thoughts race, the testament of survivors.

On Tuesday and Thursday nights he takes classes at the University of Toronto. Its centerpiece, a sprawling sandstone structure positioned among the commons, emerges from the earth like a medieval castle. Tulsi gets chills each time he passes through the ornately arched entrance. Even the classrooms are elaborate, with exposed rafters and long rows of wooden pews. Tulsi feels as though he's in church. Not simply a place designed for learning, but for the divine implications therein.

Some of his credits from Pittsburgh have transferred. It will be a long road, but he is already registered for summer classes. Starting in June, he'll take Introduction to Civil Engineering. It is a field-based course, and there is even a camping trip meant to teach the basics of land surveying. When Tulsi thinks of it, he can hardly wait.

•

There had been no word of his sister in the months since he arrived. For a while, after he first moved to the hostel, he'd blanket the Nepalese neighborhoods. Hours spent wandering through Rexdale and East York, scanning faces as he had for so long. He still has a picture of Susmita, creased and tattered but clear enough: dark eyes shining, smile frozen in place. He showed it to shopkeepers and mail carriers, elderly residents smoking on their stoops.

Once, a man in paint-splattered overalls smirked at the photo.

"You all look the same to me," he said. "Who can tell you apart?"

Tulsi stood facing the man, unblinking. His hands trembled. As it had so many times in the past, all the pain and loss that had led him to that moment cascaded through his mind. And behind it, like a canvas upon which those memories were painted, was the familiar sensation of reduction, of being made to feel inhuman.

"What?" the man said, hunching his shoulders as though it were all in good fun. "I'm just sayin'."

To slug the man. To cock back his fist and unleash rage. To throw away these last good months and become the person the world had spurred him to be. It is a precipice he stands on, so near the edge sometimes he can feel the void beneath his toes. How sweet it must be to succumb, to release oneself to the weightlessness of free-fall.

Instead, Tulsi folded the photo and replaced it, faced the man squarely, proudly.

"I can tell," he said, and then walked off. Later he felt satisfied with how he handled the encounter. Finally, the burning ember inside of him had cooled. His anger not gone but guarded.

●

On Wednesday, Tulsi takes the bus to the dialysis clinic where Prajun receives treatments. It is a brightly lit space with curtained stations for added privacy. The ladies at the sign-in desk know him and point to a closed-off area in the corner. Prajun sits inside meditating, his arm attached to the churning machine that siphons the blood from his body before cleansing and returning it. He is dressed in his traditional work uniform of shirt and tie, his sport coat folded over the back of his chair. Even now he tends to the needs of the Community Center, stopping in daily. Tulsi stands watching for a moment before speaking.

"Are you dead?" he asks. The old man's lips curve into a knowing smile.

"I'm not sure," he says. "Did you unplug the vampire?" He opens his eyes, dimmer than when they first met but still sharp, perceptive.

Somehow, against all odds, the two have found themselves friends, a banter between them like old drinking buddies.

"You visit every week. Why waste your time at this holding station?" Prajun asks.

Tulsi takes the seat opposite him. "Why waste yours?"

"Devi insists. I have two choices: come here and die slowly or refuse and have her kill me." Prajun shakes his head and raises his free hand in feigned exasperation.

"Kill you and risk going to jail?" Tulsi says. "She would never."

"She might. Stranger things have happened."

"Yes, like us sitting here together."

"That is not so strange. You are young and naïve. Ignorant in the ways of the world. I am old and wise. You are here to learn from me, to glean what little you can from my vast intellect and experience." Prajun pulls the lever on the side of his seat and his legs swing upright. "So let us begin," he says. "Try to keep up."

"Actually," Tulsi says, opening his book bag and removing a folded copy of that day's newspaper.

"Not this again," Prajun says.

Tulsi rifles through the pages until he finds the crossword. "It's the best way to master the language and learn the idioms."

"By the time I master the language, they'll be offering me last rites."

Tulsi takes a pen from his pocket and uncaps it. "At least then you'll understand them."

Prajun smiles, but Tulsi can tell he is already tiring. "You have become too quick for me, Tulsi Gurung. Our verbal sparring has grown one-sided."

Tulsi rests a hand on his forearm. "Never." He looks back at the crossword and is about to begin, but when he glances up, Prajun's eyes are squeezed shut.

"Are you in pain?"

Prajun shakes his head and opens his eyes; they are deep with apprehension. "There is something I need to speak to you about. I joke because it is easier than addressing serious matters, but I am too old for avoidance. Dying men are not meant to procrastinate."

"Unless they are putting off dying," Tulsi says, but Prajun remains stoic. He leans over the side of the recliner and clicks open his briefcase, then lifts out a padded FedEx envelope.

"If this is about your will or some…"

"Tulsi," Prajun says. Something in his voice tells Tulsi to listen.

That it is not the time for him to speak. Prajun holds the envelope in his lap.

"In spite of my shortcomings, my… prickliness, I have been blessed with several lifelong friends. The closest is a man named Dal. We knew each other first in Bhutan and then in the camps. He had the good sense to leave long before myself." Prajun taps the envelope softly. "I say 'good sense,' but that is not right. It was courage, to admit what I could not: that we would never be permitted to return home." Prajun stares at the curtain as he speaks. Through it, the sounds of the clinic filter in: the beeping and whirring of medical equipment, chairs scraping the floor, the clacking of a keyboard. "Dal is a smart man, and savvy. Unlike many who possess those gifts, he chose to use them for others."

Prajun pauses at the sound of approaching footsteps. A moment later, the curtain is yanked back and a tall nurse enters. Her hair is pulled up in a bun, a pencil skewered through it.

"There's my favorite patient," she says, bending to read the display on the dialysis machine. She presses a button and straightens. "Oil's almost changed, honey," she says, patting Prajun on the knee. And then she is gone, pulling the curtain shut behind her. Prajun turns back to Tulsi.

"I'm sorry I did not mention my friend before, but I did not want to plant false hope. Dal works in Washington, for Amnesty International. Last year, when you came to me, I wrote to him. For months there was nothing, and then, this past week…"

Prajun lifts the envelope and hands it to Tulsi. It is still sealed. On the shipping label the recipient is listed as the Community Center. Tulsi is about to point this out when he notices "Care Of" written beside it. His own name rests a line above.

"Dal is a meticulous man, and one with resources. But…" Tulsi watches Prajun, sees the care with which he chooses his words. "He is also forthright. The world has demanded it from him." Prajun motions toward Tulsi's hands. "I do not know what it contains."

"Probably nothing," Tulsi hears himself say. He feels faint, uncertain; he stands without meaning to. He looks down to see Prajun saddened.

"I would not blame you for believing so. You may be right. It could very well be nothing."

"I'd bet on it," Tulsi says. He leans down and places the envelope in his open book bag. "Don't get me wrong. I don't mean to be ungrateful. It's just...."

"I understand."

Tulsi zips the book bag and straightens. "I should run. Early day tomorrow." He opens the curtain and, for Prajun's sake, forces a smile. "Thank your friend for me. Really." He steps into the shared space of the lobby, then turns back. "I'll visit next week," he says and points to where the newspaper sits opened to the crossword puzzle. "Have that completed or I'll tell Devi you're slacking." Prajun nods as Tulsi leaves.

•

At home, he digs the envelope out of his book bag and leaves it on his kitchen counter. It's where he keeps his mail and textbooks, the place he sticks Post-It notes when he has something important to remember. Now, he walks into his room to begin readying for bed. Prajun told him he did not know what the envelope contained. Tulsi reassures himself it is nothing: resettlement forms for those with names similar to his sister's, generic statistics regarding family reunification. The chaff of a fruitless harvest.

In the bathroom, Tulsi turns on the water and undresses as the mirror fogs with steam. He stands beneath the showerhead and lets the hot water soak in, warm him to his bones. On Thursdays, he opens the bookshop, and so must be up at six. Between school and work, sleep is at a premium, and he takes advantage when he can. He dries himself off and dresses.

In the kitchen he heats a mug of tea and glances at the envelope, its corners tattered. What had Prajun said about why he chose not to mention his friend? Something about planting false hope. Tulsi imagines rocky terrain, an arid landscape. To satisfy a general education requirement, he was taking a course on Roman History. While lecturing on the Punic Wars, the professor had described how, after defeating Carthage, the Romans plowed the city with salt so nothing would grow there. Tulsi was stunned not by the act, but by the spite required to commit it. To sow one's hatred into the earth itself. The professor had gone on to tell them that the practice was largely symbolic, that despite popular belief, such a large quantity of salt would be required that in all likelihood, it would not have turned the land barren.

Tulsi takes a final sip of tea, then dumps the rest in the sink. He shuts off the overhead light and heads to bed.

•

He wakes suddenly, the room around him pitch black. He feels cold and pulls the covers to his chin. He thinks to check the time on his phone but is afraid to reach for it. There is something palpable there with him, someone or something he cannot quite pinpoint. He is awash in fear.

"Hello?" he asks the darkness. But it is not the darkness he is afraid of, and all at once he recognizes the source of his terror.

He sits staring at the envelope. He lifts it slowly; feels the heft he took for granted earlier. Flipping it over, he pulls back the strip fastening it shut. Inside is another envelope, this one from an organization named Catholic Charities located in the Diocese of Harrisburg.

In his years in Pennsylvania, Tulsi never made it to the capital, never had occasion to go. All he knows about Harrisburg is that it is located nearer to Philadelphia, another place he has never been.

He reaches into this envelope and withdraws a file folder emblazoned with the organization's logo, a cross standing at the center of a church. The thought occurs that this is all he will find: folder after folder containing nothing. A set of Russian Dolls meant as some cruel joke.

He opens the folder. Inside is a note typed on the church's stationery. He lifts it and holds it close in the dim light of the kitchen.

Dear Mr. Maharjan,

As discussed we are happy to be of service regarding your inquiry. Every year, our Diocese welcomes hundreds of refugees to Central Pennsylvania. As a small, often understaffed organization, we do our best to provide job and housing placement, language classes, and other basic needs. We have no record of ever having assisted a Susmita Gurung or Khalishar.

Tulsi stops and looks up. Disappointment, familiar as an old friend, mixes with relief. At least the news is not bad. Alongside this there exists a strange reassurance: that in a life of uncertainty and struggle there is still a constant he can count on. *No record.* The words like a reminder to keep his expectations low. To ask for something is to be made vulnerable. To ask for too much is to beckon misery. It is a lesson he has learned the hard way.

He catches his reflection in the dark of the microwave: eyes puffy and hair mussed from sleep. In the morning he will be tired. He should have resisted the pull and stayed in bed, practiced the techniques he's learned to abate fear. He looks back down at the letter.

In addition, we have no record of having assisted a Tulsi Gurung. It is for this reason that the letters initially caught our attention. Since it is located in our state's capital, our Diocese has at times served as a catchall for various forms and petitions from asylum seekers. Matters such as those, however, are routinely rectified, as we are able to point those in need in the right direction. In this case we were unable to do so as we had not assisted, and had no record of, either party. Please accept our sincerest hope that the enclosed correspondence finds its way into the correct hands.

Sincerely,

Linda Meehan, Director of Development

Tulsi rereads the final sentence, the words suddenly a jumble on the page. *Correct hands.* He pictures a mother cradling her infant. It is the nearest he can get to what he thinks was meant.

He sets down the note. Beneath it lies an envelope, smudged and wrinkled as though handled indelicately. It is made out to him at an address in Harrisburg, what he imagines must be the location of the Catholic Charities office. There is a strangeness at seeing his name there, listed above the address for a building he has never been to in a town he has never visited. But there is something else, an intimacy to the script. It echoes back to him like a face he can't quite recall. He sets the envelope down and lifts another, studies the handwriting there. Compact, elegant, and neat, it is nearly identical to his own, as though he had addressed this to himself. It is the penmanship of the camps, the way he was taught to write at the Blooming Lotus School in Goldhap.

He feels the stifling heat of the cramped classroom, the hard bench upon which he sat listening for hours. Hands trembling, he lifts another envelope, one of dozens he sees now. He slides a finger beneath its flap but finds it already opened. A sense of intrusion settles and surprises him. He removes the letter and unfolds it carefully.

Dear Brother,

I awoke tonight abruptly, the breath robbed from my body. I cannot say why, the nightmare vanishing before my eyes were opened, a cowardly apparition retreating to its cave. Still, I was so unsettled I could not return to sleep. Instead, I sit here writing you. I sit here wondering.

Across the room, my child dreams. A girl, Tulsi, a perfect little girl. She is tiny as you were. A delicate seed made whole. We have named her Nilaya for she has given us what we never had. A home.

Brother, I wish you could see her. I wish you could hold her in your arms just once, hear the strength of her cries. She is so alive that sometimes I tremble simply watching her. It is awe I feel. Gratitude.

Tulsi, would you forgive me if I made an admission? One that has burdened me for too long? Regardless, I must. Brother, there were times I could not bear to think of you, to imagine where you were, or even gather the courage to wonder if you still lived. There were many times when my strength failed me. When hope felt false. Forgive me my weaknesses, brother. But uncertainty is a cruel companion, constant and unyielding.

Yet, what I have thought lately differs, fills me with a kind of peace. It is a funny notion, even for me, and yet I cling to it. What I have thought lately is this. Who is to say I am not with you and you with me? Who is to say I do not carry you with me in my heart? That I do not watch over you still? Brother, the world is larger and stronger than either of us, but perhaps what it possesses in might it lacks in spirit. For living or dead, ten thousand miles distant or more, I can still feel you with me. As real as the ground I stand upon. As real as the air I breathe. Brother, I hope you have found your place. Your peace. I hope you are not wary as I once was. There is no need, Tulsi. For you are here with me. I am sure of it. And I with you.

Your Sister

Tulsi waits in a corner of the elevator, ascending. The ride is so smooth it feels as though they are standing still. Only the rapidly changing floor light and sudden pressure in his ears signal otherwise. Speed, he thinks, efficiency. Hallmarks of his desired field.

He imagines himself rising, the distance between him and the earth growing exponentially. The feeling this thought produces is both scary and electrifying, like the sensation of hiding as a child.

The elevator halts suddenly, the barely detectable movement obvious in its absence. Tulsi opens his mouth wide and his ears comply, popping crisply. The doors open onto the CN Tower's broad observation deck, a wall of rectangular windows opposite him. He waits for the others to emerge, then steps out.

Children run through the enclosed space, chasing one another. A mother holds her toddler up to the glass, showing her the scene below. A pair of teenagers lean their weight against the windows, hands behind their backs, noses pressed flat.

Tulsi finds a spot away from the others. The sky is slightly overcast, so he's surprised it's as busy as it is. He holds the railing and peers down, the city in miniature below him. Cars and buses like toys on a paper map.

That first night, he'd read his sister's letters until the sky beyond his window paled from black to gray to true daylight. He held them delicately, turning and studying them like relics of a lost world. He read them one after another as they were stacked, out of order; Susmita's story unfolding like chapters torn from a book and tossed in the air. She too had faced great difficulties. She too had mourned things she'd never known. In word and thought, she had sought him out. What he now knew was that in her own way, and long before he understood it, she had found him.

The final postmarked letter listed as its return address a PO Box in Vancouver. Tulsi considered it closely. Sitting there in his kitchen, the old urge to uproot his life had returned. Here was confirmation that his sister was safe, that somewhere in the same country she worked, and ate, and slept. He could find her now; he was sure of it. He'd even pulled his duffel from the closet and began to pack before something within slowed, told him to stop. All those years, the sacrifices he'd made to seek her out, to assure himself that he was anchored to this world, that another person in it knew him and loved him, had cared for him from the moment of his birth. Selfish he thought, misguided. She was safe, had told him so in her own words. She was a mother now, had a daughter who needed her more.

Taking great care, he unpacked and replaced his bag. In the kitchen, he made himself coffee and toast and sat down again with Susmita's story, not their shared one but her own.

Since then, Tulsi had written to all the local resettlement agencies and affiliated organizations in Vancouver and was awaiting word. Though there had been nothing yet, he was certain that it would come—that someday, he would see his sister again. Not at a time or occasion of his own choosing, but at one that was right. He was hopeful. That itself was something to be thankful for.

●

Tulsi lets go of the railing and leans against the window, feels his stomach drop. Here, watching the world from on high, he is reminded of his hajurba, of the love he harbored for the mountains of Bhutan, his homeland. Maybe he will visit someday, the land of his ancestry on which he has never set foot.

A few days earlier, Tulsi learned he'd been awarded a merit grant to help cover tuition. His coworkers found out and surprised him with a cake, the sugary smell of frosting filling the tiny bookshop. Devi prepared an elaborate dinner. She insisted he invite a friend and so he did, a girl with auburn hair from his civil engineering class with whom he sometimes studies. Her name is Lucy. At twenty, she is younger but full of ideas that intrigue him with their beauty and originality. He likes watching her read, has caught her watching him. He is happy to have met her, excited where it might lead.

In the distance, a ferry inches toward the Toronto Islands, its wake a smear of chalk against the flat blue of the harbor. He tries to pinpoint the people standing at the ferry's railings but they are too far away.

You are always looking. Rest your eyes.

The words come from some other place, somewhere he cannot name.

He leans his forehead against the cool glass and repeats them to himself.

People walking behind him reflect in the glass. A couple holding hands. A security guard. A woman with dark hair. He does not turn, but remains still, listening to the wind whistling past the tower. Twenty-four years old and so much already behind him, so much wake of his own. He tries to imagine what awaits him and cannot. For once, it is a good thing.

Rest your eyes.

The words come again, and this time he accepts them gratefully, like a gift.

ACKNOWLEDGMENTS

This book would not exist had I not had the great honor of meeting and working with the Bhutanese community in my hometown of Erie, Pennsylvania. Every moment spent listening to their stories and learning from them was a gift, and I'm forever in their debt. Thank you to Scott Taylor for the introduction, to First Alliance Church for the resources, and to DZANC Books for their commitment to community service and literary outreach. For the important work they do, I'd like to thank the International Institute of Erie, Catholic Charities, the Sisters of St. Joseph of Northwestern Pennsylvania, St. Martin Center, and all the other organizations who continue to serve by helping to make a place for others.

Sections of this book originally appeared in slightly different forms in the following publications: "Miss Me Forever" in *Glimmer Train* and anthologized in *Voices on the Move: An Anthology by and about Refugees*; "Miss Me Forever: A Novel Excerpt" in *Narrative Magazine*. To Linda Swanson-Davies, Susan Burmeister-Brown, Carol Edgarian, Tom Jenks, Roxana Cazan, and Domnica Radulescu, thank you for your insights and acceptance, both of which kept me going. Thank you to Yaddo for your generosity in having me and gifting me with the time and space to write.

I'm incredibly indebted and beyond grateful to everyone at DZANC Books. Thank you to Dan Wickett and Steven Gillis for your continued kindness and support, which have meant the world to me. And to Michelle Dotter and Chelsea Gibbons, thank you for working so closely with me. Your encouragement, grace, and discerning edits made this an experience I'll treasure.

And, finally, to my family: Kelly, Beckett, Reece, and Clementine. You're my whole heart. On the love.

ABOUT THE AUTHOR

EUGENE CROSS IS THE AUTHOR of the story collection *Fires of Our Choosing*, which was named the Gold Medal winner in the Short Story category by the Independent Publisher Book Awards. He's taught creative writing at Northwestern, Penn State, The University of Chicago, and other institutions. His stories have appeared in *Glimmer Train, American Short Fiction, Story Quarterly*, and *Callaloo*, among other publications. His work was also listed among the 2010 and 2015 *Best American Short Stories'* 100 Distinguished Stories. He is the recipient of scholarships from the Bread Loaf Writers' Conference and fellowships from NBC, the National Hispanic Media Coalition, the Yaddo Artists' Colony, and the Sewanee Writers' Conference. Eugene writes for TV and lives in Los Angeles with his wife and three children.